THE SEVEN
DEADLIES

BOOK TWO OF THE TRILOGY OF THE FALLEN

GREG STOLZE

"The foliage was not green, but dingy black;
Not smooth the branches, but entwined and gnarled;
There were no fruits, but venom-laden thorns"
—Dante, *The Inferno*, Canto 13
(Lawrence Grant White trans.)

Chapter One

Reverend Matthew Wallace was preaching, he was testifying, he was sharing the Good News of Our Lord Jesus Christ, but he wasn't particularly "on." He was warming up the crowd with a joke.

"…but then the Devil looks at Saint Peter and says, 'Yes, but we've got *all* the umpires.'"

He waited for the laugh, and it was a good peal—but not great. Even on the worst day of his life, Matthew Wallace was a splendid speaker. He had a full, rich, booming voice that was equally suited to low, intimate intensity and loud, joyous proclamation. Today, however, he was distracted.

"…always the way, isn't it? When you can't win, you change the rules. We see that every day. I've heard you sports fans in the audience grumble about the two-point conversion. I've heard you discuss the designated hitter…"

He looked out over the sea of black and brown faces over white and colored shirts, but he didn't really *see* them. His sermon today was clicking along like a freight train—powerful on its tracks, but predictable.

"…in electoral scandals, we see people cheat! In the disgraceful, murderous deeds of terrorists, we see people *cheat*! Am I wrong here?"

"No!"

"Is there some other explanation?"

"No!"

"No, what we've got is a group who know they can't win a straight fight, so they get dirty. Can't lick our soldiers? Then they attack our accountants, our stewardesses, our *children*. They cheat!"

A few days ago, Reverend Wallace had spoken to a demon. As his freight train voice rolled along, carrying its usual load, half of his mind kept returning to that fact.

"...cheated when they handed over Christ! 'Oh no,' they said. 'We can't execute this man. That would be unholy; that would make us dirty. Why don't you Romans just do that thing for us?' They cheated!"

He stood up and paused, and this was a familiar stop on the Matthew Wallace Express—a little refueling station before he switched that rambling, leisurely engine for a powerful bullet train.

"But you can't cheat God."

Here and there, people said "Amen." Not too many. You don't set off all the fireworks at the beginning.

"You can't cheat... God!"

More noise.

"You *can't* cheat God!"

"No sir!" "Amen to that!" "I hear you!"

"You can't cheat God because God cheated death! Because even your cheating is part of God's plan, like when the Israelites handed over His son; like when they tore down the sacred Temple of Christ's body! They cheated, but you can't sneak behind a God who is everywhere. You can't hoodwink a God who sees all. You can't *break the world* when it's held in His omnipotent grasp."

He was really rolling along when the train derailed. One minute, he was preaching like there was no tomorrow and he wanted to finish his sentence before the Rapture took him to Heaven. The next moment he just stared, eyes wide, face slack. His voice—that unstoppable voice, that magnificent voice, that voice like thunder, like waves on the shore, like a mother's loving caress—just trailed off.

Confused, the congregation turned and saw Matthew Wallace's son Noah standing by the entryway.

To grasp the shock of the minister and his flock, it's important to understand three things:

First, Noah Wallace had repudiated his father. Strayed from the fold. Abandoned the faith. He'd told anyone who'd listened that the Bible was full of contradictions, impossibilities, myths, fables and outright lies. He'd become an atheist and gone off to grad school and refused to answer his parents' letters or phone calls.

Second, Matthew Wallace had shared this, all of it, with his congregation. Since his Sunday services were videotaped, edited and broadcast in syndication, that also meant that Noah had found out (secondhand initially, but he'd eventually been unable to stop himself from watching). Matthew had never tired of praying for the return of his fallen offspring, his prodigal son.

Third, and this was something only Matthew knew, the figure before him in the shape of his son was actually the demon with whom he'd spoken.

Gaviel, called demon, called Namaru, called fallen and rebel and God's forsaken, had possessed Noah Wallace's body when the minister's son experienced a moment of pure, unadulterated confusion and despair. The first time Gaviel touched the doors of Matthew's church, the resident faith had scalded his hands.

Today, walking down the aisle, he could feel it pressing in on all sides. The belief. The passion. The devotion. The fear and contempt and righteous anger at the idea of creatures like him.

Each step was torture, but it didn't stop him: He'd been in Hell. He understood agony all too well. If his steps were hesitant, if there was sweat on his stolen face, if his eyes were maybe too bright and his face too stiff as he battled to hide the pain, well, it was all good theater. All grist for the mill. All part of convincing people that he really was Noah, the failed intellectual, his prideful education broken by the embrace of his father's simple (albeit loud) faith.

Funny how things work out, he thought. *In the beginning, God walked with the first man and woman every day, in the cool of the evening. They needed no faith, for He was simply there, simply present. We, the angels, were unseen as He commanded, hidden away from His precious children. But now He has cloistered Himself, and we walk among them. The wheel has turned indeed.*

"Noah? Is that really you?" A parishioner, an old woman with artificially brown hair and gray roots gaped up at him. He gave her a brave little smile and a nod. He played at nervousness to mask his suffering.

In the war, we used their blasphemy, their faith in us, as our finest weapon against the Holy Host. Their belief gave us strength to contend with the mightiest of seraphim. Now the loyal ophanim are withdrawn, and humanity's faith turns against us. He felt a flash of anger and let his mind follow it, nursing it for strength.

They are His favored children, whom He abandoned and neglected. We were His servants—like field hands, sent to work the soil on behalf of sons and daughters who would never see our faces. What did He fear? That mankind would be corrupted by lust for us? Or that we would pervert them by our love, that we would give them the gifts that they would need to defy Him? It all came to pass. But now the weapons we gave them are turned on us.

He had reached the front of the church. He opened his mouth. Noah had a voice like Matthew when he cared to use it, and Gaviel's true voice could break men's souls. But at this moment, like the minister, his words came out in a whispery croak. He cleared his throat and spoke again, rough and raw.

"I've come back," he said. "Can I stay?"

"What the *hell* were you thinking?"

The third word came strangely from Reverend Wallace's mouth.

"I thought I was returning to the warm cuddle of God's forgiveness," Gaviel replied.

The two of them were facing the Mulesboro Municipal Floral Clock. Matthew had told the demon that he needed to talk right away and suggested it as a place where they could do so unobserved.

It was an overcast, chilly autumn afternoon, and most people were at home with a good book, a load of laundry or a pre-game football show. Sitting on a wood bench overlooking withered flowers and a stilled fountain, the pair could watch the dark clouds boiling across the sky.

"God commands us to be as innocent as doves but as wise as serpents," the reverend said. "Matthew, Chapter Ten. I'm willing to help you, but I haven't forgotten what you are."

"What does that mean?"

"It means I'm not willing to hand over my entire congregation."

"Hand over? I hardly think they're yours to dispense."

"I don't want you there."

"It's too late for that."

"I know, and I think that's exactly why you did it." Matthew turned on the bench and glared at the devil beside him. "I think you knew that if you did it in front of the entire congregation—"

"In front of God and everybody?"

"—that I'd be forced to take you back. That I'd have no choice but to invite you back in and let you be a part of the faith life of the church."

"And what's so wrong with that?" Matthew turned away from the defiant face beside him. "You'd prefer it if I just sit in the back of the salvation bus? After all the decent Christian gluttons and hypocrites are done worshipping, I can meet you—their *adulterous* minister—to accept their leftovers? I think you've got the church confused with your marriage, Reverend."

"You go too far!"

Gaviel raised his hands. "Sorry, sorry. It's just infuriating to see other sinners receiving relief while I'm left on the outside, nose pressed against the glass."

"That's not the issue. You're trying to distract me. I know we're not perfect—I know *I'm* not perfect—but don't try and sidetrack me from what really matters."

"My salvation through Jesus Christ doesn't really matter?"

"What really matters is that they all think you're Noah Wallace, the boy they grew up with, *my son*, while I know you're—"

"Don't." The demon held up his hand and glanced across the landscape as lightning flickered from cloud to cloud. "Don't say the name," he whispered, and the thunder rolled in.

Matthew glanced out at the clouds and then back at his companion. There was an uncertain look on the minister's face. Did he...? "I'm not impressed by cheap theatrics," he grumbled.

"But your viewers are, aren't they?"

"You leave *them* out of this," Matthew said, his protective instincts roused again.

"Actually, that was snide. I apologize again. But you must admit, the return of the lost lamb is a riveting trope. Makes for some good TV."

"My *ministry* is not *theater*! Don't think you can influence me just by dangling ratings in front of my nose."

"It's only theater if my return is insincere. Do you think it is?"

There was a long, quiet moment. "I don't know," Matthew said at last. "I think that if you wanted to fool me, you probably could. If you wanted to *make* me trust you, you could probably just do that, couldn't you?"

Gaviel nodded. "But I didn't."

"You didn't. So I have to make up my own mind."

"Burdensome, isn't it?"

They sat in silence for a while, then Gaviel asked, "What are we going to do about Zola?"

"You stay away from her!" Matthew answered.

Gaviel just nodded. Zola was Noah's mother, Matthew's wife.

There was more silence. "I guess we have to tell her something," Matthew said at last. He was thinking how much it would hurt her if her son returned to him but scorned her.

Gaviel nodded again.

"She wouldn't believe the truth."

"I could show her. Like I showed you."

"It would break her heart."

"Oh?"

"Knowing that her son was..." Matthew gave Gaviel another suspicious glare. He didn't mean to, but when he thought that the demon might be somehow holding his son prisoner... Gaviel claimed that Noah was dead, but Matthew clung to his doubts, which were also his hopes.

"Let us say 'unavailable,'" Gaviel finished for him. "It would be a terrible strain. Especially right after seeing him return."

"After *thinking* she did. You are not my son. Remember that, okay? Whatever you are, you are not my son."

The devil took this in silence. But like the minister, he began to frown.

"So why here?" Gaviel asked at last.

"Sorry?"

"Why meet at the floral clock?"

Matthew shrugged. "Father Warwell showed it to me," he said, nodding at the church on the corner behind them. "We were working together on the interfaith food-pantry drive—"

There was a soft *whump* sound behind them. A moment later, Matthew frowned and asked, "Do you smell smoke?"

It was too late for Rosemary Nevins.

She'd come out to Hollywood like a thousand other pretty American girls, dreaming of stardom but waking up to waitress jobs. Instead of swimming pools, they wound up in typing pools. Instead of the envious gaze of the fans, they caught the cynical eye of spinster landladies who'd seen it all before and had found a good, parasitic niche selling space to this year's crop of hopeful dreamers.

Rosemary Nevins had wanted stardom, but it was too late.

Many of the girls, shiny bright and magnetic, drawn to LA's iron inflexibility, found other dreams to chase. Dreams of marriage, motherhood or even just independence on their own terms. Some dreamed those dreams real, and some were happier that way than they would have been as stars, distant, trapped in the telescope gaze of producers, directors and fans.

But for Rosemary Nevins, it was too late for those lesser, realer dreams.

No few would-be starlets went from dream to nightmare. Too unstable or silly, or worse somehow, too proud to be ordinary, some girls scorned part-time jobs and standard romance and the dreadfulness of being *normal*. They found prostitution or drugs or other marginal, criminal lives, and they hated themselves and everyone around them, but more, hated the thought of being defeated. Even as they popped pills in by-the-hour motels or endured the stink and shame of a bang against an alley wall, they reached for the dream, planned their comeback, imagined the scene's description in their unauthorized biography.

Rosemary Nevins would not achieve even that fate.

Instead, she would gain fame at last, but only after her life's last moments. Her picture would appear in the papers, and her name would whisper from lip to Angelino lip in hushed and confidential tones: "Rosemary Nevins. The fifth victim of the Hollywood Ice Pick."

She died in 1957.

The two Wallaces, Matthew and Noah—or, perhaps, Matthew Wallace and the demon in his son's body—stood and turned when they heard the crackle of flames. Matthew took a moment to stare while Gaviel immediately bolted toward the church.

When he recovered from his shock, Matthew's first instinct was to mutter, "No, not again." He started to say a prayer as he dug out his cell phone. He paused in the middle to dial *911 and say that St. Timothy's in Mulesboro was on fire. He stayed on the line with the dispatcher as he ran across the street, where he could see a few people staggering out, eyes wide, coughing. As

Matthew got closer he saw a woman talking to the demon and pointing. He heard her say, "Lynn! Lynn's in there, in the church office!"

Gaviel stripped off his jacket, flung it to the ground and ran toward the flaming door.

"Noah!" Matthew called. Then he started his prayer again.

Gaviel wasn't afraid of the fire. Previously, when he had been a minister of the world, flames had been like goldfish — something you tended to, something you ignored when inconvenient, something pretty to look at. They were not something that could actually *hurt* you.

Of course, Matthew had no way to know that — as Gaviel was well aware.

He felt the heat as he got closer, and a small smile crossed his face. He had Noah's instincts, human instincts, the fear of the blaze, but he wasn't human. When he spoke, the words were in the primal tongue of reality itself. Then he frowned.

The flames had refused his order to step aside. His imprisonment had been long and horrible and he'd lost much, but surely his sovereignty over fire…

Again he spoke his words beyond words, a question this time.

The flames grew brighter and hotter, despite his request to the contrary. He glanced over his shoulder and saw Matthew, and that decided him.

"It's only heat," he muttered, then took a clean breath and charged into the burning church.

What got him first were his eyes — a dirty and immediate pain started digging into his sockets. Next he felt his lungs seize up as the smoke filled them. He coughed and, prompted by one of Noah's vague fire-safety memories, dropped down low, where the air should be better.

Me, kneeling to fire. That's ironic, he thought as his hands and knees blistered. With an irritated grimace, he repaired them. Another frown, and the shape of Noah Wallace was cast aside.

Gaviel's true form—a body of sculpted light and majesty— was both more and less comfortable than Noah's flesh and blood. It was a relief to be free of that mortal shell with its hungers and farts and instinctive fears, but to become a god incarnate in an agnostic world was no easy feat. He could feel the weight of logic and reason smothering his grandeur, just as the smoke and flame had smothered his body. But he could bear the load... for a while.

Wings of sunset swept him forward at a sprinter's pace, then faster still. He guided himself, not by human senses, but by an angel's instinct for worship. There was only one source remaining in the building—a weak source—and it wasn't in the church office but the women's bathroom.

Plowing through the door, he saw a woman standing by the sink, splashing water all over herself and coughing hard. She looked up at him with panicked eyes and said, "I want to live!"

You sure picked the wrong place to be, then, Gaviel thought, but what he said was, "HOLD ONTO ME!"

Even at her most calm, the woman could not have refused that call. Driven by terror, she clung like a limpet.

Stupid-ass bitch, Gaviel thought as he swept them through the church proper. The smoke was lighter here, and the pews had not yet caught flame. The woman (Lynn, he assumed) was clutching him and weeping hysterically. He resumed his human shape as they reached a back door.

He staggered out and nearly ran face-first into a firefighter.

"Here, take her!" he said, shoving Lynn at the woman in the red helmet.

"Your pants are on fire!" the firefighter said, pointing at Noah's smoldering trouser cuff.

"Damn," he said, coughing. "These are Italian."

Then he said, "Ooh."

Then, unexpectedly, he passed out.

When Joellen O'Hanlon walked down the street, she ignored the whispers and the occasional catcall. She was used to it.

"Hey, crazy lady!"

Teenagers, mostly. They did the yelling. Most of them too young to remember, ignorant of the truth (but they were all ignorant of the truth, young and old, all of them except her and her son, and even he didn't know it all), only acting out in public what their parents muttered in private.

She went into the grocery store and concentrated. Joellen didn't make much money, and it was hard enough to get by stretching coupons and food stamps and cash. Even if you were good at math, it would be tricky to figure the best deal. Is it the store brand of oat cereal, which was a dollar cheaper when you bought a smaller box, or the bigger box of Cheerios with a dollar coupon? She had her list and her calculator, she had $40 worth of food stamps and $11.15 in cash, so she could buy $51.15 worth of food and not one cent more. She had to count, keep careful track, add and subtract, and people muttered as they watched her writing numbers and erasing them. They thought she was crazy, but all she really was was poor.

Her son, Black Hawk, always wanted to shop for her, bless his heart, but she wouldn't let him. She wasn't going to give in and let the whisperers make her hide. Let them hiss behind their hands. Let them make her blush and feel stupid and weak and cry herself to sleep some nights. She knew the truth and they didn't.

More, she knew they were afraid when they looked at her.

Gaviel woke up irritated, as he often did. He didn't care for sleep. As an angel, he'd never needed it, and wasting eight hours a day incommunicado seemed terribly inefficient to him. He knew humans needed the rest to knit up bodily injuries and to process unresolved psychological conflicts, but he could deal with physical harm directly. As for psychology, none of his battles on that field were internal.

Matthew was sitting in a chair in what Noah's memories identified as a hospital room.

"Are you all right?" the minister asked, but his wonderfully expressive voice wasn't full of concern. It was guarded. Not quite suspicious, but... close.

"I think it's pretty clear that I'm not," Gaviel replied. "But don't worry. I'll mend fast."

"There are reporters who want to talk to you."

"Pah," Gaviel made a dismissive gesture. "Please, no."

Matthew nodded. Then, squinting, he said, "Lynn Culver told the paramedics that an angel rescued her."

Gaviel's face and voice were as cool as iced tea in July. "Sounds like hysteria to me. Or smoke inhalation. Or some combination thereof."

"What did you do there?"

"Isn't that obvious? I went into the church and dragged Ms. Culver out." Wincing, he sat up. "And I must say, she could use a couple hours a week at the gym."

"Why?"

"Well, because she's carrying at least twenty extra pounds and... oh, you mean why rescue her?" Gaviel shook his head. "You'd prefer it if I left her to broil in her own hamfat?"

"I suppose you're used to flames."

"Matthew, come here." As the minister moved nearer, Gaviel pulled up his nightshirt to reveal blisters on his shoulders and back.

"How'd that...? I mean..."

On the spur of the moment, Gaviel decided to lie. "Do you remember what happened the first time I touched *your* church?"

"You burned."

"Holy ground, father."

"Then..."

Gaviel waited while Matthew figured it out.

The reverend took a deep breath, then stopped, then squared his shoulders and said, "I'm only going to ask this once: What *really* happened at that church?"

"I thought you saw."

"I mean..." Matthew bit his lips, then said, "You didn't have anything to do with it?"

"What?" Gaviel's question was very, very quiet.

"You have to admit, it's pretty suspicious."

Gaviel said nothing, just stared, face blank.

"I mean, just as you're trying to convince me that you're back on the straight and narrow, trying to come back to God, there's this perfect chance for you to save a life and look like a hero. Come on, anyone would think it."

"Come here."

Matthew edged closer. Gaviel reached out and slapped him across the face.

"I don't *believe* you!" he said. "You think I burned that church to *show off*? You pathetic, suspicious little worm! Ignoring the fact that *you* picked where we were going and the fact that I hurt myself for a *mortal* and the impossibility of me knowing that anyone would be too *stupid* to escape, do you really think that you could *outsmart me*? That if I wanted to impress you that I'd try such a hackneyed charade? Lucifer's wounds, rescuing someone from a burning building? That's so derivative it would make a B-list Hollywood screenwriter roll his eyes! If you can't grant me heroism, at least credit me with some *subtlety!*"

"Look, I'm sorry, but—"

"Get out of here!"

"I just—"

"BEGONE!"

And like Lynn, Matthew obeyed without question.

The reverend felt guilty for accusing Gaviel, but he told himself he was dealing with a *devil*, that he was right to be suspicious. The thought that the demon had done it nagged at him every time he saw a news report about the church burning—the first in the county since 1999. It tormented him when he tried to sleep, and he wrestled with it when he preached sermons against racism and hate and division.

Two weeks later, a man named George Lasalle walked into the Mulesboro police station, side by side with Father Deon Warwell, and confessed to the arson.

The police arrested Tim Grady in September of 1957. They tried to keep it quiet, but the Hollywood press had a thousand ears to hear and bottomless pockets to pay for dirt. A scandal-sheet extra announced the capture of the Hollywood Ice Pick more than twenty-four hours before the cops did. By that time, every paper in town had printed its exclusive—his landlord, his neighbors, the officer who'd processed him, anonymous sources close to the arrest and in the DA's office. One enterprising reporter even talked to prisoners in Grady's same jail, and when the drunks and hopheads and wife-beaters told him only that Grady was in isolation and the guards seemed more tense than usual, he made up salacious rumors about strange threats and scuffles and unusual injuries, then printed a retraction five days later, buried in the classifieds and apologizing for trusting slick, lying criminals.

When the buzz of sensation and publicity cleared, the real Tim Grady was revealed. He wasn't the monster everyone had feared and privately wanted him to be—no woolly-haired giant Negro with a murderous lust for white women, no beatnik pot-smoking communist Jew. Just a little man with a bland face, flat features and mild, pleasant brown eyes.

He was quiet, kept mostly to himself—no, even the label of loner wouldn't stick, because Grady was known and liked in his neighborhood. At least, he was liked until he was accused of murdering five beautiful young girls by stabbing their left eyes out with an ice pick. Even after, there were a few who defended him: a man whom Grady had helped to move heavy furniture up steps, a woman to whom he'd given rides to the store when her car was in the shop. They said the police had the wrong man, that Tim Grady was no killer.

But he was.

Gaviel had visited Lynn Culver in the hospital once, but they hadn't talked long. She'd been doped up, and he'd been in a bit of a hurry that day. The first time he went to her apartment, after Lasalle's confession, he was much more relaxed.

"You really don't need to keep checking on me," she said as she ushered him in and offered him coffee. He waved off the drink and sat.

"Have you heard about the ancient Chinese belief that when you save someone's life, you're responsible for them thereafter?"

She wrinkled her nose. "Shouldn't it be that *they're* responsible for *you*?" He shrugged. She sat too, stirring a coffee cup that had a teddy bear printed on it.

"How are you doing?" he asked.

"Oh, well, I still have a pretty bad cough," she said, and her gravelly voice lent the claim credence. "All in all, though, I can't complain. Thanks to you. What about you?"

"Full recovery." For some reason, the urge to end that statement with *praise the Lord* floated up through Noah and was only bitten off at the front of his mouth.

"That's nice." For a moment they sat in silence.

"Have you met George Lasalle yet?" Gaviel asked. Lynn suddenly seemed to have trouble drinking her coffee.

"Um, no," she said. "No, I haven't."

"I understand he's been attending services quite regularly."

"Yes, it's really something."

"Quite a conversion. Not so surprising after Reverend Warwell spoke up for him at the trial, but still..."

"Yes."

Another pause.

"He got a suspended sentence, right?" Gaviel asked.

"That's right, yes. Conditional on, you know, counseling and... uh, good behavior. I guess."

"Very quick trial."

"Well, they, you know, I heard they wanted it taken care of quickly. To quell any... tensions. In the community. You know?"

"Oh, I know," Gaviel replied. "White man burns a church with a black minister? Yeah, I know about the 'tensions in the community.'" He tilted his head. "Have you forgiven him?"

"Well, I... I mean, I..."

"You were the only person hurt in the fire. It could look like you were holding out. You know, holding a grudge."

"I certainly don't... I mean, I... you know..."

"Can you forgive him, Lynn?"

"Of course," she said weakly, too quick, not meeting his eyes.

He leaned in. "Or is it that you don't think he needs forgiveness?"

"Every… everyone needs forgiveness," she said.

"Even for sins they didn't commit? Crimes of which they are innocent?"

"What do you mean?"

"Did you hear about an angel coming to George Lasalle? Telling him to confess to the crime?"

"No." Her voice was barely a whisper.

"He must not have told many people." He leaned back again but kept his eyes fixed upon her. "And you told the paramedics that an angel rescued you."

She gave a short, unnatural laugh. "Well I… I inhaled a lot of smoke. I was pretty worked up. I know it was you, now. Really. I mean, I know it was really you that saved me."

"Is that what you saw? Me?"

She said nothing.

"Is that *all* you saw?"

Her lower lip began to tremble.

"What do you want?" she asked, her voice low, pressed down by awe and terror.

"All I ask is that you believe."

Chapter Two

Charles Rodriguez didn't like the new kid, Mitch. Mitch was a gringo, which wasn't a phrase Charles (who was "Chuck" to his intimates and friends) used with every Anglo he knew. Lots of whites were all right, perfectly fine, good people. Some of them had a certain unearned assurance and arrogant blindness about them, though, a false sense that they were exempt from the perils to which others were subject. A few whites had that vibe, that easy sneering confidence that said, "Everything has always gone my way, and it always will." That (in Charles's eyes) made them goddamn gringos.

Even gringos could be okay in the right circumstances. If you didn't take them too seriously or expect them to return your calls, they could be fun; could get you into good clubs and parties. Chuck had even dated a gringa chick for a while, and (as he'd told his buddies) the bedroom was a great place to be fool-proud and careless.

But Chuck, and now Mitch, worked at an asylum for the criminally insane, and that was a bad, bad place for misplaced white-skin confidence.

Mitch had already told Charles how much he could bench-press and how many girls he was dating. Mitch had been a prison guard in Colorado but had come out to Los Angeles to break into movies. Charles just nodded at these revelations and went on showing the new kid around the asylum. They were almost done.

"This is the infirmary," he said. "This is where we bring sick patients."

"I thought they were all pretty sick," Mitch said, half-laughing at his own joke. "You know, like that one guy you were telling me about with the dogs? That's pretty sick, y'ask me."

"When a patient seems ill, he's placed in four-point restraints on a gurney and brought down here while the on-call doctor comes in. Two guards put him in restraints, minimum. The bite plate goes on and stays on."

"Just like Hannibal Lecter, right?"

"One guard stays with the restrained patient at all times. If the doctor decides he's too sick to return to the population, he's placed in one of the quarantine cells here. Can you give shots and put in an IV?"

"Sure, I got the certificate for that."

"Good. Sickroom duty is usually okay, long as you're careful about the body fluids. It's only the freshies you gotta look out for." Chuck had explained the concept of freshies already. A freshy was a new patient, one who hadn't had a chance to get used to his new residence. One who hadn't had time to grow soft and weak on a starchy diet and a regimen of sedatives and little exercise.

Mitch nodded. He looked bored. Charles felt like he shouldn't care, but some part of him wanted the little punk ass to be impressed.

"Here's our most famous inmate," he said, gesturing to the infirmary's Cell Two. "Take a look."

Mitch was gratifyingly cautious as he peeked through the wire-reinforced glass on. Then he frowned.

"That old fuck? Who is he?"

"That's Tim Grady."

"Who?"

"Tim Grady, man! The Hollywood Ice Pick?" Seeing Mitch's confused look, Chuck shook his head. "He killed five women in the '50s. Jabbed their eyes out! Claimed in court they'd all asked him to do it. He's been here ever since."

"So he's what, seventy? Whoo-hoo, I'm real scared."

"Yeah, he ain't much now. The doctors here, they been doing a real job on him. For the first three months he was here, he was getting electroshock every week. Once he quit trying to escape all the time, they dropped it back to every month, but they didn't stop jolting him until 1959. He tried to run away three more times in the '60s and '70s—the last time he even made it far as the front gate before he got spotted by a part-time cook who remembered him from the papers."

"Yeah? So he was some kind of badass?"

In the light of Mitch's interest, Chuck warmed to his story and relaxed his formal tone. "Back in the day, yeah. Fought his way out of a three-nurse pileup once, ran down the hall and got halfway through a reinforced window before they sedated him again. In the '70s they started keeping him drugged all day, only letting him pace his cell at night." Charles scratched his head. "That was after he stopped talking, I think. Turned into a total caveman. They figured out that it was women set him off—old women, young, whatever—so they doped him during the day when there were ladies around and made sure to only hire guys for the night staff. His chart makes for some interesting reading."

"He sure don't look like much now."

"Yeah, he ain't done much in the last twenty years. He'll have a freak-out every now and again, but he's so old and frail that he can't even do that right. He got cancer in the '90s, and they had to do a bunch of surgeries on him. He's in remission now, but that took a lot of the fight out of him. Whenever he gets sick, he can't shake it, so they put him in here."

Mitch frowned. "I'd've thought they'd keep a sickly guy like that in the infirmary all the time. I mean, this is where all the sick people go, right?"

"Well, you know Dr. Gould, the chief of staff? He's been here forever, and I heard Grady got at him during his last escape attempt, back in '76. Supposedly, that's why Gould walks with that cane."

The two orderlies paused for a silent moment, looking in at the peacefully resting form of Tim Grady. Neither thought anyone was watching them.

But someone was.

Back at his apartment, Gaviel looked around. Such a human place. He didn't care for it. Too much clutter. And dust. He dusted every week, but his keen senses still saw it everywhere. He'd have to simplify—getting rid of the stereo and CDs would be a good start.

He sat on the futon. For a moment, he just sat, back straight, hands on his knees palms up. He sat and thought, doing nothing *but* thinking, in a way that most humans could if they wanted, but which most were too impatient to pursue.

He was contemplating his situation.

Matthew suspects me, he thought. *Despite my best efforts. But I've worn him down. He'll permit me to work in his church, grudgingly. I'll have to go slowly there. And I'll have to backslide so that he keeps his confidence, and so that he has a chance to invest himself in saving me. Once he does that, it will blind him.*

Unlike most humans, Gaviel could also think wordlessly, contemplating facts and issues without using the crutch of a verbal framework. For about five minutes, he did that.

Lynn has poor faith, but it's enough for a little while, he thought, when he'd decided that verbal thinking was again a useful organizational tool. *I must get better worshippers eventually, but for now, more like her will suffice.*

When Lynn had opened herself to him, believing fully, it had been bittersweet. Inside her was a faded, guttering spark — a pale ghost of the light that emanated from God the Most High. Before his rebellion, it had been Gaviel's duty to shape the light of God's will into forms that could safely touch upon material reality. The faint glow of will within Lynn Culver was so very close to nothing... but then, so was she. Reorganizing her untapped potential had been fairly simple once Gaviel accustomed himself to working on such a miniature scale. With her willing faith, he'd been able to give her the strength to resist her personal "demons" — alcohol, impulsiveness, habitual shame and self-hatred, the puppet master behind her problems. He showed her own light to her and told her it was from God — which was not even a lie, really. But if she'd known it was in her all the time, she would never have believed.

He'd stolen half of it and returned the rest, and she'd thanked him profusely.

They'd also had a long discussion in which they decided it would be best for her to move far away — Minnesota, perhaps — and start over without so many memories dogging her shadow. With her newfound, newly given, strength of character, she had the courage to do so.

She would, of course, publicly forgive George Lasalle before going.

Gaviel hungered for stronger faith — more to steal and consume, but also more to work with. Lynn was poor stuff, unfit material for a celestial artist. Matthew Wallace, however... Gaviel could reshape Matthew's soul into that of a hero, a savior, nearly a god on Earth. Or he could drain it deeply and grow fat and powerful.

If Matthew would let him.

He sighed, then frowned. He didn't like sighing when there was no one around. It was all right as a nonverbal emotional control gambit, but doing it by oneself smacked of humanity. That was the last thing he needed.

He leaned forward over his coffee table and opened the rolled-up paper bag upon it. He removed its contents and put them neatly on the table. It wasn't much: a tinfoil ashtray he'd picked up at Denny's and a package of Camel cigarettes.

There was no lighter, nor were there matches.

Noah hadn't been a smoker, before. He'd tried it once or twice but didn't like the thought of his teeth turning yellow.

Gaviel tamped down the filter and stared at the tip of the cigarette. Then he addressed it, once more speaking the primal language of the cosmos.

Nothing happened. He tried again, different words, different phrasing.

Still no response. He spoke again, trying charm this time.

Nothing.

There was a distinctly uncomfortable sensation in Gaviel's mind—something alien to his experience as an angel, but one he knew from his imprisonment in Hell. He had hoped that his return to the physical world would mean the renewal of his full faculties, but clearly that was not the case.

It was infuriating.

He was not a creature made for loss of any type, but it was increasingly obvious to him. He'd forgotten how to talk to fire.

Mitch Berger really didn't much care for Charles Rodriguez. The guy seemed touchy and uptight and badly in need of an enema—or, as they called it out here, a "high colonic." Any time

Mitch said something to him, Chuck just gave him a look like he (Rodriguez, that is) was about to take a nap. Sometimes he threw in a sad little head-shake, too.

Mitch didn't much care—there were a lot of orderlies at the asylum, and the schedule juggling didn't leave him and Chuck together often. And it wasn't like the guy was incompetent or anything, just *boring*.

They stayed separated for most of Mitch's first two months, but they both drew infirmary duty one night. The infirmary, like most orderly posts, was staffed in overlapping eight-hour shifts—when you signed in, your partner had already been there four hours, and he checked out after another four. That way, there was always one alert, fresh guard on duty. In theory.

In practice, most duties at the asylum were mind-death boring almost all of the time and horrible in one way or another during the remainder. Still, it paid a lot better than flipping burgers.

Rodriguez already looked tired when Mitch came in.

"Yo," Mitch said. "What up?"

Chuck gave him That Look. "We got a freshy in room five," he said. "He's got some kind of stomach flu."

"Wait," Mitch said. "Don't tell me. It's Squirt, isn't it?"

Charles gave a tired nod. Mitch cursed quietly.

Dean "Squirt" Ellis was a five-foot-two, one-hundred-forty-pound homeless schizophrenic and scatophile who didn't respond well to medication. He'd gotten his nickname not only from his size, but from his habit of chewing up a mixture of his own feces and urine, then spraying it from his mouth at the asylum staff. He was not well liked.

"Please tell me he's sedated."

"He's sedated," Charles said. "He's s'*posed to* come out of it in the morning, but given the track marks he had when he came in, I wouldn't be surprised if he shakes it off early."

"Cripes. Stomach flu you said?"

"Not real surprising, is it? Given his diet."

"An' I bet he ain't real careful where he pukes, either."

"Oh no, he aims. He aims."

Mitch gave Charles a surprised look, then laughed. Chuck laughed a little too, and both men relaxed a little, even though they hadn't realized they were tense.

"There's more, too," Charles said.

"What, Squirt's got AIDS or something?"

"No, it's the Ice Pick. He had a fit this afternoon."

"Yeah? What kind?"

"Usual manic episode—moaning, running around, flailing his arms and banging his head."

"They sedate him too?"

"Yeah, but nothing heavy-duty. After the cancer recovery, they had a real scare with phentobarbital—almost stopped his heart. It was touch-and-go for a while. Lucky for him Dr. Gould wasn't around. Anyhow, since then, all we've used on him is diazepam, but he's so used to it he can toss it after a couple hours. Sometimes he shifts over into REM sleep, but you can't rely on it."

"Whee."

The two men sat and filled out some paperwork, but mostly they kept an eye on Cells Two and Five.

Mitch had been there three hours when Tim Grady started to moan.

"Damn it," he muttered, standing. "Time to prick the Pick."

"You want me to take it?" Charles asked.

"I'll do it."

"I don't mind. I'll be out of here in an hour—you still got five."

"Thanks, man."

"Hey, it'll wake me up for the ride home." Charles unlocked the medication cabinet, prepped the sedative shot, then locked the cabinet up again.

As he was unlocking the door to Cell Two, Grady fell silent. Chuck paused.

"You think he knows you're coming?" Mitch asked.

"Could be," Charles said, frowning.

Then Mitch turned quickly, looking behind his back down a long, dim hallway.

"What?" Charles said.

"You hear something?"

"Nuh uh."

For a moment, both men just stood, alert, staring. Neither said anything, but both competently palmed their canisters of pepper spray.

Nothing.

Finally, Charles broke the silence. "Okay, I guess I'll go take care of Mr. Grady."

"You want me to back you up?"

At that moment, they heard stirring from inside Cell Five.

"Fuck," Mitch said. "Should we get backup?"

Charles looked in the window at Squirt. "He's still in the straps," he said, shrugging. "Must be a full moon."

"All right. You take care of Shady Grady. I got your back."

Charles unlocked Cell Two while Mitch stood behind him, shifting his glance warily between the two occupied rooms. Then, when the door opened, he heard something again—a quiet fleshy slap from down the hall.

He looked, and this time he saw.

She was naked, barefoot on the grubby linoleum, making no attempt to cover herself. Her features were lovely, as were her red-gold locks, lustrous even in the washed-out fluorescent light. Her skin was pale as cream, or leprosy.

Mitch just stared, stunned. *But there are no female inmates*, he thought. Then he thought it again.

She didn't come any closer, and he saw a tear mar her stark, sad, beautiful visage. A strangely dark tear, almost chocolate brown in the harsh, buzzing tube-light. But he knew, somehow, that the tear was blood.

"Charles, come out here man," he said.

"Charles?"

He only took his eyes off her for a moment to look back at Cell Two. Just a glance, back and forward again, then he just stood there while he bobbed his head around twice more, trying to process two unthinkable thoughts at once.

The first was that Charles was slumped in the open doorway.

The second was that the woman was gone.

Black Hawk O'Hanlon—"Blackie" to just about everyone—made pretty good money as a journeyman electrician. He ran conduit and tested circuits and paid his union dues even though money was tight. He couldn't afford to be a scab—people were wary enough about hiring an O'Hanlon as it was. Times were never great for him and Mama, but now they were really feeling the pinch. Construction had slowed down lately. People blamed the stock market, the Arabs, the Republicans and Democrats. Privately, Blackie thought they'd just built too many goddamn buildings when there weren't enough people around, but he kept that to himself. Working in the construction trades, you didn't really want to badmouth growth.

In any event, the jobs were thinning out, and he had to work twice as hard and twice as well to make people feel good about hiring "one o' them crazy O'Hanlons."

When he'd been a teenager, Blackie had resented his mama, his grandpa, the whole family, the whole family thing. He didn't ask to be born from a pack of hayseeds without the good sense to go to the same church as everyone else. He just wanted to be normal, but instead he grew up hearing about his granddad and uncles shooting it out with the cops and FBI and state troopers.

It had happened during May of 1981, so it hadn't gotten a lot of national news play. (People wanted to hear about the Pope getting shot, not some kooky rednecks playing Cowboys and Indians with Johnny Law.) He'd been five years old, and it was mostly a jumble of sensations in his memory: the noise, the broken glass, the smell of gunpowder all through granddad's farmhouse. He thought he'd seen blood (when he thought about it at all, these days, and he tried very hard not to think about it), but the only part he remembered clearly was Mama carrying him out. It had been a really bright day, and he'd been blinded by the sun after staying in with the curtains drawn. He remembered, too, the look of hatred and terror on Mama's young face, the feeling of her gingham check dress under his hand as he clung to her and she came out waving her free hand, screaming, screaming something at the cops.

"Hey long-hair. Blackie! Earth to O'Hanlon!"

"I heard you the first time, Bill," Blackie said, lifting a layer in his very tidy toolbox. He handed a Multimeter to the other electrician. "What happened to yours, anyhow?"

"The boy got into it, dropped it down the basement steps."

"You really ought to keep your kid out of your workshop."

"That's rich."

"What?"

"You giving me child-raising advice." Then Bill looked up, a sudden, jerky movement. "I mean, on account of you not having any kids of your own! That's, that's all I meant, Blackie."

O'Hanlon nodded. All of a sudden, he felt tired.

The two men worked quietly for a while, checking the connections where the office cubicles would go, and when Bill was done with the Multimeter, he thanked Blackie more politely than usual.

Bill was older than Black Hawk. If he hadn't grown up around the O'Hanlons, Bill probably would have been very angry about the FBI at Ruby Ridge and the ATF at Waco. Not to the point of joining a militia, but probably he'd have gone as far as talking about them approvingly.

Initially, Bill and his father and older brothers had been loudly indignant about the way the Feds (or, as some derisively called them back in the '80s, the Revenuers) had treated the O'Hanlons, who were just minding their own business, weren't doing anybody any harm.

Then the FBI found the bodies in the O'Hanlons' back soybean field. Drifters, transients and runaways, apparently. Over the next few years, identifications were slowly made. None were local to Tennessee, leading to speculation that Blackie's uncles had traveled as far as Iowa and Florida looking for people to kill.

"So, Blackie. You get hired for the Lanwell job?"

O'Hanlon shook his head. "I guess they don't need so many."

"You want me to put in a good word for you?"

"Yeah, that'd be all right."

"Better you than some scab, right?"

"Thanks, Bill."

At that moment, the site foreman came around the corner. "Blackie?" he called. "You better come down here."

"What is it?"

"Phone call. Something's happened to your mama."

Going to church wasn't easy for Gaviel. Every time he stepped inside, he felt the scalding heat of faith. Taut lines of powerful belief knotted at that place, lines anchored deep in the past and stretched out across Missouri. Those tight strong threads convulsed when he disturbed them, excoriating him, *hating* him, knowing him as a thing that should not be.

But he kept going. Week after week he went for *The Hour of Jesus' Power*, secretly (shamefully) glad it was so short. He could take it. He could handle sixty little minutes of the world's anger. After all, he'd handled Hell.

And when it was over—ah, that was the sweetest time. When he could walk out knowing he'd faced it, faced God's anger (or, at least, humankind's profound faith in God's anger, which was not nearly the same thing but still painful) and that it was *impotent*. He was still there, still standing. He had violated the holy sanctum and emerged again, insolent and whole. Perhaps the bottoms of his feet were charred in his shoes, and all the meat on his bones sore and stinging from the radiant rage, but that was simple to fix outside. Just a shrug and a twitch, and his borrowed flesh was good as new.

That moment of triumph was his second favorite part, and the *very* best thing was right after.

Matthew proceeded out of the church first, with his acolytes behind and then the choir (led by Matthew's mistress, Gina Parris) singing a variety of zesty hymns that all sounded the same to Gaviel. He came out after them and quietly stood behind Matthew, with Zola, as the parishioners emerged to shake the minister's hand and mouth faithful platitudes and make teasing jokes about how they always knew Noah would grow out of his atheist phase.

Gaviel smiled and nodded, and in the privacy of his devil heart he examined their souls.

Too self-satisfied, he might think of one, a businessman who was prosperous but not rich, and who took *pride* in his fortune's modesty. Ronald Stone was a generous donor to the poor, who delighted in imagining himself as a benevolent god to them. He had faith, but it was not a faith untainted.

Another Gaviel might judge too afraid, looking at the weathered form of a woman who had suffered and endured much. Nana Flanders had buried her husband in World War II and lost her two sons as well—one guarding an embassy in Beirut and the other to alcoholism. She believed as well, but mostly because she'd given up on her world and clung to the hope of God's world. Hers was a warped faith—though not one he'd disdain to steal.

So many flawed, damaged people shuffled out into the sunshine, smiling and shaking hands, and he could sense how Matthew's words, the reverend's very presence, buoyed and bolstered them, giving their armor of faith an extra bit of spit and polish to resist another week's tarnish in the ordinary world. Lives half empty, but souls half full, and Gaviel watched and did nothing.

The business with Lynn worked out for the best, he thought. The sustenance he leached from her, even hundreds of miles away, was a mighty thin gruel, but it kept him from starving. He could watch the luscious feast of richer conviction pass him by and have the strength not to devour it. Indeed, he relished the denial, enjoyed the anticipation, basked in the knowledge that by waiting, he would make his ownership of them far more complete.

Ah—and now the fairest of them all, he thought, with something of an air of a dieter sniffing around outside a gourmet chocolate shop. The Carter family approached.

Valencia Carter had a good soul—solid and strong, buttressed by a lifetime of positive habits and love and meaningful family ties. Her faith was bright and uncomplicated and perhaps a little complacent, but all in all an impressive edifice of trust in the divine. Her husband Stefan was not quite so stout in his religion, but he was a decent man, intuitively generous and sensible, and his tendency toward kind actions made believing easier for him that it might otherwise have been. Both were fine believers, much better than Lynn, and either would make a fine treat for any demon cunning enough to divert their feelings from God to itself.

But Gaviel only had eyes for their daughter May.

May had gone to high school with Noah and had (he knew) labored hard under a terrible schoolgirl crush. Noah knew her as shy and quiet and homely and uncertain, but Gaviel could see inside. He could see that her faith had been tested and had survived, not with outside support (like her mother) or by a natural inclination that almost made belief lazy (like her father) but by simple, humble strength. May was genuinely modest, and she placed her trust completely in the Lord. She was simple and clean; unstained and pure.

"Good morning," he said to her, and she smiled shyly. She'd gotten her teeth fixed some time in the last six years.

"Hi, Noah," she whispered. Then the Carters were past, and the next family was shaking hands with the Wallaces. Matthew remembered their names as he remembered every parishioner's name, but Gaviel's eyes were on May as she walked away.

She looked back and inside he exulted.

Virginity is the ideal of those who want to deflower, he thought. It was something from Noah's mind, a quote from Karl Kraus, and upon consideration, the demon disregarded it as unimportant.

Blackie went to the hospital only to find his mother already sitting up and arguing with the doctor.

"...don't need your needles in my skin, invading me the way your ice-eyed asshole ancestors took this land from my people."

"Mama?" he asked. The doctor gave him a glance.

"Mr. O'Hanlon," he said, "If you could please ask your mother to take these?"

Blackie looked between the medical authority and the parental authority. "I've never met a man could make Mama take medicine she didn't want," he said. "You best just let her be."

The doctor glared at him. "Perhaps we should discuss this outside," he said.

They left Joellen talking to herself about totem guides and the Trilateral Commission.

"Your mother is clearly manic," the doctor began.

"Manic? That means excited, right?"

"Yes, she—"

"So why not just wait for her to calm down?"

"I'm afraid it's not that simple."

Blackie shrugged. "Look, I know she gets… spells. But she'll calm down if you let her go on for a while. Just come back in fifteen minutes, and she'll be out of steam."

"I don't think—"

"Why's she here? On the phone they said she collapsed?"

"Yes, she was in the supermarket when she apparently blacked out. She came to in the ambulance and has been haranguing anyone who'll listen."

"Do you know why she conked out?"

"We haven't been able to… not with her so frantic," the doctor said.

"But you still want to sedate her?"

The doctor paused. He wasn't that much older than Blackie, and had only completed his residency three months earlier.

"Fifteen minutes, huh?"

"I'll stay with her."

Joellen was still crabby when the doctor returned, but she consented to let him examine her and take a blood sample.

"This is all coming out of Medicaid, you hear me?" she said. "I ain't payin' for any of this out my own money!"

Nothing seemed to be wrong, and rather than let the doctor do more tests, she insisted on being released. He grudgingly agreed, though he pressured her strongly to see her own physician soon.

"What happened, Mama?" Blackie asked as he opened the car door for her.

"I can do it myself!" she replied, slapping at his hand. When they were inside the car, she lowered her voice. "I had a vision," she said.

Blackie got a sick, crawly feeling in his gut.

"I saw it son, the Lightning Tree, the Tree of Knowledge, the Tree of Nothingness... I felt it again for the first time in... in years and years."

Blackie swallowed and glanced over at his mother and felt helpless. When she wasn't around, he could almost dismiss her beliefs, which were a confusing amalgam of misremembered Native hooey, tabloid New-Ageism and murky muttering about the government picked up from the Vietnam and Desert Storm vets at the town's least reputable bar. When he was alone, he understood how people could call her crazy.

But when he was with her, hearing her voice, seeing her eyes... she didn't seem crazy. Not normal, certainly, but he'd felt that same vibe pouring from the eyes of the police when he came out of the farmhouse in 1981. He'd known it when his buddy Rick fell in love and then fell out of love and then found out the girl was pregnant. He'd heard it in Ronna Dunkirk's voice after her daddy died. He'd sensed it coming off people who'd been grabbed tight by tragedy or faith or joy or something else bigger than they were, something they couldn't resist or ignore. Maybe it was madness that had his mama in its grip, but he couldn't *feel* that. It didn't act like a delusion. The only things he'd seen with such power were things that were *more* real than the everyday, that were bigger and more important, not spooks and phantoms and imagination.

If he'd tried to explain what Joellen O'Hanlon believed — about the Tree and God and humanity and the whites and Indians — he'd have blushed and stammered and shown without speaking how ridiculous the ideas were.

But deep down, he believed them too. Not with full and forceful faith, but the way a child believes in the bogeyman under the bed. He believed against his will, and somehow when he fought it, the faith got stronger still.

"...got to leave, I can see it now. It's *in the world* now, Black Hawk."

"Wait," he said, braking at a red light and turning to look at her. "Leave? What do you mean, leave?"

"Pay attention, boy! You're always woolgathering, head in the clouds, no practical sense! We got to get our money together, pack our things and go! The tree is *here*! It's *awake*, or almost, and we have to go, have to help it."

"Go where?"

"West," she said. "To our ancestral lands."

(Joellen insisted that she and Black Hawk had Indian blood and, therefore, a right to be in America that few others possessed. She was rather murky about exactly what tribe they were from, but she insisted that her son's hair go uncut and, despite some struggles when he was a teenager, it was so. Unbound, it came down to his knees.)

"Where out west?"

"I'll find it. I'll know when the time comes. I'll see it, somehow." As he put on the parking brake in front of their house, she turned to him with her eyes bright. Joellen was a plain woman, and her face had more lines and more wear than most others in their forties, but at that moment, it was lit from within. Fired by faith, she was beautiful, not the way a woman is, but like a sunset.

"The High Priest is coming," she said, and she was radiant.

"Um, yeah..." her son weakly replied. "Let's go inside first."

"I'll go, I'm fine. I'll start packing. You get your stuff and meet me back here. Pack light! We can't bring much."

"Mama, do we have to go today?"

"Why not today? This is the day the Lord has made, let us rejoice and be glad in it!"

"Yeah, but... I mean, it's so sudden. I mean, you just had your, your thing in the grocery store."

"My *vision*, son, my *inspiration*! That's *why* we have to go now, don't you see it?"

"It just seems that... y'know, maybe I could finish off this job, save up a little more money... uh... sell off some of our stuff, maybe buy a truck instead of a car..."

She looked at him, and it was a look that would have made him flinch when he was eighteen. But now he was twenty-seven, he made more money than she did, and he'd faced worse things than stern glares.

Seeing his resolve she said, "Why don't I call Clara up? We'll talk it out in front of her and see what she thinks."

Immediately, Blackie felt better. Clara lived up the street, she was a wizened old great-grandmother who still made her own way and who didn't give a damn what anyone thought. Clara was (in Blackie's mind) one of the few stable elements in his mother's life, and she'd never given bad advice to either of them.

"That's a fine idea."

So they called her, and while Clara crept down the block with her walker (she wouldn't let anyone help her), Joellen started packing, frantically rushing around the house, upending boxes and jars looking for hidden money. She'd made a habit of hiding cash, squirreling away fives and even tens inside vases, under the coffee-maker, between the pages of a copy of the *Bhagavad-Gita* she'd gotten somewhere. She was also flinging her clothes into suitcases with wild abandon, wrapping up shoes in pantyhose and chucking them in boxes, dithering over whether she should take scrapbooks (because they might provide essential documents for the followers who were coming) or leave them (because they were ultimately only vain sentimentality, a distraction from the True Tree).

Blackie opened the door for Clara who took one look at the disarray within and said, "Ooee, your mama havin' one of her spells, then?"

He nodded.

"Clara!" Joellen said. "Thanks for coming. I need you to talk some sense into this stubborn mule boy of mine."

"I'll talk sense," Clara promised.

"Do you want some tea, or some lemonade or something?"

"Lemonade sounds nice, sugar."

While Joellen darted into the kitchen, Clara gingerly lowered herself onto the sofa while Blackie sat in a battered rocking chair facing it.

"Mama's got this idea," he said. "It's about the Tree."

"Oh Lawd, the Tree."

"Uh huh. She says she had a... you know, a vision of it. Out west. And she wants to go to it, right now."

"Oh my word."

Joellen bustled into the room, a tall glass of lemonade with ice on a plastic tray.

"Sorry about this, hon," she said, then picked up the glass and upended it into the back of the old woman's dress.

Clara shrieked and arched forward, just as anyone does when they unexpectedly get ice down their spine.

"Mama, why'd you—"

Blackie was astonished, but he was even more surprised when Joellen picked a paring knife off the tray and slit Clara's throat from ear to ear.

A nice woman in her thirties slowed down when she saw an old man by the side of the road. She was from out of town, and she'd gotten lost, and that maybe made her more receptive to helping him, because he looked more lost than she could ever be. Or perhaps she was hoping against hope that he was a local who could tell her how to get back on the highway. She'd been driving all night to get to her brother's funeral in Los Angeles and had been quietly berating herself for the last hour for not taking a plane.

"Hi," she called out hesitantly. "Can I... D'you need some help?"

He turned without poise, with the loose, unconsidered movements of an animal. Looking at the blankness of his wrinkled face, she had second thoughts. But then the man seemed to pull himself together. It was dramatic: Instead of the vacancy, a sharpness filled in his eyes and his posture straightened up. He walked cautiously toward the car.

"Yes, I... I hope you can," he said. His voice was strange, scratchy. "I don't know where I am, I... I got lost?"

Up close, she could see he was wearing gray clothes, pajamas maybe, and no shoes. Absently, she turned off the car radio.

He must have wandered away from an old folks' home, she thought. Part of her wished she'd ignored him, or better yet, never seen him in the first place, since saving him would certainly put her behind schedule again and she'd yawn all through the funeral. But she was a nice woman, and she knew she'd never forgive herself if she left a confused old man out wandering at... what, one in the morning?

She unlocked the door and, stiff and hesitant, he sat beside her.

"I'm *so* glad you happened along," he said, and something about his tone made her give him a quizzical look.

"Well, to tell you the truth, I'm lost myself."

"Oh my. Where are you trying to get?"

"Back on the highway, really."

"Ah. I think I can help you, though this has all changed so much since my day."

Maybe he's just entered a lucid phase, she thought, hope rallying within her.

"What about you? Are you from... er, where should I take you?"

"Just take a right up here... my, my, this all used to be dirt roads and nothing. I think the old Union Pacific station is still up ahead, though."

"Is the highway near that?"

"Mm hm." He looked down at the radio and started fiddling with it. She thought about asking him to stop, decided not to bother. He played with the slides of the air conditioner and pushed in the dashboard lighter.

"Just take a left here," he said.

"I don't see any signs for the highway."

"This is where I get out."

"But I don't see..." She looked around at the train station, searching for something that might be a group home. She heard the clunk as the lighter popped out, but paid it no mind until the old man jammed it against her neck.

She screamed and recoiled. Then she shoved him back, good and hard. He popped his door open and stumbled his way out, waving the orange-glowing lighter to keep her back. She slammed the car into reverse, not really thinking, and pulled away. He lurched off toward the switching yard.

Gingerly, she touched her neck, then pulled her fingers away. It hurt terribly. Tears of fear and pain and confusion welled up in her eyes and she quickly closed the passenger door. Then she locked herself in and kept searching for the highway.

Eventually, she found a 7-11, and the clerk inside gave her directions. He also let her use the phone to call the cops about the aged psycho who'd scalded her neck. She went to the funeral the next day exhausted and sad and bandaged, and she heard on the radio that she'd been attacked by an escaped mental patient—the infamous Hollywood Ice Pick.

The police descended on the Union Pacific station as fast as they could, but it had taken the nice woman a good twenty minutes to find the convenience store. By the time they arrived, Tim Grady was on a slow train hauling dry goods east.

Back when she was a teenager, Joellen O'Hanlon had worked the bleed rail at the local meat-packing plant. After the FBI raid, the slaughterhouse had quietly let her go.

That was years back, but the professional way she unzipped Clara's neck showed that, like riding a bicycle, throat-slitting was a skill one never really lost.

"Mama!"

"Now can we go?"

"Mama, *why*? She was your friend, why… *why*?"

"Friendship is nothin' next to the Tree. She's nothin' next to the Tree. None of us is *anything* next to the Tree. You wanna know why she's dead? Because you wouldn't get off your ass! Now you got a choice. You can hand me in, hand your own mother in to the cops, or you can light out quick before anyone misses her." As she spoke, Joellen went to the front window and closed the blinds.

"You did all them up in the soybean fields, didn't you?" Black Hawk asked it very quietly. It was something he and his mother had never, ever discussed.

"Some," she replied, very matter of fact. "Others your granddad killed." She went into the kitchen to wash her hands, though she'd made the cut so fast and clean that very little blood had spilled on her. No time.

Blackie sat there, stunned. He tried hard to think, but he couldn't think. The part of his brain that handled logic and reason was just shut down, shorted out, numb. He couldn't think but he had to decide.

Face blank, he got up off the recliner. Then he went out to his car and opened the trunk. Wordlessly, he and his mother began filling it with her things.

By eleven o'clock the next morning, Mitch and Charles were drinking beers at O'Fallon's Tap, the nearest place that would serve them that early.

"It's a raw deal, man," Charles said.

"A raw *fuckin'* deal," Mitch agreed. He'd been put on indefinite suspension, pending a review of his actions the night before.

Charles had shaken Mitch's hand the first day they met, and hadn't touched him since. Now he reached over and clapped the other man on the shoulder.

"Listen. If you'd chased down the Ice Pick and I'd been... you know, if there'd been a bubble or, or something... they'd have *still* bitched you out and I'd be *dead*. Maybe." Chuck was having trouble putting his thoughts in order. He still couldn't remember how he went from having the syringe in his hand to having it jammed in his neck. The diazepam had gently knocked him out, just like it was supposed to, and he was still feeling fuzzy and lost. But he knew Mitch had checked on him, made sure he was okay, instead of chasing Grady, and he felt guilty.

Besides, he had a sinking suspicion that Gould and the doctors and the administrators wouldn't be too impressed once they figured out that he—a two-hundred-pound man in his late thirties with training in Humane Restraint, armed with sedatives and a can of pepper spray—had somehow been overpowered by an unarmed, one-hundred-thirty-pound septuagenarian.

"I just don't get it," Mitch said.

"Sometimes it's like crazy people don't have to play by the same rules," Charles said. "You work asylums long enough, you'll see some freak-ass shit."

Mitch opened his mouth to speak, then decided to finish his beer instead. "Funny you should..." he started, then gestured for another. While the bartender was off refilling his mug, Mitch leaned in and lowered his voice.

"Funny you should mention that, 'cause right when it happened I saw something really, *really* weird."

"Yeah? What?"

"Well, you know how I'd said I heard something up the hall? I heard it again, like a footstep, and I turned..."

At that moment, Mitch's low muttering was swallowed up by a low hum that became a buzz, then a rattle, then a rumble. He furrowed his brow and looked for the sound, but it was all around. It came from the bar and the salt and pepper shakers and the bottles, everything was vibrating and humming and starting to jiggle and jump.

"What the...?"

"This your first quake?" Charles asked. "Shit, that's all we need." He sighed and said, "Man, this one's picking up..."

Then suddenly, the floor of O'Fallon's tap ripped free of its foundation and dropped down to a crazy tilt.

Chapter Three

Officer Rebecca Ellison was naked except for her uniform cap. She was kneeling in front of a man she'd known for less than two hours, fellating him with fierce intensity while her thoughts scattered in a dozen different directions.

One level of her mind was shocked and appalled that she was going down on a guy who'd insolently asked, "So, what time d'you get off duty?" while she was writing him a speeding ticket.

Another part was focused on the fact that he was black and she was white. Then there was also her worry about the part that was contemplating the racial dilemma—did it mean that she was a racist because she was thinking about it? Or did it mean she *wasn't* a racist because she was *doing* it? Plus, she was uneasy about not using a dental dam—not that she'd ever *needed* one before, because this was the first time ever, *ever*, that she'd gotten intimate with a *complete stranger*.

But the bulk, the majority of her mind was lost in the fulfillment of the act, an incongruous but overwhelming sense of rightness, a blissful feeling that this was what she wanted, needed and *deserved* more than anything in the world.

Gaviel idly reached down and patted her on the back. His mind was also operating on many different levels, but since he'd done so for ages, he was more at ease.

One could chart his attention on a continuum with "Noah" on one end—not the actual Noah Wallace, but the remnants of him, memories and instincts and habits, which Gaviel shared with the imprisoned spirit of his unwilling host. (For Noah was not, as Gaviel claimed, gone beyond recall.) On the other end of the spectrum was "Gaviel" the demon, the devil, the celestial being who had arranged the situation.

Noah had fantasized about this very thing—about getting a blowjob from a white policewoman, specifically after being pulled over—ever since he was fifteen. The most Noah-like part of Gaviel's mind was marveling that it had finally come true, but he was, somehow, a little disappointed. Another part, still on the Noah end of the scale, was analyzing that disappointment and considering that Officer Ellison was broad-waisted, flat-chested, plain-faced—fit, and not *ugly*, but no centerfold. Still, she was going at it with gusto, and that made up for a lot.

Along the mid-range of the Noah/Gaviel consciousness was contemplation of the act *qua* act, which Gaviel was enjoying in a less personal way than Noah. Not the racial/ authority/ submissive element—any human act would need to be exceptionally baroque to even raise one of Gaviel's eyebrows—but the pure physical sensation, which was pleasant. Gaviel had found many human experiences quite satisfying, and this one was right up there with a medium-rare steak and an unbruised gin and tonic. Possibly even nicer.

Over her shoulders, he was watching CNN, which was a minor part of Noah's fantasy. Gaviel was mildly interested—it was about the Golan Heights, and that part of the world loomed large in religious history.

Mostly, however, Gaviel was thinking back over his afternoon, which had been spent in East Saint Louis.

His weeks of playing it cool at *The Hour of Jesus' Power* had left him feeling itchy, antsy and eager for action. He'd just gotten his resources back in order after a disastrous episode with a local politician named Maryanne Prisco: He and she and another demon from Florida had gotten involved in a very intricate exchange of favors and promises and obligations and—despite everyone's best efforts to look out for their own selfish interests—in the end, no one had wound up better off than before. In fact, in one way or another, each of them had lost something. (In the case of the mortal, Maryanne, it was her life, but that was neither here nor there.) After that, he'd diverted himself somewhat with solo work, some Chamber of Commerce-level politicking in Ladue—nothing overtly supernatural, just keeping his hand in—and his urge to get involved had finally led him to impulsively set out for what was, historically, one of America's poorest, saddest and least sanitary cities.

What he'd found there had shocked him. Even the *Gaviel* part of him.

It hadn't taken much poking and prodding to learn that something unnatural had beaten him to the punch. It wasn't demonic, of that he was sure. He didn't know *what* it was. Something strong and infectious and inhumanly crafty, since its infrastructure of servants and observers was sophisticated enough for Gaviel to respect. He'd sniffed around for four hours before he was attacked. He'd judged the attack to be a feint, a tentative strike to benchmark his abilities. He'd evaded the assault rather than show his full power and call down a serious response.

Driving back from that at three in the morning, he'd gotten pulled over by Officer Rebecca Ellison, and the opportunity had been too good to pass up.

(At some level, Gaviel wondered if his actions had been taken to salve his own wounded pride, but he dismissed that idea as impossible. It would take more than a human body and human memories to drag him down to *that* level of pathetic behavior.)

Rebecca was slurping and stroking and, for some reason, she was humming "You're a Grand Old Flag." Noah's body was rolling along toward its ultimate response when the CNN anchor broke in to announce that Los Angeles was in the midst of a major earthquake.

For several years afterward, people asked one another, "Where were you when you heard about the Devil's Quake?"

Harvey Ciullo was at work at the hardware store when the manager stuck his head out of his office, face white, and said, "I just heard on the radio! Sounds like California just dropped into the sea!"

Thomas Ramone was also working, washing dishes at the sandwich shop. The DJ broke in, right during the guitar solo of "Get Free." The other busboys and cooks crowded around as he turned it up. Their boss was mad at them until they told him it was LA, told him what happened, and then he got really quiet and said, "I got nieces and nephews out there."

Sal Macellaio was clocking the pickups at a credit union's ATMs. His first instinct was to scrub the job, figuring that all the cops would want to be extra heroic.

The demon Sabriel (also known as Christina Vadrudakis or Angela Meyerhoff) was right in the middle of seducing Nate Kowalski when the news came on NPR. It was a complete sexual buzzkill, but she recouped the lost ground on the emotional front, sitting by him on the couch, holding hands and drinking hot chocolate while the horror unfolded on every network.

Teddy Mason was eating his breakfast, and he just stared, aghast. He called the store where he worked, but they said business as usual. Which, really, was nothing more than what he should have expected.

Usiel, the Reaper of Souls, heard about it on his car radio. With an irritated grunt, he put in a cassette tape. Since his escape, he found that music was the thing humans did that annoyed him least. Talking about their suffering, or the suffering of others, annoyed him most.

As for Officer Ellison, she lied whenever she was asked that question. And blushed.

"Mitch? Hey Berger, can you hear me man?" Charles's own voice sounded muffled to him—he was hearing it only through bone conduction in his skull. His eardrums were numb, overwhelmed by a sound that had filled the whole world, the sound of the earth's crust beating like a tom-tom, the scream of the ground beneath his feet.

Chuck, a lifetime Angelino, had gotten to a doorway and braced himself, but he'd seen the kid sliding down the floor before a cloud of dry white dust billowed up and in from somewhere like a magician's trick and—poof!—Mitch had disappeared.

The earth was still and silent, but Chuck wanted get the kid somewhere safe before any aftershocks kicked in.

As he cautiously made his way through the jumbled tables, he heard something. Even through the ringing, he heard Mitch's howls.

Berger looked like he'd been dusted with flour. He was clutching his left leg and his mouth was open like a wolf under a full moon. Red blood was seeping out of the gap in his leg and pooling, pushing the white dust aside and clotting it up around the edges. The shinbone was poking through the skin.

"Oh shit," Charles said, not nearly loud enough to overcome Berger's screams. "You're gonna be okay kid. You're gonna be all right."

He knew moving him could just make it worse—that Mitch could have back trauma worse than the leg, just less visible, but as he got near, he felt the floor tilting and giving. He decided that he just had to get him somewhere safe.

Poor gringo, he thought as he slid his hands under Mitch's armpits. "This is gonna hurt," he warned, then pulled the younger man free, up toward the doorway.

Mitch thrashed, but weakly. Maybe it was blood loss. Maybe some part of him realized Rodriguez was helping him. They reached the edge, where the floor of O'Fallon's sat angled below the concrete steps outside.

"You stay there," Charles said. "We're gonna get you something, then we're gonna bandage and splint that, okay?"

Weakly, Mitch nodded, biting his lip.

From outside, they heard and saw a fiery explosion.

"Oh *fuck,* what now?" Mitch cried.

"Probably a gas station, a gas main, something. Someone rear-ended a Pinto, shit, I don't know. Don't worry about it." Charles went to the bar and grabbed a bottle of whiskey. He was turning back when someone seized his wrist.

"Didn't take long for you spics to start looting."

Turning back, Chuck saw the bartender. The man looked crazy. He held a nickel-plated snub-nosed revolver.

"It's for him," Rodriguez said, pointing at Mitch. "He's really hurt."

"Just put it down."

Seeing the glaze over the fellow's eyes, Charles complied. "Do you have any first aid supplies at least?"

"Not for you. Those are for my family. You two can just get the hell out."

"Alright, we're going." Charles couldn't quite believe this. But then, he couldn't really believe the earthquake, either. "I'm just going to splint and bandage him, all right?"

"Get going!"

"You cum-guzzling shitwhore!" Mitch bellowed. "You crazy fucked-up assjab! I gotta fuckin' *bone* sticking out my fuckin' *leg*, shithole! Let him fuckin' *help* me!"

The bartender flicked his mad eyes from Chuck to Mitch and back again. "Okay. Patch him up. But then you two are *outta* here."

"Right. Thanks man."

When news of the earthquake was getting out, Blackie and Joellen O'Hanlon weren't hearing about it. Even if they had, they wouldn't have much cared. They had fallen into the hands of Grant Dagley, who was quite possibly the worst sheriff in the United States of America.

The US certainly has some bad sheriffs. The ACLU could tell you horror stories about Joe Arpaio in Phoenix, whose cheerfully brutal policies toward prisoners have cost the city millions in lawsuits. Or there's Sydney Dorsey of Dekalb County, Georgia, who got a life sentence for having Derwin Brown assassinated after Brown beat him in the 2000 election. But while Sheriff Arpaio might have housed prisoners in tents during the scorching Arizona summer and broadcast detainees over a webcam before they were ever convicted of a crime, he at least had the excuse of thinking he was serving justice. And Sydney Dorsey was a murderous crook, but he never went out of his way to be sadistic. He might extort or kill you, but it was never personal.

Grant Dagley became a cop in the '70s because he liked the idea of beating people, and by the time he met Blackie and Joellen, he had been elected county sheriff uncontested for four terms running. No one was brave enough to run against him, not after what he did to the last two who had any chance. Besides, Grant had made some powerful friends with his willingness to look the other way. There were people as far away as Memphis and Indianapolis who knew that you could take a guy to Springer County, Illinois and murder him, as long as you gave Sheriff Dagley ten grand. For twenty grand, he'd even pull the trigger himself.

Grant had been an alcoholic for years and didn't really bother hiding it. He did conceal his habit of sniffing the fumes from the isopropyl alcohol in his patrol car's first aid kit—he was worried people might think he was weird. He did not, however, give a good goddamn about justice. He really didn't care much about anything. He was a vicious bundle of impulses that he gratified whenever they arose. He wasn't even *smart*, but he'd found that an excess of cruelty could cover for a lot of dumbness.

He decided to pull Blackie's car over when he saw that the driver was a man with long hair. Trying to think up an excuse, he noticed that the license plate was obscured by mud. That would do.

When Blackie slammed his foot down on the gas and took a two-wheel turn onto a back road, a good cop would have called in the state troopers, set up roadblocks, gotten a whirlybird in the air. Dagley just smiled and decided a challenge sounded fun. He gassed his own car and took off in hot pursuit.

Whatever other flaws he had, Dagley was a great driver, even drunk. (Plus, his patrol car had a much burlier engine than Black Hawk's aging Oldsmobile had.) He made the turn with one hand on the wheel. He unsnapped the holster on his revolver with the other and thumbed off the safety catch. His cruiser had power windows, so when he pulled even with the other vehicle he could lower the one on the passenger side and fire cleanly through it.

The bullet missed both O'Hanlons, but it shattered the driver's-side window and the front windshield. Blackie instinctively flinched away from it, pulling off the road and into the ditch. His car didn't roll, but it slammed to a sudden stop against the earthen bank. Both seatbelts snapped tight with bruising force, but Blackie's forehead still rebounded off the steering wheel.

Blackie's mind was just starting to regroup when Grant Dagley yanked open the door and shoved a pistol right under his chin.

"Don't move, hippie," Dagley said.

He reached across Blackie's lap with his left hand, unbuckled the seat belt, and then grabbed a tight fistful of hair and dragged Blackie out by it.

"You leave him alone!" Joellen screeched.

"Quiet, you," Grant barked. Then he did a double take.

"Holy shit," he said, shifting his aim to her as he forced Blackie face-down in the dirt. "You're whatsername. The killer redneck from out east. An' I'm the lucky one who found you."

"You made a mistake," Black Hawk said. Dagley stomped on his forearm, hard, making him howl.

"Shut up," the sheriff said, but Blackie couldn't stop his shrieks. "You," Grant said, gesturing at Joellen, "Hands where I can see 'em."

Grudgingly, she complied, leaving her sharp little paring knife in the crevice between seat and door.

Dagley chewed his lower lip and said, "This must be your son down here, hm?"

She didn't reply.

Grant put the boot into Black Hawk's side.

"Yes!" she said, tears spilling down her face. "Yes, he's my son, don't... don't hurt him."

"Uh huh. Wow." Dagley started to chuckle. "Of all the cops trying to catch you two, I'm the one who gets lucky. Heh. You're a plain little thing, ain'tcha? How 'bout you just get out the car, nice and slow, keeping your hands where I can see 'em. You try and run and, damn, your son's gonna suffer."

She did it, but she had to lower one hand to open the door. As she did, she recovered the knife and slipped its tip into the top of her shoe, then pulled the cuff of her jeans down over the handle. It was all done quick.

Dagley talked her around the corner of the car and had her brace her hands on the hood, legs spread, while he frisked and handcuffed Black Hawk. The whole time he kept reminding her that any sudden move would spell doom for her boy.

He found the knife when he frisked her and shook his head. "You're just a dumb little cunt, aren't you? And you're coming with me."

He didn't take them to the station.

He took them to an old abandoned barn.

Officer Ellison blushed and wouldn't meet Gaviel's eyes as she dressed.

"I'll probably never see you again," she muttered.

"Not unless I contest the ticket," he replied. He took his eyes off the TV for a minute and gave her a hard, frank look. "Why? Do you *want* to see me again? Do you want me to call and send you flowers and chocolates and a bottle of mouthwash? Would you like this to turn into a *relationship*? Do you think it gets better, hm?"

She still had her head down and away when he took her chin in his hand and gently—but firmly—brought her eyes around to see his.

"Don't make more of this than it was," he said. "But don't make it less, either. And for Pete's sake, don't tie it in to the earthquake. It had nothing to do with that. It just was what it was, and that's all it has to be. And that's not a bad thing... is it?"

Her face was wracked with confusion, but she shook her head.

"You've learned something about yourself," he purred. "And isn't knowledge to be treasured more than diamonds?"

She shrugged, and with that, departed.

Noah took the top off a bottle of imported chai and sat down to watch earthquake footage. He also set out his pack of smokes. After several tries, he went to get matches.

It was an old barn, out in the middle of nowhere, abandoned so long that the smell inside was dust and fresh air instead of hog or cattle. Many weathered boards on the roof had blown off in windstorms or had warped enough to let in shafts of golden sunlight, which lit up the dust inside like rays from a saint's halo. It would have made a beautiful subject for a Grant Wood still life. Instead, it belonged to Grant Dagley, and it was where he took people he was sure no one would miss.

The iron hitching ring was rusty, but still solid, and the thick center pole was still firm. That's where he chained Black Hawk, at gunpoint.

"You got a front row seat," he said.

"You're crazy," Blackie muttered. Dagley's gun butt crashed into Blackie's mouth, knocking two teeth right out and staggering the big man down. He only caught his balance because his handcuffed arms held him painfully upright.

"Just don't know when to keep quiet, do you?"

He spun as he heard Joellen charge him. Her hands were bound behind her back as well, but her look was madness, a pure madness of rage and hate. If he'd shot her, she still might have gotten to him, she looked that crazy... but he stepped back and put the gun to Blackie's head. The threat to her son stopped her faster than a bullet. That made her sane again. Perhaps it was the only thing that would have.

He took her over to an old pigpen. There were three railings slung between each of its posts. With threats and slapping he got her positioned, bent over the top rail, hands cuffed around the middle one. He cut her pants open with the paring knife, then went back to his cruiser for the first-aid kit. He opened the bottle of rubbing alcohol and took a deep sniff.

Although Blackie and Joellen had no way of knowing, this meant that he planned to kill them.

The sheriff pulled on rubber gloves and began to violate Joellen with items from the first-aid kit and from his equipment belt—the grip of the scissors for cutting gauze, his baton, even the handle of her own kitchen knife. Now and then he asked Blackie and Joellen for suggestions, but neither O'Hanlon responded. Black Hawk was just crying, helplessly, while Joellen prayed and prayed for the Tree to give her strength and salvation.

The sheriff had fetched his six D-cell flashlight when his mobile phone rang.

He looked at it and sighed. "God damn it," he said. "I got to take this call." Tucking the flashlight under his armpit, he fumbled open the phone.

"Hello," he said. Then, "She what? What? No, don't... no shit. All right. I'll be right there. No, I'll... I'll be right there."

He closed the phone and looked at the two of them, and suddenly all the fire seemed to go out of him.

"Fuck," he muttered. He sighed and drew his pistol. Then he seemed to remember the flashlight and tried to one-handedly transfer it from left armpit to left hand. He dropped it instead, and grunted as he bent down to retrieve it. He looked aimlessly at the scene, Joellen quivering with terror (or maybe rage), Blackie sobbing helplessly, pieces of first-aid gear scattered here and there. He'd just heard from his secretary that an investigator from the Illinois Office of the Attorney General was there with a clerk of the court, asking pointed questions. It was a surprise he didn't like, and it was going to steal a lot of time he'd planned for cleaning up after himself.

"Fuck it," he muttered. With the mood swing of a classic boozer, he decided to ignore the O'Hanlon problem for a while. He'd intended to make the hippie dig the graves—he didn't really want to do it himself. He'd kill them later and deal right now with the trouble that was right up in his face. It would all work out. It always had.

"Don't go nowhere," he muttered at them. He flung the items from the first-aid kit back into their carrying case, took one last huff from the isopropyl bottle, then dumped it all in his trunk and drove away.

In his boxcar heading west, Tim Grady whimpered like a kicked dog and stared up at the naked, accusing form of Rosemary Nevins.

Tim had killed her the day she'd done a really lousy job at an audition, and the whole thing had seemed (to her) like the unfair capper on an unfair day in an unfair life. He'd talked her into a few drinks, then knocked her out, and she'd woken tied up in a basement with him soothingly explaining how he could tell she was unhappy and he was going to take it all away. Give her *solace*. That was the exact word he used, "solace." And then he poked that prong in her eye and killed her.

Rosemary Nevins died angry, and that anger gave her the strength to remain. It took her a while to learn how to use her strength, but Rosemary's ghost soon became a familiar sight to Tim Grady. Just a shadow at first; then a shape. And then a still, chill form pointing at him in accusation, at night, when he was alone in the dark.

That was how he got caught. She spooked him so bad he got careless. He was carrying victim number six out of his car when he was spied by a busboy taking a forbidden smoke break in the alley. The busboy, Connor Collins, drank on the anecdote of that smoke break for the rest of his life, and the arresting officers Smith and Smythe made similar advantage of the arrest. Victim six became a brief overnight sensation and wound up marrying her psychologist. And Tim Grady was institutionalized.

At first, Rosemary hoped he'd get the chair, but by the time he was on trial, she was learning that of all the hardships of being a ghost, the worst possible fate was to be forgotten and cut off from everything. Grady was her link to the living world, a world much warmer and more real than the lands of the dead, and part of her was relieved when he was imprisoned instead of killed.

With Grady and her minor notoriety to keep her anchored, Rosemary had lingered and grown stronger. She'd learned new tricks—how to overlap herself with a human body and feel once again the warm embrace of skin over blood, the firmness of objects. She'd learned how to control a body too, a skill she practiced most often on Grady. For she'd never forgiven him for stealing her body away and leaving her a wisp, a vapor, an outsider. She paid him back in kind, making him act out and then leaving before he was punished.

Tim tried to escape—tried to run from her and from his imprisonment, but either alone would have been too much for him. Together, Rosemary and Dr. Gould had him forever.

Then the storm came.

She'd feared being forgotten. She'd feared never touching or hearing or screaming or feeling again. She'd feared slowly fading into nothingness. The storm was worse, woven from ill winds, charged with all the bitterness and hate that humankind had ever forgotten.

The storm hit, and she'd been unprepared, and the wicked winds had pulled her down with more strength than a hungry ocean. She'd felt herself falling, failing and right before she was finally unwoven into nothing, she'd said, "No."

Why should she cease? No. When others got to *be*? No. Should she rest forever, while the world ticked on ignorant and happy and deluded and doomed?

No, no and no.

Rosemary had risen up changed, and she'd helped Tim escape because she wanted other women to see what she'd seen, learn what she'd learned and die as she'd died. It was unfair that she'd suffered like that, so she'd make it fair by making them suffer. If they died, and just died, good enough. If they stuck around, like her... that would be much, much better.

She got Tim out, and he seemed desperate to go east. It was as good a direction as any.

Even after her years with Tim, Rosemary had no idea what had really led him to kill. But that was not necessarily surprising. Until the day he escaped, Tim hadn't really known either.

Joellen choked down her sobs and brought her writhing face under control through sheer will.

"Blackie," she said. Then, more sharply, "Black Hawk! Stop your cryin'!"

"Oh Mama, Mama…"

"I'm all right. I'll be okay. Son! You got to quiet down!"

It took great effort, but he obeyed. For a moment, they both just listened, occasionally snuffling or choking on a smothered sob.

"Okay, he's gone." Joellen had paid close attention while the sheriff drove away. Sound carried a long way on the prairie on a still day, and she could still hear the faint buzz of his cruiser.

"What're we gonna do, Mama?"

"We escape, that's what we do. How tight he cuff you?"

She heard the jingle of short chain. "Tight."

"What about that ring? It's tight?"

Behind her back, she heard the sounds of effort and movement. "It's screwed in. I can't even shift it." He grunted though, and kept trying.

"It's okay, I may be able to get out."

"Do you remember where our car is?"

"Uh huh. Go up the dirt road, second left, right, second left again, then along there. How many miles you figure?"

"Don't know."

"Well, we gotta get out of this first, then we'll find the car." She frowned.

"He didn't take the car keys, did he?" Blackie asked.

"If he did, you can hotwire it. You're an electrician, right?"

"You really think you can get free?"

Joellen lifted her left foot. Underneath it was her paring knife. When the cop had dropped it so he could stick something else in her, she'd covered it up and he'd forgotten about it. She could barely believe her luck.

"I think I can reach the knife," she said. Carefully, she scuffed it over the hay-strewn floor. Bending as far as she could, her fingers brushed the handle… but she couldn't grab.

"Mama, just jump the fence!"

"Hah!" With a bitter little laugh, Joellen started climbing carefully over. "If my hands were free, I'd slap my own head. Looks like you're good for some thinking after all."

Once she was over, she could easily lower her hands and grab the paring knife. She slid herself over to the side of the slat and started hacking at the wood.

For ten minutes, the two O'Hanlons were silent. When Joellen said, "Shit," it wasn't loud, but it seemed loud in the still.

"What?"

"This ain't workin'. The blade's too flimsy and short… if I keep scratching, it'll just snap off. And the slat ain't even any looser."

Blackie slumped lower. He'd been leaning forward, tense, but now he looked beaten. "So that's it?"

"Naw, there's another way. But it ain't pretty."

Joellen took a deep breath and put the base of the blade against the base of her left thumb. She spread her fingers wide, flexing her thumb and feeling the tendons beneath the skin tighten. She was trying to figure out the best cut, the least damage that would separate the base of her thumb from her wrist. That was the widest part of her hand. If she could cut that thumb joint free, the cuff would slip off. She had no idea how it was attached though. And she knew from experience that the best way to cut deep isn't with pressure, but with a keen edge and a long speedy draw. With her hands together, there was no way to do that. She'd have to saw for it.

"Please lady Tree, give me the strength for this ordeal," she prayed, then went to it.

"Mama! No!" But Blackie was easy to ignore. The pain was hot and itchy and grinding as she went through skin and tendon, but she was used to pain, she was used to making herself numb, and she pretended it was just a tough ham hock, she and Blackie didn't get big cuts of meat all that often, she just thought how good ham tastes once you cut it off the bone...

Her skin tore as she pulled the cut against the steel cuff, but the blood greased it up and she popped free.

"Okay, son. Now you," she said as she reconnected the shackle to her good hand.

Mitch Berger wouldn't stop twitching and quivering, and Charles was worried that he was going into shock, but the bartender was a clear and present danger, even if he did give in and sell Mitch — at normal prices! — a couple of double whiskeys to take the edge off.

When they finally left the bar, they saw what had caused the earlier explosion — as Chuck had guessed, it was a gas station. The flames were so high and hot that they didn't even waver. They shot twenty feet in the air with the steady intensity of a blowtorch flame.

"Jesus Christ," Chuck muttered, looking at the carnage. Buildings all along the other side of the road were simply flattened. He could see a vast crack in the earth with the flimsy remnants of plasterboard strip-mall buildings sticking out of it, like leaves from the mouth of a sloppy salad eater.

The parking lot for the tavern had partially collapsed, and there was a surreal cross-sectional view of the pavement, the gravel beneath it, packed soil under that, then a layer of dirt before you hit the basements and conduits and sewer lines.

Charles shook his head. No time for gawking. He had to get Berger to a hospital — though, shit, they were all going to be swamped — and that meant getting a car. His own was ass up, trunk to the sky and nose pointing at China. But Berger drove a Jeep—*Gringos and their Jeeps,* Charles had thought—and he blinked as he saw that it had a no-shit winch on the front.

"That's a piece of luck," he muttered, gently lowering Berger to a less-broken piece of pavement while he went off to try to loop the end of the winch cable around something that wouldn't simply tip over or wrench out of the ground.

When the Jeep had pulled itself up, Chuck helped Mitch into the passenger seat and continued to reassure him. "You're gonna be okay, amigo. You're gonna be just fine. It's a clean break. You just have to be tough, all right?"

Miserable, Mitch nodded.

"Shit man, what've you got a winch on your Jeep for, anyhow?"

"Earthquakes," Mitch said, and gave a rickety grin. Charles laughed out loud—maybe a little too loud, but it felt good. "Naw, seriously? I did some off-roading. Plus it looks tough, y'know."

"Tough. Yeah."

They were pulling up in front of a Walgreen's pharmacy when they saw a short figure entering it. He looked unhurt, and he had a makeshift club in one hand. The other held a Slurpee cup.

"Oh fuck," Charles said, pulling out his pepper spray.

"What man?"

"Squirt just went in the drugstore."

"Squirt? *Our* Squirt?"

"The one and only."

"So the mixed nuts have spilled. That's just fuckin' great."

"You gonna be okay out here?"

"I guess I gotta be."

Charles frowned, hesitated, then gave Mitch his pepper spray. He got out and approached the pharmacy cautiously. *If it's empty,* he thought, *Squirt will probably just go into the back and get himself some junk until he passes out or ODs. This could go pretty smooth.*

Then he heard a woman's scream and he started to run.

Inside the store, he didn't bother with stealth—she was hollering loud enough to cover any noise he might make. He grabbed one of the grocery carts at the front and pushed it ahead of him, its wheels vibrating in time with his running footsteps. They were back by the prescription counter.

She was just a girl, really, face obscured by Squirt's namesake pollution. A man with gray hair and a white uniform crouched nearby, clutching his head. The escapee waved his club like a caveman would, tearing at the girl's soiled clothes with his free hand.

Charles rammed the cart into Squirt's side as hard as he could. "You want restraints?" he shouted—an empty threat, but one that would cow a lot of the older inmates.

Squirt, though, was a freshy, and he swung his club overhand. Charles danced back, but like a lion-tamer with a chair, he kept the cart between him and the flailing madman. He grabbed the end of the club as it slammed into the wire frame handles—it was just a thick chunk of splintery wood— and tried to wrench it from the inmate's grasp.

But Squirt had turned his back on his intended victim, and she wasn't standing still. She grabbed a rack of reading glasses off the pharmacy counter and brought it down on his head with a clatter of plastic frames. She had one hand on the top and one on the bottom, and she hit him hard enough to crack it in half.

"Mr. Moriarty!" she screeched. Apparently it was the gray-haired man's name, and it stirred him to action. He stumbled up and threw his arms around Squirt's waist. While the two employees struggled with Squirt, Charles was able to get to the side of the cart and yank the club free. By then, the Walgreen's duo had the lunatic on the ground. Charles thought about interfering, but he didn't as Moriarty stomped and kicked at

Squirt, who was sobbing and getting into a fetal position. With grunts and curses, the girl yanked the heavy computerized cash register up off the counter.

"That's enough!" Charles said sharply.

She'd raised it to chest level and was ready to smash in her assailant's head. But instead she put it back.

"Give him some pills," Charles said. "Dilaudid. About double the normal dose should knock him out."

"How do you know?" Mr. Moriarty asked.

"I'm from the asylum." He reconsidered his statement. "I mean, I work there."

For a moment, the trio just stood there, trembling and hyperventilating. Inanely, Chuck noticed that the girl's nametag said *Tansy*. He wiped his face, flung away the club and said, "Uh, when you got a minute, my friend out front is hurt bad."

Mr. Moriarty nodded, and Charles could see a huge goose-egg forming on the front of his forehead. "I'll… I got this. Tansy, you go get cleaned up, all right?" He went back into the pharmacy area for the pills.

"All right." She started walking unsteadily toward the back. Halfway there she turned and said, "Thanks, mister. What's your name?"

"Charles Rodriguez."

"That's a nice name."

Black Hawk had an easier time of it. His mother had learned from her first attempt, so she had him hold his cuff up against his hand, where she'd had hers down on the wrist. She could take a good long sweeping cut with the knife, and her sure-handed bleed-rail instincts took the edge deep and true. The wound gapped a little as he popped free of the cuff, but there wasn't as much tearing as she'd endured.

"Can you make it to the car?" Blackie asked as he cut up his shirt and bandaged his mother's hand. It was hard: He kept trying to use his aching left hand, but the thumb wouldn't obey. He knew that his thumb was disconnected, but he kept trying to use it by instinct.

"The car?" she said, when it was her turn to tend him. "Fuck that. We wait until that sumbitch comes back and see how he likes getting things shoved in *him*."

Blackie paused to wipe snot on his sleeve and give his mother a look of dread.

"Oh Mama, no. No, we gotta go."

"You go if you want, chicken belly. I'm staying here to put that bastard paid."

"Mama, he's a *cop*. He's a police officer. People are gonna notice real fast if he goes missing. Plus he's got a gun, Mama, and we're both hurt bad."

"He thinks we're chained up. We lay in wait—or I guess *I* do—and get him when he ain't lookin'."

"Lay in wait where?" Blackie licked his lips and said, "The Tree, Mama. That's what matters, ain't it? Ain't that what's important?"

Seeing doubt flicker in her eyes, he pressed his point. "Look, you said we had to go to the Tree, get there fast as possible. Nothin' matters but that, right? And we got no way to know when he's coming back. And no way to know someone else won't find us first, and then what? They gonna believe us over their sheriff? No, we gotta get to the Tree first. Please."

Joellen looked like she was tasting something sour, but she said, "I suppose you're right. We'll go to the Tree." There was a grinding noise as she gritted her teeth. "The Tree of Nothingness will give me revenge."

The water in the bathroom wasn't working, but Tansy washed up with bottles of Evian, Suave shampoo and Neutrogena antibacterial soap. She grabbed a US flag T-shirt from the promotional items aisle and changed into that.

When she emerged, she saw that the crazy guy was unconscious and that the other guy—Charles, apparently—was securing him to a bolted-down steel couch. It was in the prescription area, for customers to sit on while they waited for their meds. Charles was using electrician's tape (aisle four, Automotive and Repairs) to secure the inmate's forearm to the couch arm, and his leg to the couch leg. He was wrapping it over and over, so that the man wouldn't even be able to turn his limbs.

As she got closer, she saw that the crazy man's feet were bare and bloody. Charles looked up.

"I tried to call the cops," he said, "But of course the phones are out."

"Try my cell," Tansy said, then saw that there was no carrier available.

"I don't think he'll be able to get free. At least not for a while." Charles set a couple of two-liter bottles of juice on the couch beside him, along with three loaves of bread. "He won't starve."

Tansy shrugged. "I wouldn't cry if he did."

"He can't control himself," Charles said, but without a lot of passion. He stood. "I gotta go check on my friend. You want to come?"

"Better than staying in here with him," she said... though her eyes flicked to aisle four's small knives, way up at the top away from the hands of grabby toddlers. As they walked out, she took one and started stripping away its plastic and cardboard packaging. Charles said nothing.

Outside, Mr. Moriarty had moved another man to the back of the Jeep. "What happened to him?" Tansy asked.

"Broken leg."

Moriarty looked up. "You did an okay job on the splint, though I got a walking cast and put that on instead. I can't set the bone here, but I slowed down the bleeding a lot and cleaned out the wound. I got him crutches, too. And he's not feeling any pain."

"Hey," Mitch said, his eyes glassy. He grinned a big druggy grin. "Lucky Chuckie. Who's your friend in the wet T-shirt?"

Mr. Moriarty flushed. "Sorry Tansy, he's... he's flying high," he said.

"He had a couple beers and some whiskey before coming here," Charles clarified. Moriarty's eyes widened.

"I wish you'd told me that."

"Dude, you're cock-blocking me," Mitch said in a stage whisper. "Don't want Tandy to think I'm a *drunk*."

Tansy just shook her head and gave a short chuckle. *If he wasn't drunk, stoned and covered in blood, he'd actually be kind of cute*, she thought. Then he leered at her and said, "I'll salute that flag any time, baby." *Well, maybe not*, she thought.

"What do we do now?" Charles asked.

Moriarty shrugged. "Your friend here needs a hospital, though he's not in immediate danger. I'm probably going to stay with the store."

"Even with Squirt inside?"

"You call him Squirt?" Tansy asked. "Ick."

"All the more reason," Moriarty said.

Charles nodded. "Scripps-Lamley trauma center is probably the closest place, right?"

"Mm, closest as the crow flies, but you'd have to get on the freeway. I'll bet you fifty bucks the onramp's collapsed."

"The Jeep can go off road."

"Do you really want to jiggle your friend around?"

"Do I really have a choice?"

"Scripps-Lamley, that's west of here, right?" Tansy said. "Can I come along?"

"Why? Are you hurt?"

"No, but my house is that way and I want to... you know. It's where I want to be. I want to make sure my dad's all right."

"He doesn't work at O'Fallon's, does he?" Mitch asked. "'Cause if he does, he's an *asshole*. He ain't hurt, though."

"No," Tansy said, confused and disdainful. "He sells cars for Hammond Chrysler Mercury."

"We can drop you off, I guess," Charles said. "You ready to go?"

At that moment, there was a second rumbling. The pharmacist bolted back toward the Walgreen's while Charles and Tansy went to pull Mitch out of the Jeep. But when Tansy saw the source of the sound, she froze.

It was maybe twenty feet high at the shoulder, and she saw it as something like a mastodon. It wasn't, really. It wasn't like anything she'd seen. But her mind needed some answer that fit with what she was seeing, hearing, *feeling*. As a child she'd seen a mastodon skeleton and life-sized statue in a museum, and that was her mind's touchstone image for brute power from an age long past. The image she saw looked like a figure from a fever dream or a hallucination, but in her heart and thrilling through her bones, she knew it was real in a way that even she, perhaps, was not.

So, a mastodon, or something like. But instead of flanking a trunk, its huge tusks emerged from a bearded human face the size of a dinner table. It was galloping along, and its gait and weight made the earth shudder. As it neared, Tansy could see details. It was a uniform slate-gray color all over—even the whites of its no-pupil eyes were gray. It looked like stone and caught the light like stone; it shook the ground like its mass was stone, but it moved like flesh and hair. Seeing stone move like hair seemed, to Tansy, somehow more horrifying (or horrifying in a different way) than everything else she'd seen that long day.

That's where the earthquake came from, she thought. *That thing woke up in the ground and pushed its way up.* She had no idea where this notion came from.

As it passed, she could see that one of its back legs had been chopped off below the knee, making it run like a three-legged dog. The stump looked like a cliff face—all rock, but craggy and jagged.

What could hurt that thing? She wondered. Then she saw.

The second thing—and again, to some part of her it wasn't a "thing," it was an *idea*—was shaped, in her sight, like a man. But seeing it, she was struck by the feeling that men were shaped like it. It was not a thing that was compared to other things: Other things were compared to it. It was the original. It was the source. Men were shaped like it. A sunset was glorious like it. An eagle or an oil fire had beauty like its wings. A missile strike or lightning bolt was terrifying like the spear it held. She looked at it and tried to fit the ideas of glory, hugeness, the beauty of men and the beauty of fire together, tried to tie them in all at once with a sense of power that would dwarf the earthquake. She failed. The best she could do was a glorious titan, winged with flames and holding a spear.

As it showed forth, some instinct made her turn away and shield her eyes from it, but Charles didn't have that instinct. He was staring, entranced, his face lit by its glow and shaped into an expression of utmost rapture.

Then she saw him point and heard him yell, "Look out!"

Eyes low, she turned to see what he meant. She looked past the legs of the magnificent spear-carrier and saw something that could only be a fit enemy for such a being.

The third thing was long, low to the ground—something like a snake or an insect or an oil slick. It had a face and *was* a face that was unearthly in its beauty and its malice, while at the same time it was a vast centipede with a four-jointed jaw that opened like a flower.

Its mouth was gaping open now, like it was hissing, and then it turned itself inside out.

That was the only way she could think of it.

Like a sock being inverted, only quick and with a massive thrumming rattle, it was striking at the beautiful giant with a great spur of bone that emerged from its throat and must have been at the base of its tail as it vomited itself completely reversed. But somehow she saw, and felt, and smelled, and just plain *knew* that it was pollution and purity both, that it was perfect serenity and boiling chaos at the same time, unified opposites. That its strike was not a blow but a cutting of what could be; it was somehow trying to make that glorious titan *impossible*.

The burning apparition spun and swept the spear with such speed that it seemed to be a vast fan of flame in its hands. The monster shrieked (as well as it could when gagged by itself), and the sheared-off tip of its tail crashed to the ground, dissolving instantly into muck and grime.

The creature pulled its wounded stump back inside like a snail retracting a poked eye, and it tried to back away, but with all its many legs it couldn't retreat fast enough. The giant flapped his wings, leapt into the air and landed on the creature spearhead-first.

At its impact, ten-foot tall clouds of flame billowed out in every direction. Tansy turned aside again and saw that even the mesmerized Charles threw an arm over his eyes. But when it reached them, the flame didn't seem to be flame, not real flames. Perhaps it was only the idea of flame, or something best symbolized by flame.

Nonetheless, they coughed and fell.

Chapter Four

Two days later, the LA quake was still the main news story. If anything, coverage had intensified.

Initially, Americans were shocked (except for the cynics, who were never shocked by anything) at the widespread death and destruction caused by what was later determined to be a 7.2 on the Richter scale. But the quake, it turned out, was only the beginning. With the collapse of the power grid and the extensive damage to the sewage system, people were quickly plunged into an existence that was nearly pre-industrial. At first, lines formed at gas stations as people tried to flee the area. Then, as they realized the pumps weren't working, they started to steal gas by siphoning it from the tanks. This took even longer, and the people in line at the stations became more upset, and eventually started stealing gas from parked cars. Or they just turned violent.

Terry Cook, the owner of LA's biggest cab company, told all his drivers that if they wanted to go home, they could, but that people who stayed would get time and a half pay for as long as they wanted to work. They weren't going to charge fares. They were just going to take stranded people where they needed to go, as much as they could.

Tansy, Chuck and Mitch saw an impossible sight in front of a Walgreen's pharmacy, and they weren't the only ones. With phones down and cell towers out of commission, word was slow to spread. But it spread nonetheless.

That was the first day.

The area hospitals were quickly overwhelmed with the broken, burned and traumatized. Ambulances ran day and night, straining the hospitals' reserves of fuel—fuel which was also needed for generators to keep blood chilled to storage temperature, and to run the lights in operating rooms, and to keep the water pumps running so staff could wash their hands before treatment.

Every police officer in the area was mobilized, but it wasn't enough. As the gas riots (which were now also food riots and water riots and general lawless looting riots) spread, rumors spread with them—the police were shooting black people on sight, the hospitals were turning away any Latino without proof of US citizenship, the fire departments had written off entire sections of Watts, Inglewood and Compton and weren't even responding to calls there.

In reality, the fire departments were (arguably) the worst off of the severely compromised emergency services. Not only did they have communications snafus (due to the lack of phone lines) and spotty access to their central 911 computer (thanks to erratic power generation) and limited gasoline (like everyone else) and trouble getting to the fires (because of the badly damaged roads) but they had the additional problem of having to carry in all their own water since they couldn't rely on fire hydrants to work.

The governor called out the National Guard and declared a state of emergency. It didn't seem to help.

After a day of random riding and a couple of carjackings, Terry Cook reconsidered and called the local hospital. He told them how many cars he had and said they were at the hospital's disposal, along with his dispatchers and fuel reserves. He said the hospital could use the cabs as long as they needed to and as long as there was someone to drive them.

That was the second day. It was also Halloween.

Even in the face of increased rioting, heroic linemen and power plant workers pulled twenty-four- and sometimes forty-eight-hour shifts trying to restore electricity to hospitals, police stations and fire houses. In the process, they brought power back (off and on) to other parts of Los Angeles.

A couple of different segments of shaky, blurry "Lucifer footage" got shown on NBC the first day, but were quickly denounced as tasteless hoaxes. Nevertheless, rumors and stories had already hit the streets in the first two days—apocalyptic scuttlebutt and wild-eyed tales of Armageddon that didn't seem nearly as implausible in a world of violence, destruction and chaos. Once they saw the footage, many took it as confirmation of *all* the stories.

The cab drivers took a lot of people to the hospital before their gas supplies finally ran out. Some of them hadn't even thought how they were going to get home themselves, so they wound up bunking down at the cab lot.

LA was lost in an orgy of blood and fire and looting; rage and helplessness and misery and loss. People around the nation watched on TV as the natural disaster turned into an epic human tragedy, and they were shocked. (Except for the cynics, who shrugged and said, "I told you so," until ABC started carrying a story that Brian Dennehy and the actress who played Sister Agatha on the soap opera *Hearts in Bondage* had been murdered in their homes. After that, even the cynics seemed baffled.)

That was the third day.

After that, more National Guard troops showed up. Los Angeles was declared a Federal Emergency Zone. A cordon was placed around the region to keep people from going in unless they were bringing in approved and needed emergency supplies. A curfew was imposed, and martial law was declared within the city limits.

It wasn't until after the fifth day that things started to calm down.

It was on the fifth day that Lucifer appeared on national TV.

Mitch was out in a parking lot that had been converted into an open-air ward for people whose injuries weren't life-threatening. He saw Lucifer as a pillar of flame rising into the sky, felt him as a music that chilled him to his core... but he shook his head and told himself someone was shooting off fireworks, that he'd heard something on someone's radio, that he was still feeling aftereffects from shock and drugs and deprivation. He told himself these things but didn't really believe them.

Charles Rodriguez, who was camping out at a Red Cross site near the hospital, saw the Morningstar as he had seen him before, and recognized him rising into the sky, and his heart yearned while a blissful smile crossed his face.

Right near City Hall, where the Morningstar revealed himself before leaping aloft, a woman hiding in her gray car saw him almost as he truly was, and her mind was broken by blows of grandeur. She went mad, delighted and miserable at the same time.

And far away in St. Louis, Gaviel watched live, grainy footage on NBC and heard the Adversary's announcement. It came across as static to the unenlightened ear, but Gaviel knew it as the primal language, the tongue of angels, sometimes called Enochian.

Lucifer's challenge didn't fit into English well, but a vague approximation would be, "I stand ready to oppose any and all."

Seeing even an image of his onetime master brought so many memories rushing back. Gaviel blinked, and he looked at his smoldering cigarette. He gave a short command in that oldest of tongues.

There was a brief flash and a puff of smoke as the whole cigarette was instantly consumed.

Later, when there were no fresh atrocities to report, Fox rebroadcast the shaky video images of Lucifer at City Hall, along with experts who pointed out that the distant light from fires in the background was visibly congruent with other, accepted footage, and that the placement of shadows on the front of the buildings was consistent with a hovering light source. NBC didn't directly accuse Fox of sensationalism, but they continued to apologize for showing "obviously staged and false video." CNN covered the story in terms of the dueling networks' credibility, but it was CBS that ran an announcement from a CGI artist who claimed he'd worked on the "original" Lucifer footage—though he said he had no idea who'd spliced it into footage from the LA quake, or how it had been stolen from his (destroyed) special effects lab.

The ghost of Rosemary Nevins was furious when Tim got off the train. She'd left him temporarily to go back to Los Angeles and inspect the scene. While Tim was her best bond to the living world, he wasn't her only one. Certain sites, crucial to her story, also kept her from being swept away. Or they had. The place where she'd died, where Tim had gotten caught, where he'd been tried and imprisoned… all were rubble and soot. Without the tours of jaded thrill seekers who took pictures of her death spot, in between going to where the Black Dahlia was found and the hotel where Fatty Arbuckle fell from grace, without that attention and emotion and Schadenfreude, she was that much closer to being forgotten and being banished from the lands of the living altogether. It made her all the more protective of her last link to the world—but when she returned to her murderer, she found he'd jumped off the train when it slowed for a curve and had set out into icy desert night.

"You couldn't kill yourself *before* me?" she screamed at him as he trudged through gray sand. "*Now* you do something this suicide stupid? Now, when you're finally good for something, you decide to wander off and freeze?"

Rosemary didn't expect Tim to respond. He'd stopped talking (unless she possessed him) some time back in the 1980s. Even before that, he'd learned not to respond to his victim's phantom. It just got him sedated or, worse, put in restraints.

Tim's treatment had reduced him to a skeleton of a human spirit, barely better than an animal. From her jaunts inside his skin, Rosemary knew this. But to her shock, this time he actually spoke.

"Tree."

"*Tree?*" she repeated, incredulous. "You jump off a moving train the middle of the night in a desert with no goddamn water because you saw a *tree*? Shit, we were in Los Angeles, you saw hundreds of fucking trees. If you'd stayed on the stupid train until Vegas, you'd have seen hundreds more. Not only that, Tim: women. Uh huh. If you'd just kept your nutty head on straight and stayed put for a couple more hours, you'd have had your pick of showgirls and strippers and cocktail waitresses. You could have killed them all. *We* could have killed them all. But nooooo. You had to go off on some psychotic tangent in the middle of fucking nowhere and *doom us both!*"

As she ranted at him, Tim trudged steadily south. The sun was starting to rise, taking the bitterest edge off the sandy night chill. In twenty minutes, Tim wouldn't be able to see his breath anymore. In two hours, it would crest eighty degrees. An hour after that, the sun would slam off the gritty sand below it, radiating killing heat in every direction.

But now, in the predawn chill, Tim was making pretty good time for an escaped madman in the depths of senescence.

Rosemary stepped into his skin and tried to take control. If she remembered the Nevada map right, the highway wasn't too terribly far. She could turn him around, walk him there, maybe find shade under a road sign and hope someone other than a cop would pull over. She entered and commanded, but he resisted her with unusual ferocity.

Long ago, she'd decided not to destroy his soul and steal his body permanently: Being a man (especially an old man) didn't appeal to her. Besides, it was more satisfying to have him around to punish. She knew that the moment he died, he might slip from her grasp and plummet down to destruction. Unlike the vengeful living, she could think of many fates worse than death. Letting his soul survive, however—even in its weakened condition—meant that possessing him wasn't automatic. And she'd tired herself out trying to kill that bitch in the car with no weapon but his arthritic bare hands.

Failing to seize his gross motor controls, Rosemary stepped back. For a moment, she just watched him stumble across the dusty sand.

"You better hope you die all the way!" she screamed. "When you snuff it, you better *pray* that Hell gets you before I do! 'Cause if you stick around, you're gonna be *my* slave, *my* victim, and I've learned a lot of bad things that can happen when you're dead!"

He wasn't paying attention. He'd reached the top of a hill and was looking down at a small stand of scrubby pines.

"Tree!" he said again, and his face lit up like a child when it sees mommy.

"You crazy old fuck," Rosemary said, disgusted... but she felt something.

It wasn't a ghost—she could always see them, and there weren't any around. It wasn't human though, that was for damn sure. It was... lifelike, but not alive. Or alive in a different way. Or perhaps it was dead in a way like nothing she'd ever encountered. Whatever it was, it was definitely *there*.

In fact, it was definitely in the goddamn tree toward which Grady was charging.

He fell down twice getting there, but when he reached it, he flung his arms around the trunk and kissed the rough, dry bark.

Rosemary felt the... the presence, the mystery... respond. Just a little. She got a sense of terrible age and terrible depth. The thing was mostly still, but not completely. It was like looking into the ocean's deepest pit and seeing only a brief ripple on the water's surface. Like some great prehistoric beast, perhaps, twitching a cheek during a long hibernation.

She felt that tiny flicker of response from it, then watched as Tim Grady sank into the ground. The look of rapture was still on his face, and then he was gone.

ABC was interviewing the first National Guardsman to be wounded in Los Angeles. A sniper had shot him while he was out enforcing the curfew.

"Oh yeah," he said. "I was in Desert Storm, and this was lots, lots worse."

"Worse how?" asked a news co-anchor, concern writ visibly on her intelligently pretty face.

"You kidding me? No artillery, no armor and not much air support. Really limited visibility..." He shook his head a little and shrugged. "Plus, everyone you shoot at is an American," he added.

"American soldiers shooting civilians," Matthew Wallace said, shaking his head.

"It's Kent State all over again," his wife Zola said.

"I don't think so," Gaviel replied. "I mean, Kent State was political. This is just criminal. The troops weren't there because of demonstrations. They were there because of looting and riots. And besides, *he* didn't shoot anyone. He *got* shot. There's the major difference right there."

"Do you really think the soldiers didn't shoot back?" Matthew asked. "We just don't hear about it because of the media quarantine."

Gaviel shrugged.

"Let's not talk politics, okay?" Zola said. She turned to her son. "Would you like some more ice in that, honey?"

"No, Mom, I'm okay." He smiled back. "And if I did, I could get it myself."

"It's all right. I like doing things for my men."

"In that case...?" Matthew held up an empty glass and shook the melting ice cubes.

"All right," she said, getting up to refill his tea.

When the two men were alone, Matthew gave Gaviel a look. "What?"

"Calling her 'Mom.'"

"Do you not want me to? Do you want me to act cold and aloof? Would that be *better*?"

Matthew gritted his teeth and said nothing. Gaviel sighed.

"So," the demon said. "What are we going to do about Los Angeles?"

"What do you mean? We'll pray, probably take up a collection for the Red Cross..."

"Is that all?"

Matthew ran his tongue over his front teeth but politely asked, "What would you suggest?"

"I suggest we send missionaries."

"Missionaries? It's LA, not the Andes or Micronesia."

"Relief workers, then. Volunteers. Raise money, get food, take them out there and distribute them."

"Uh huh." The reverend narrowed his eyes. "And what's your *real* reason?"

"To alleviate the suffering of our brothers and sisters in need. Isn't that reason enough?"

"There are brothers and sisters in need everywhere. What makes you want to go to Los Angeles in particular?"

Gaviel grinned. It wasn't entirely free of bitterness.

"All right, I'll confess. You think I have a secret reason? I don't. But I do have a reason to go *there*, instead of any other swamp of human misery. If you scrunch up your brow and think hard, I bet you'll even guess what it is."

"Lucifer unbound," the minister said.

Gaviel tapped his nose.

"You want to go find your leader."

"He's not *my* leader. Not anymore. But if he's there, there's more going on than you see on the surface. And the surface, as you may have noticed, is pretty appalling."

"So why get involved?"

"Matthew, don't play devil's advocate. It suits your poorly. If I don't go, who's going to, hm? Do you think some weekend warriors from Kenosha are equipped to deal with the plans of the Adversary himself? He raised rebellion against the Ancient of Days and swept a third of the stars from Heaven. Do you think the Red Cross and the National Guard can handle him? They couldn't even *understand* him."

"But you can? You can face him?"

Gaviel laughed. "Head to head? I wouldn't have a marshmallow's chance in Mount St. Helens. He was smarter and stronger than any of us even before the defeat. Even before we were cast down, stripped of our might, bound and imprisoned…" His voice had become low, with a seething undercurrent, and the light in the room seemed to be gathering redly in his eyes. "He never suffered that indignity, though. He was never humiliated before Heaven's court, shorn of his glory and made to kneel."

At that moment, Zola returned.

"What are you boys talking about?" she asked.

"Los Angeles, Mom," Gaviel said.

"It's so awful," she said, giving Matthew his drink.

"What do you think we should do?"

"Oh, I'm sure I don't know," she said.

Matthew got a speculative look in his eye. "Noah wants to go there," he said.

"What?"

"It's true, Mom."

"Oh honey, what… I mean, why?"

"Isn't it obvious? I think I can do a lot of good. Especially if Dad helps me. If the church helps me."

Zola wasn't looking at her husband, so she missed his reaction to the word Dad. It was brief anyhow.

"But it's so… so violent and dangerous."

"Well, I wouldn't go right away. We'd need time to raise money, get people involved. It's not like we don't know anyone there, either." He turned to Matthew. "Who was the guy you talked to out there? The one from the Million Man March? Reverend Perdue?"

"You've got a good memory."

"You called him just the other day, right? I remember you saying how hard he and his have got it right now."

"Uh huh."

"We could put out a call for donations and goods and take it to his church."

"But Noah, is it safe?" Zola asked.

He shrugged. "If no one goes and helps them until it's safe, is it ever going to *get* safe?"

She put a hand to her mouth and looked at her husband. He said nothing. She looked back at her son.

"This is just so... It's awfully sudden, isn't it?"

"So was the earthquake."

"I'm a little surprised, I have to say," Matthew said. "I remember when I had to practically drag you along on service missions before."

"Yeah, when I was fourteen and sixteen and it wasn't my idea. I admit it. I resented being asked if I wanted to go, when it was clear that I had to go. I'd actually have respected both of you more if you'd just said I had no choice... but that was a childish resentment." He smiled, a sweet smile. "When I became a man, I put aside childish things."

"It almost seems that you're a completely different person," Matthew said, and the sourness was subtle enough that only one listener caught it.

"I just... I don't know what to think," Zola said.

"I want to help them," Gaviel replied.

It worked. Zola went to him and flung her arms around him, tears welling up.

"But I just got you back!" she said. "I just got you back, and I don't want to lose you again!"

He returned the hug, slow and gentle, but strong.

"I'll stay if you don't want me to go," he said quietly. "But I want to go."

Gradually, she pulled herself back. She put her hands around her son's handsome face and stared into his eyes.

"I'm so proud of you," she whispered. Then she bit her lip and dabbed at her eyes and excused herself to fix her makeup.

For a while, the minister and the demon just sat and looked at one another.

"I like the way you used your wife as a weapon against me," Gaviel said. "It was almost devilish."

"Shut up."

Owen Milk wasn't smart, but in his job, brains would be more of a liability than an asset.

Owen was a clerk at a gas station and convenience store in an area of Kansas colloquially known as "the middle of goddamn fucking nowhere." It was a Shell Oil on a long stretch of state highway that cut through flat, endless plains of wheat going on as far as the eye could see—and, given that the tallest hill for miles around had an elevation of one hundred feet at best, the eye really couldn't see all that far.

A man of average intelligence would probably sit at the job and listen to the radio (though only two stations came in clear— news/ talk and country/western), read magazines, maybe steal a beef jerky or two now and then, and quietly get very, very eccentric—maybe actually insane—as a result of extended boredom.

A man of great intelligence would most likely bring great books and read them all day behind the counter, occasionally pausing to stare off into the fields and silently ruminate. After a few months, this hypothetical brilliant man would have an existential crisis about wasting his life doing one of the dullest jobs on Earth in one of Earth's dullest corners. Then he'd probably go off back to school or sell insurance or try to make money through a complicated wire-fraud scheme.

But Owen Milk was conscientious and stupid and quite boring himself. He drove half an hour to work every day, opened up, listened to country music until Rush Limbaugh came on, and looked at the pictures in the magazines. He sometimes took a candy bar or a Yoo-Hoo off the shelf, but he always paid for it out of his own pocket. He had not one dram of ambition in his entire body, and he'd held the job for ten years.

The Shell station did okay. Maybe five or ten cars an hour went down the highway, and maybe one or two stopped. The prices were surprisingly high, as they tend to be when there's no competition.

When the woman came into his Shell station and asked for the bathroom key, Owen gave it to her without much thought.

The theoretical clerk with average wit might have thought she looked familiar, and that might have drawn his attention to her poor appearance. Now, you get all types at a roadside gas station, but this woman looked (and smelled) a little more disheveled than even the most toothless class of back-road traveler.

Thus, when the woman came back in and said the key wasn't working and could he please help, the average-smart clerk might have been suspicious enough to just tell her to try it again. He might have then noticed that she had her left hand in her purse, held a way that seemed stiff and unnatural.

The conjectural smart man wouldn't feel like he'd seen her, because he'd consider *America's Most Wanted* too lowbrow for his refined tastes, but he'd certainly pick up on her rank aroma, and on her eyes. Those eyes, they were a weird combination of intense and vacant. When she fixed that vacantly intense, or intensely vacant, gaze on him, the smart man would get very uneasy. He still might have gone with her after thinking too much and concluding that he was exhibiting class-based prejudice. On the other hand, if he'd really been on the ball (not reading something in translation or working on a crossword puzzle), he might have picked up on the fact that there had been a man in the car with her when she pulled up, but that the man was nowhere to be seen now.

In any event, such speculation is useless. It wasn't a smart man, or even an average one. It was Owen Milk, and when he went with Joellen O'Hanlon he suspected nothing. Blackie got behind him and hit him under his short-ribs with a tire-iron.

Poor Owen crumpled and started howling, and then Joellen tied up his wrists and ankles with electrician's tape. Black Hawk took care of gagging him (actually apologizing the whole time) and then the pair shoved him into the bathroom and locked him in along with the only key.

Owen was lucky, because he was conscientious about keeping the bathroom clean.

Owen was also lucky because Joellen had told Blackie that they'd just immobilize and rob the clerk, while she secretly planned to kill him "for safety's sake." When Blackie locked the key in with Owen, however, her plans were foiled and she couldn't even berate him for it. She did seem pretty grouchy the next day, though.

The O'Hanlons were not having a comfortable journey. Being chained to a pigpen gives one plenty of time to contemplate one's rapist, and Joellen had thought about the sheriff's phrase "all the cops trying to catch you two." She'd decided that they couldn't risk recognition by going to a hotel, and *certainly* not a hospital for their damaged hands. They were simply going to have to drive the whole way on back roads, sleeping in shifts and buying food from drive-ins when they could.

Their car smelled worse than a boar's den during high rutting season, and both of them were feeling like absolute fevered crap. Each tried to hide symptoms from the other, but Blackie had several times gotten the sensation that the car had just lifted off the ground and was drifting along in a cloud of uncomfortably hot air while he was driving. As for Joellen, she'd had to pull over a couple of times because she was getting tunnel vision and shortness of breath.

Their infections made them feel paranoid and obvious, so they'd cut down on food and water. (Plus, the roadside stuff was *so damn expensive!*) But the hunger and thirst had made them reckless and desperate, and that was when Joellen came up with her plan: They'd go to a roadside convenience store, lure out the clerk, overpower him and tie him up. Then they'd steal all the money, gas, food, aspirin, that fancy-pants bottled water… everything they needed.

While Owen Milk struggled against his bonds, the pair grabbed chips and cookies and Wonder Bread one handed, rushing back and forth between the car and the convenience store deliriously. Blackie paused to tear open a Moon Pie, only to have his mother sharply tell him there'd be time for that on the road. The store had a small supply of fresh fruit, and she grabbed it all. They got lunchmeat, cheese, crackers and a small jar of mustard. They got pre-made hoagies and a couple of hot dogs. There was a small display of over-the-counter medicines: They took them all. They took Diet Coke and 7-Up and Starbucks brand mochachino. They took Perrier and Red Bull and a variety of Elements.

They were four miles down the road before they realized they'd forgotten to rob the till. But they were so happy to be eating and drinking that they just laughed it off.

Chapter Five

"Los Angeles," Matthew Wallace said, looking out over his congregation. He paused. He said it again. "Los Angeles.

"You know, a lot of people call LA the new Babylon. You heard this? They say that LA is a venal place. A wicked place. They call it the new Sodom, the new Gomorrah. And if you've been there, sometimes you can see their point."

Another pause as he turned thoughtful eyes to the camera, but only for a moment.

"You can drive down Hollywood streets and see harlots of every nation, every race and creed, plying their trade in their sad, ridiculous high heels and stockings and fake-leather vinyl skirts. You don't have to seek this out, you can see it driving from your hotel to a drug store 'cause you forgot to pack a toothbrush! And you can shake your head and cluck your tongue and say, 'What a baaaaad town.'

"You can go by Paramount and Universal Pictures and see the ads for the movies they make—movies packed full of murder and vice and lewdness; adultery for fun and crime paying plenty. You see that filth everywhere, at any theater in America, any theater in the world, but you know it comes from Hollywood and you say, 'What a baaaaad place.'

"That's without going into the pollution and the political corruption and the racial-profiling policemen and the ghettos. Ghettos that gave birth to gangs as we know them, ghettos that innovated the modern crack trade in our cities, ghettos so full of pain and despair that people embrace the lies and *death* from drugs rather than face the true suffering of life! LA is all that.

"What a bad, baaaaad city."

He paused.

"And let's not forget the traffic."

The timing was spot on—a one-liner that produced enough laughter to cool things down a degree without completely chilling his meaning and mood.

"Los Angeles. City of *Angels*. But if you follow the news, it looks like a city of devils.

"Yeah, you know what I'm talking about. The Lucifer Tape. The Evil One spotted, coming out of a Los Angeles restaurant, film at eleven! And one group on the news wags their heads and says, 'It's fake, it's all fake. There's no devil in Los Angeles.' And others, they say, 'It's real, it's true. Satan is alive and well and living in California!'

"Who's right?

"Is there real evil, incarnate, stalking the streets of the City of Angels? I don't know. And what's more, *I don't care.*"

He paused to let that one sink in.

"Is it the Adversary himself, or a special effect turned tasteless prank? I don't care. Beelzebub, or bytes and bits? I don't care! The Great Beast or more Hollywood hogwash? I do not care!

"And do you know why?"

"Why?" asked a parishioner.

"Do you want to know why?"

"Tell us!" "Tell us why, Reverend!"

"If you want to know why, I'll tell you why. I don't care because it doesn't matter! It doesn't matter if the Devil is there with cloven hooves and wings of fire! It doesn't matter if it's just some giggling nerd with a fancy computer and a taste for practical jokes! It doesn't matter if Satan is there because *evil* is there, my people! Suffering is there! A million souls cry out in pain, while we sit around trying to guess if it's live or Memorex!"

Murmurs were echoing back at him from his congregation, and it lifted him, buoyed him up, and his arms came out as if to pull his voice louder.

"We love to be smug, sitting here a thousand miles away saying, 'Oh, that baaad town. Oh, that evil city, it finally got what it *deserved*!' Hollywood partied into the wee hours, Hollywood snorted its cocaine, Hollywood drank its champagne, Hollywood threw up in the swimming pool, and now we'd like to sit back and watch when the landlord comes down to the new Sodom saying, 'Uh, someone's gotta pay for this.'

"Someone's gotta pay.

"We love to watch Hollywood, that wicked city, that smog bank on the Pacific, get its comeuppance. We'd love to see the Devil come and cart the whole place off, love to watch it fall into the sea. Wouldn't we?"

He turned to where his family was sitting.

"Now, those of you who've been with me a while may be familiar with my son Noah."

The camera panned in, and Noah's face was embarrassed.

"This boy of mine went off to college, got a load of education, learned everything 'postmodern' and 'hypertextual.' He learned everything about 'deconstruction' and what was that word son?"

"Which word?" Gaviel asked, playing the straight man, a boom mic right out of the camera's range dipping to catch each lovely syllable.

"That word you said last night."

"I don't know what you mean."

"Some word, big fancy word... German word, you said it meant 'taking a cruel pleasure from another's misfortune.'"

"Schadenfreude."

"Shadden-froyd," Matthew repeated. He shook his head. "Now that's what I call a five-center. Shaddenfroyd. Uh huh. I got another word for that.

"I call it sin."

"Amen!" "Tell it, Reverend!"

"*I* call it *sin*."

"Hallelujah!"

"I call it *sin* to sit here, in the comfort of our homes, maybe with some salsa chips and a beer next to the remote, watching *earthquake footage*, and *smiling*! I call it pride! I call it pride and sin! We sit here thinking, 'I'm glad it's them and not me,' when we see some poor soul who's got no home, no food, drinking water from a busted sewer pipe 'cause that's all she can get! We sit here watching that earthquake footage, and it's just like a movie, ain't it? A real Hollywood blockbuster. It's got explosions, it's got guns going off and crime and drama of every sort, and we watch! We watch, and it's okay because it's real? Is that how this works? Because it's *real* suffering, *real* death, *real* horror, it's okay for us to watch? We shake our heads over the fake stuff, roll our eyes at the slasher flicks and *Halloween* and *Hannibal*, but when the blood's *not* fake and the people *aren't* actors, we can't get enough!

"It's a sin."

"Oh Lord! Merciful Lord!"

"We sit and watch, and all we need is some curly white wigs, 'cause we're *judging* them. We can watch LA go to hell because some part of us thinks, 'Oh, the Devil would never come to *Saint Louis*. The Devil would never come and blow up Jefferson City. The Antichrist wouldn't arise to personally annihilate... oh, for example... Florissant, Missouri.'

"You know what I say to that?

"I say, 'Judge not, that ye be not judged.'

"I say that every city, every town and village and tarpaper shack, lies under the shadow of the Devil's burning spear. I say that we are all, in this life, subject to his cruelty. I say that this world, the world of the flesh, is under his dominion, and that anyone who denies it is delivering himself, herself, unto Satan."

"Save me, Lord!" cried a woman from the pews.

"You tell it, sister!" Matthew replied, a hand darting out and back to point at her. "This woman knows! She knows! She knows from whence her mercy comes! Because we don't pray, 'Oh Lord, give me some temptation to resist!' We pray, 'Lead us not into temptation!'

"Who are we to judge the people of Los Angeles? Who are we to sit so smug and say, 'Well *I* wouldn't do that.' Do you know? Has a movie star ever offered to do some lines with you? You ladies think that if Denzel Washington cocked his eye your way, you'd be so strong? You *know* it? Or you fellahs, if Halle Berry said, 'Oooh, could you put some lotion on my back with your big strong hands?' — are you so sure you'd be such a good, righteous, Christian man?

"We are sinners all, and weak, and we should praise God right now for not tempting us more."

"Amen!" "Hallelujah!" "Praise the Lord!"

"We watch LA suffer and we go, 'Well, someone had to pay.' And we feel so holy and pure because we never got tempted like them. But we're no better, and they're no worse, and the sins of the new Babylon were paid for two thousand years ago.

"Yeah, you know what I'm talking about. You know. What we see in LA now, it ain't justice, my people. This ain't God coming down and saying the rent is due. What's going on out there, is the Devil's double billing!

"The sins of the world are paid in full!"

"Amen!"

"The sins of the world are washed clean!"

"Praise the Lord!"

"The sins of the world are gone, outta there, lights out, game over! The sins of the world, yours and mine, died on the cross with our Lord and Savior Jesus Christ!

"So what does that mean?"

"Tell us!"

"What does it mean?"

"Tell us what it means!"

"What does this mean, for us, and for Los Angeles, for that poor beat-down city of angels? It means it could be us. It means their suffering is unfair. That's what's wrong, that's the evil, that's the Devil in the city, and that's what *we must fight!*"

"Amen!"

"Who wants to fight?"

"I do!"

"Who *wants* to *fight* that evil?"

"I'll fight it, Rev'ren'!"

"I hear you, my people, and we all gotta fight it. We all gotta fight the good fight, and today that fight is in Los Angeles! Who's gonna fight it?"

"We are!"

"Who?"

"WE ARE!"

"Hallelujah! Every one of you here can fight this! Every one of you here can put on the armor of righteousness and roll out against the suffering and pain of this world! There is not one of you, no, not one, who does not have something to offer Los Angeles, poor LA, the fallen city! Certainly you can offer up your prayers. We're all praying, every one of us. Maybe you have more. Maybe you can give 'em money! Maybe you can give 'em food! Maybe you can go out there, take a trip with us and *The Hour of Jesus' Power*, and give 'em some comfort and help first hand! Because we're not sitting still here! We're getting ready to go! It's sudden, yes, but God moves in sudden ways.

His moment comes like a thief in the night, and you gotta be ready to go! And we're going, my children! *We* are *going* to *Los Angeles!*"

After the service, Gaviel sat behind a desk in the foyer, taking names, collecting pledges. People were enthusiastic, everyone was coming by and signing up for something. He knew, from Noah's experience, that some would just forget their pledges of cash and canned goods. Once, that had bothered Noah, but Gaviel just accepted that some people didn't pull through, for whatever reason. Others would back out of the journey when they thought about it more—when they gave their fears a chance to rebut the reverend's encouraging words. That was fine too. If anything, the demon within Noah had even lower expectations for mankind, and it was... sweet, almost, to see them care. Even to see them *wanting* to care, it was like a sigh, like a song—and not one of those human songs, they were all the same to Gaviel, might as well be the sounds of cats fucking—like the angel songs he could not quite remember. The songs of purity and devotion; the songs that were silenced forever by the war and still absent from the world they'd made.

"Good morning, May," he said. He put a tiny touch of shyness in it—not too much, because Noah wouldn't be shy around her normally. Just a pinch. Just enough to make her wonder why.

May was shy, too. She was always shy. She looked down at her feet. "Hi, Noah," she replied.

"Are you going to sign up for the trip?"

"I don't know if I can get off work."

He nodded, understanding.

"When do you think...? Oh, never mind," he said.

"What?"

"Uh, well… I was going to say, or ask… when you would know. You know. So you could call me and let me, uh, know one way or the other."

"Oh. Well, I could probably find out on Monday."

"All right. Good. You'll, uh, call me Monday?"

"Okay. Are you at your parents' house?"

"No, I have a place in St. Louis."

"Oh."

"Yeah, it's in University City. It's all right. I transferred to Wash U to finish off my degree and be closer to home." He blushed and looked behind her. "Look at me, chewing your ear off when there's a line forming."

She stepped aside and let people sign up to be kind. But she and Gaviel continued their conversation.

The devil couldn't be sure, but he thought that maybe the pain of being in the church wasn't so bad this time.

Black Hawk O'Hanlon didn't realize he was in an utter daze until his mother snapped him out of it. He was driving the car, he'd been driving the car for… how long? He didn't know how long. He'd been driving. Driving the car. The highway was flat and empty. It had been empty and flat for a long time, then they'd gotten closer and closer to Las Vegas, and they'd switched off outside Vegas, his mom had driven because you needed a fresh driver when there were people around, couldn't do anything weird or suspicious that might get the cops' attention, because the radio said there was a nationwide manhunt for him and Mama, they'd found the guy at the convenience store and he'd identified them, and there were pictures from the Shell station security cameras, and the man on the radio had read out their license plate number and everything.

Mama had driven around the outskirts of Vegas, and there'd been a lot of cars. She cursed and hissed at the drivers while she tried to keep to the speed limit, and then things had trailed off, and they'd been out in the desert again, more hills this time, but still dry and dusty and full of nothing.

They'd switched and he'd driven... and it had become day. The sun had risen at some point, and he hadn't even noticed, he just drove, straight and flat and thoughtless, as if he'd been driving forever, as if he was going to drive forever, and then his mother said, "Stop! Turn around!" He slammed his foot on the brake.

The car squealed and slid, and he counter-steered, and it was like waking out of a sound sleep and finding yourself on top of a roller coaster. He ran the steering wheel back and forth, trying to stay in control, and then they were in the ditch, surrounded by a thick dust cloud the color of French's mustard, and all was still.

He realized that he still had the lights on, so he turned them off. Then he realized that the radio was on, but no station was coming in, just static.

Was I driving in my sleep? he wondered. He turned the radio off. Only then did he realize that his mother was yelling at him.

"...the high hell is wrong with you? When I said stop, I meant stop *proper*, not stop like a goddamn fool!"

"Sorry, Mama, but you shouldn't yell at me like that. You startled me."

"Well, here we are in the ditch now, bright boy. Again. Good job. Oh, I swear..."

"It's not so bad. The car has four-wheel drive. I'll just push us out." As he opened his door, his wounded left hand tapped the door frame and he winced. It had swelled up under its unchanged bandages. It was at least an inch thicker and wider than his right (which still had both of the sheriff's cuffs attached to it). The rags wrapped around it were stiff, with pus leaking out the bottom edge. It smelled like the garbage bin behind a Burger King on a hot summer day.

"Why'd you yell anyhow?"

"We're almost there."

"Yeah?" The idea of a destination had slipped his mind completely. For days, he'd just been running. Even the notion of running away had faded, blanked out by fever and fatigue.

It was awkward pushing the car with just one hand, but he got his shoulders and back into it and they got back on the road. Three cars drove by while he was pushing, but none stopped.

Joellen stayed behind the wheel and turned off onto a dirt road, then she turned off that and parked the car by a low rise. They climbed the hill, and both were too befuddled by illness and fatigue (and, in Joellen's case, religious ecstasy) to notice Tim Grady's footprints, several days faded in the still desert dust.

They walked to the tree and touched it, and like him, they were pulled into the depths of the earth.

Chapter Six

A bout six months passed.
Gaviel went to Los Angeles with a gun and a plan and a bus full of the faithful. He came back happy, having stolen a briefcase full of money and a suitcase full of cocaine. He'd also managed to betray and kill two other demons, one of whom he'd devoured with delicious ruthlessness. Killing a human by stealing her soul had been the best part of the trip. He never even learned her name, and that anonymity actually made the experience even more titillating. He did lose the gun there, but that was okay.

The ghost of Rosemary Nevins searched for her killer but found him nowhere in the lands of the living or the dead. That scared her. She went back to Los Angeles to see if her places of memory were being repaired, but she periodically returned to the desert, to the tree with the ominous sense of power and presence, to the site where the most important person in her world had vanished without a trace. She had a lot of years of hate built up in her and she remained strong, able to slip between Nevada and California without the effort eroding her into nothingness. But if Tim was gone for good and the site of her death remained buried and unremembered in light of far greater tragedy, well those were not good prospects for Rosemary Nevins. She spent altogether too much of those six moths being afraid.

Mitch Berger wound up in an emergency aid camp administered by FEMA. His leg got set, but the break was worse than Mr. Moriarty had thought, and he was on crutches for a long time. After that, he used a cane. He got part of a relief settlement and he got workman's compensation. (This despite his leave of absence the day of the quake. The issue was quietly dropped because two of his superiors were killed in the mass escape.) When his leg finally healed, he set out looking for Chuck Rodriguez.

Chuck was a guest on a lot of talk shows and news shows and radio call-in programs, where he loudly and frequently testified that the Lucifer footage was genuine in all particulars. He was cheered on Springer and hissed on *The View*, and one caller to Larry King swore to "kill him deader than shit." ("Shit" was of course bleeped out with the five-second delay.) There were rumors about him getting a book deal. Then he disappeared.

Terry Cook's cab company lost a lot of money during the three days they gave rides away, but the good press more than compensated. No, what bankrupted the company was a pair of lawsuits. Two people who'd been transported to the hospital in cabs died, and their surviving relatives sued Terry Cook for not transporting them correctly.

Terry turned out OK, though. He declared bankruptcy, went on talk shows—sometimes with Chuck Rodriguez—and received enough cash donations from outraged and sympathetic Americans to settle with the relatives. His ghostwritten book, *Cook's Cabbies: Blue-Collar Heroes and the Devil's Night Quake*, stayed on the bestseller list for three weeks. When Artisan made it into a movie, he was played by Brian Dennehy, who had not been killed after all.

Mr. Moriarty tried to keep his store open during the civil unrest, but he got shot by a Satanist when he sold first-aid supplies to both Satanists and Christians after one of the many brawls and riots that occurred between cliques of the faithful. The bullet lodged in his spinal cord and doomed him to impotence, a colostomy and a wheelchair for the rest of his life.

Tansy wasn't so lucky. She died in the riots. So did Squirt. So did the soap opera actress.

The Reverend Matthew Wallace made a concerted effort to keep the seventh commandment, but the flesh was weak. After six weeks, he again committed adultery against his wife, Zola, with Gina Parris. He also tried to remain strong and skeptical against the demon that wore the face of his beloved son.

Joellen O'Hanlon slept in the timeless ground beside Tim Grady and her son, Black Hawk. They felt nothing, knew nothing and were unaware that they awaited the coming of the High Priest.

Lynn Culver, the sad and confused woman who set fire to the Catholic Church in Mulesboro, moved up north to Oswego, Illinois, and started a new life. She worked for the grounds-keeping office of a local community college, typing and filing and answering the phones. It was okay.

George Lasalle, who took the fall for Lynn's arson, continued to attend services at the church he'd allegedly ignited. He showed up every Sunday just before mass began and left right after communion. Nonetheless, several parishioners a week managed to offer him their forgiveness and understanding. Every Sunday, he seemed a little smaller, a little more ashamed and a little more withdrawn.

Officer Rebecca Ellison ran into her old high-school boyfriend at a class reunion and wound up marrying him a year and a half later. Three years later, she retired from the police force to stay home and raise their first child. She lived a content and conventional life, but she never stopped blushing when she heard about the great LA quake.

The demon Hasmed, hosted in the chump Harvey Ciullo, established himself as an up-and-coming criminal mastermind then threw away his chance to enter the Mafia so that he could save the life of sweet, innocent, three-year-old Tina Ciullo. This led him to screw over Johnny Bronco's mob for Rico Pudoto's Atlantic City gang. A war started, many gangsters died, and it looked like many more would.

Thomas Ramone got kidnapped, sold his soul for freedom, pulled a few robberies, got fired and found a new job.

The infernal temptress Sabriel (also known as Christina Vadrudakis, Angela Meyerhoff and "Keiko from Vegas") bought a bookstore, helped Hasmed steal a lot of money and accidentally began the slow and dangerous process of waking the slumbering demon Avitu.

Sal Macellaio got on the bad side of Rico Pudoto's mob war and fled New Jersey, licking his wounds and swearing to destroy Harvey Ciullo—or whatever Ciullo had become—if it was the last thing he did.

Usiel, who never rebelled but was confined to Hell anyway, waged a solitary war against any and all demons he met. But without allies or support, he was mainly limited to striking at servants and lesser fiends. Then one day, he met Lucifer.

Teddy Mason, a somewhat neurotic furniture-store manager, found that his sexual dysfunctions and general uneasiness vanished, miraculously, the night he finally remembered the name of a tree in a dream he'd had every month since puberty. He found a new sense of purpose and rightness and duty, and he took his wife and son to Las Vegas with lies about winning a family vacation.

The name from Teddy Mason's dream was Avitu, and though he didn't know it, he was destined to be her High Priest.

As for Owen Milk, he stayed on the job at the Shell station until his death, years later. He died plugging in a poorly wired coffee-maker at work. In his entire career, he'd only been late nine times and had only missed work seventeen times.

Chapter Seven

Thomas Ramone dreamed he was back in high school. He was wandering through the halls, which were thick with his fellow students. Everyone seemed to be moving along purposefully, getting to class, clutching papers and books. Only Thomas was unsure—unsure which period it was, or which class he was heading to, or if he had his homework done. He had a terrible feeling that he didn't, that the teacher was going to ask for a report and he'd just hang his head and look stupid while the other kids snickered about him being a stoner and a moron. Or maybe it was test day. Maybe that was it: There was a test in Physics or Geometry or something, and no way was he ready. But he had to go, right?

Thomas found himself in the boys' bathroom, and suddenly he had to take a shit real bad. He looked around—the place was huge but dirty. There were grungy tiles on the floor and stains from water damage on the ceiling, the mirrors had black flecks where their backing was coming loose, and all the stall dividers were covered with peeling, sickly green paint. Something stank, too.

But he had to do what he had to do, so he opened one of the stall doors, only to realize that the stalls were enormous. Each one had about five toilets in it, and each toilet was just overflowing with drippy, festering crap. Rolls and rolls of toilet paper hung out of the bowls next to yellow drizzles, and his gorge rose thinking of sitting on *that*, but damn, he really had to go, and this was the only place.

And he wasn't *alone*. There were other guys there, sitting on those filthy commodes—big guys, football and wrestling types, looking at him and waiting for him to drop trousers and do the same, like, what? Is he too good for this, huh?

Then Thomas woke up.

He moved his eyes a bit behind shut lids, then rubbed sleep out of the corners and opened them. He realized that he really, truly did have to drop a load, which he got up and did in the dim solitude of his efficiency apartment toilet.

While he was sitting there, he realized that it was finally the last day of his parole.

Gaviel listened to NPR as he drove to East St. Louis, but he paid only partial attention. It was an interview with an author who was talking about how a particular mathematical function yielded a string of numbers that cropped up again and again in nature.

"…sunflowers, for instance, almost always have 17, 21 or 28 petals. Those are the third, fourth and fifth numbers in the sequence. Albuquerque cornflowers have 14, 17 or 21—the second, third and fourth…"

Gaviel grinned. He'd known the angel that embodied that mathematical function. Her name had been Bosuile, and she'd stayed loyal to God. Her numbers recurred in flowers because, during the war, Gaviel and two Slayers had torn her to pieces over a vast field of blossoms.

But although the thought of an old kill brought a smile to his face, he was mainly concentrating on a newer one: Edasul, the demon he'd killed and consumed in Los Angeles. He hadn't gotten much of her essence, really. The feasting was an inefficient process without intimate knowledge of the victim's nature, and he just hadn't had time to do the research. Nonetheless, there was a spark of her within him now, alive and enslaved and very useful.

Edasul had been one of the Neberu, once an angel of patterns and fortune. Since the Fall, they'd become angels of misfortune, which meant that their predictions were warped and their foresight imperfect. But even a blurry glimpse at the underpinnings of fate was preferable to blindness.

Gaviel hadn't enjoyed running from East Saint Louis before, but with Edasul's stolen sight and his growing recall of fire's language, he thought he might be able to make things uncomfortable for whatever thing was lurking there. And if he made some bucks in the process, all the better.

(While Gaviel was parking his car, the Reverend Matthew Wallace was sitting down at his desk with a white legal pad to start putting together his sermon on the subject of Matthew 19:24. He'd an uncomfortable moment looking through his Bible when he came across Matthew 19:9 and its mention of adultery.)

Gaviel's foggy fate-sight led him to one particular gang fortress among several. He got out of his car, took a drag on his cigarette, picked up his suitcase and rang the bell for the second-floor apartment.

A short and suspicious conversation ensued, in which Gaviel offered to sell pure cocaine at pennies on the dollar, while the unseen man within asserted (not very convincingly) that there was no cocaine trade occurring within. Gaviel persisted. He opened his briefcase so that those in the upstairs apartment could see the blocky shape inside, and he continued to market his wares in such an aggressive fashion that, had he been a police officer, any judge in the nation would deem it entrapment.

He was admitted.

(Matthew's desk was a thing of beauty. Zola had gotten it for him when he'd signed the contract to go on TV. It was sleek and huge and dark and polished. His daughter had once said it looked like the desk Darth Vader would sit at to do his taxes. When Matthew was preparing a sermon, he sat there alone with the door closed and insisted on absolutely no interruptions. He stared at the white legal pad—he never used a yellow one—and then wrote *GREED* at the top in capital letters.)

Gaviel climbed a stairwell that was so filthy that it was impossible to tell what color its carpet had once been. There was a small landing at the top, and walking upward he faced empty beer cans, discarded cigarette butts, blackened glass pipes and a featureless brick wall. Turning to face the apartment door, another wall was at his back. There'd been a window once, but it was covered with sheet metal. He faced a sturdy steel door with a sliding slot at eye height. It was a good setup: There was no room to swing a battering ram, and anyone who got in front of the door had nowhere to hide from the perspective of a viewer within.

The slot opened, revealing a pair of eyes and the twin barrels of a shotgun.

(Matthew skipped three lines on the pad, tapped his pen against his lower lip, then wrote: *We hear a lot about greed, these days.* He frowned, switched pens, scratched out *We hear a lot* in red ink and wrote *A lot of people are talking* above it.

(Matthew used three pens to write a sermon. First he captured his initial thoughts in black ink, crossing it out in red to make corrections. The final draft was written in blue and left to sit overnight before being copied, by hand, in black, onto 3x5 index cards. He practiced with the cards until he could do it from memory.)

Following orders, Gaviel opened his shirt and dropped his pants, demonstrating that he wasn't wearing a wire. The door opened and Gaviel walked in, swinging his suitcase jauntily, looking around at the scene of squalor.

A haze of bluish smoke drifted around the ceiling. A rickety card table in the kitchenette area had piles of currency and a sorting machine. Two bare bulbs hung from cords and provided illumination. The room's only window was sheeted over with metal plate. In the living room, two wicker-back chairs faced a sofa, with a large-screen TV behind them. The TV was off.

In front of the couch was a coffee table holding a couple of beer bottles, remote controls, a smoldering bong shaped like a nude woman writhing in ecstasy, ashtrays, rolling papers, a *TV Guide* and the liner notes from a couple of DVDs. On the wall was a faded Rainbow/ PUSH poster and a lot of peeling wallpaper. On the sofa was a man.

(The three pens Matthew used were exquisite. They were fountain pens, and before he started writing, he loaded them up with ink from glass bottles. The pen that wrote in black was decorated with onyx. The blue pen was inlaid with lapis lazuli. The red pen was plated with coral. Each pen was pleasingly heavy in the hand, well balanced, suited for important documents. Matthew held them unusually far back, which meant he wrote in broad letters—his grip was a holdover from his days using Bic disposables, which tended to leak and stain his fingertips. He still used Bics for other matters, but Zola had gotten him the beautiful three-pen set as a Christmas gift, so he never used anything else to write his sermons.)

The man on the couch was young and muscular, with yellow-black skin and a nose bulbed by booze or syphilis. The man from the door stayed back, cradling his shotgun like a child as Gaviel entered. A third man stood in the hall to the rest of the apartment. He leaned there casually with one hand behind his back.

Gaviel stuck out his hand like he was at a job interview. The man on the couch ignored it, so instead Gaviel took another puff on his cigarette, then set it in the ashtray and pulled up a chair.

It was obvious the sofa man was the leader, so Gaviel negotiated with him. There was some brief verbal sparring—some jibes about a "door-to-door coke salesman," which Gaviel took with good grace. The demon spun out a plausible story about how he'd grabbed the coke in California by keeping his wits when the shit went down. He said he'd come home to St. Louis and was willing to sell it cheap because (1) he didn't pay for it in the first place, and (2) he had no other way to turn it into cash.

(Matthew made notes about the evils of greed, giving examples of people whose addiction had left them with nothing, people whose materialism had made them outcasts, people whose emphasis on the wealth of the world had drawn them away from the life of the spirit. He frowned. It seemed rather flat, somehow.)

The potential customer expressed doubts about the quality of the merchandise, which Gaviel allayed by opening his package on the table and letting the man sample. Next, the client explained that his operation already had a supplier, that their supplier did not look on competition kindly, and that dealing with more than one supplier was severely frowned upon in his business.

Gaviel said he understood those concerns, but he suggested that the supplier need never know (nor concern himself) with a little side action. The demon proposed that, instead of using his cheap coke to drastically increase their supply and sell more, that they keep the price the same and sell a purer product. This would not net them any money directly, since they'd sell the same amount at the same price, but by the same token, it wouldn't rouse any suspicions with their current distributor. The long-term effect, however, would be increased business stimulated by a superior product, undercutting the competition for a fraction of the normal cost.

There was some posturing about whether Gaviel was trying to teach the man his business, and the fellow with the shotgun put it to the back of Gaviel's head. Gaviel calmly questioned the wisdom of pointing a loaded weapon in the same direction as the man's boss, prompting the gunman to step to the side and threaten him from that position. But the exchange had established Gaviel's credibility, so the demon didn't really mind.

(Matthew rolled his eyes upward, trying to remember some line about "risking eternity to win a toy." Was it eternity? The toy part sounded right. And who said it, anyway? Shakespeare? Maybe a little too far out there for his audience.)

After a pause, the man wondered out loud why he shouldn't simply kill Gaviel right then, steal the product, lose *no* money and be able to be honest with his supplier. Gaviel shrugged and said that what he'd brought was only a small portion of what he had to sell.

There was a moment of contemplative silence.

Gaviel held his breath. He was thinking that they'd either go for the long-term deal, or they'd choose instant gratification and try to rob him.

The man on the couch made his decision.

Thanks to the little piece of Edasul that Gaviel held within, the demon knew the choice before the other two—and before anyone else could act on it.

While the boss was inhaling to order Gaviel's death, the demon was raising his left hand and starting to speak. He hadn't been holding his breath from fear, but to give himself that half-moment advantage.

He spoke a short burst of Enochian, the angel language, and with loud and dazzling pops, the two naked light bulbs burnt out all at once. The man with the shotgun fired both barrels, but not until Gaviel's rising left hand had pointed it harmlessly upward. Standing, Gaviel pulled on the gun barrel, and the man pulled back. The tug-of-war lasted only a second, though: Gaviel switched from pulling to pushing, and smacked the man in the face with the weapon.

The man on the couch was standing and drawing. The man in the hallway was stepping in, pistol in hand. Everyone's eyes were starting to adapt to the dim light seeping around the edges of the window cover. Both men were starting to aim at Gaviel.

The fallen angel closed his eyes and said a few more words in the ancient language; sang a few more notes in the ancient song.

His cigarette exploded—a harmless burst of warmth and brief light, but enough to dazzle the gunmen again for a few seconds more. Gaviel's mind held a mental map of the table, the chairs, the litter on the floor, and he took a few steps back and sideways, eyes still shut, while his enemies fired blind. He opened one eye, now dark-adapted, and watched the disarmed shotgunner reaching for the front door. He paused just a moment, timing it, timing it...

"He gettin' away!" he shouted, in a credible imitation of the boss' voice. There was just enough urgency in it to spur action without thought, and the man in the hallway fired at the silhouette in the doorway a split-second before his eyes and mind registered that it wasn't the stranger, the salesman, but his friend.

The noise and flash made the real boss turn his head, and Gaviel stepped up and swung the shotgun like a baseball bat. The man dropped, face down, back onto the sofa.

The injured man fell forward through the door, spilling dim light inside, as Gaviel pointed his weapon at the other gunman and said, "Drop it."

Instinctively, the man complied, stepping back as Gaviel approached. The demon grinned as he stooped for the pistol.

"You do realize, don't you, that this is a double-barreled shotgun? And that your jumpy friend pulled both triggers? So that you just dropped a loaded gun because of a threat from an empty one? You get all that, right?"

The man blinked and said "Aw, shit."

Then they both smelled smoke.

Gaviel heard the crackle behind him, the voice of the flames, and he could see them reflected in the other man's eyes. His human body's reflex was to turn and look, but the demon didn't do so until he'd shot the third gangster in the chest—really, just as a safety precaution. Then, gun still ready, he turned and saw.

When he'd unnaturally accelerated the burn of his cigarette, some sparks must have fallen on the table's clutter of paper and dry dust. The *TV Guide* was on fire, and the precious white powder was quickly catching.

The demon asked the flames to stop, but they ignored his request. He dropped the shotgun and reached in bare-handed to salvage what he could. Grabbing the cut-open plastic package made about half of it spill out onto the table, which was itself starting to smolder, and then the man in the doorway shot him in the back.

"Ow!" the demon yelled. He staggered forward, knocking the table over and spilling all the coke—some still burning—onto the filthy carpet.

As the man took a second shot (a miss), Gaviel turned and returned fire. He supposed it was only reasonable that the man would carry a second gun. Why hadn't Edasul's power foreseen it? Was she, perhaps, still alive in some fashion, still thwarting him? Surely not. It must just be the inherent problems of trying to predict an unpredictable world.

After all, her powers hadn't saved her from him.

Gaviel knit the hole in his body and finally struck flesh with his third gunshot. But by then the *other* injured gangster—the dumb, gutshot one from the hallway—was making mischief.

The demon stood up and strode toward him, shaking his head in disbelief. The mortal was setting the money on fire!

"What the fuck are you thinking?" Gaviel demanded, shoving the man aside and grabbing for the piles that weren't yet alight. He could only grab one-handed, as he kept the pistol aimed with the other.

"If I can't have it, you can't either," the man mumbled.

"That's a very silly and childish attitude," the demon said. He shot the man a second time, this time in the face.

(Matthew carefully capped his pens and decided he'd done as much as he was going to. It wasn't flowing. It wasn't right. He decided to go have a contemplative sit in the sauna and see if that would help him concentrate.)

At the same moment that Gaviel was chiding the gangbanger for dropping his pistol, Usiel the Reaper of Souls was in a bar, realizing that he was talking to none other than Lucifer the Morningstar.

The infamous Adversary, the angel who first declared enmity against the Maker of All and whose cry rallied a third of the Host to fight and suffer and, eventually, fall at his side. Lucifer, the Deceiver, the Lord of the Flies, stood beside Usiel in the TGI Friday's, offering to split an order of hot wings and inviting him to fight by his side against others who had found freedom from Hell's imprisonment.

Usiel responded as any good angel (and many demons) would. He turned, got off his barstool and threw a hard right hook.

He intended it as a distraction while he got his scythe ready, but the Morningstar ducked the blow and charged in, wrapping Usiel in his arms. The pair rebounded off the bar and staggered down the aisle. They slammed into the door to the short-order kitchen and then they were suddenly elsewhere.

Usiel recognized the effect—to some demons, all doors were as one, and Lucifer had certainly had ages to acquire the trick. They were somewhere sunny and hot and seemingly empty of life.

"Don't be a fool," the Adversary cautioned, but Usiel wasn't listening, didn't dare listen, wouldn't let himself hear that voice of dread command.

Instead, the Reaper of Souls touched a ring on his finger, and in an instant, the ring became the releasing tool of a Slayer, empowered to sever the bonds that tie all life to life. He gripped the scythe with both hands, one whole and one badly mangled, and he swung the shadowy blade at Lucifer's head.

The Adversary didn't even try to duck. He clapped, once, and the scythe was a gray metal ring again. It wasn't even on Usiel's hand, it dropped through the air into Lucifer's waiting palm.

"You're just wasting time," Lucifer said, but Usiel was transforming, casting aside his mortal shell and revealing himself in the fearsome form of an Angel of Death.

Then Lucifer spoke several phrases in the tongue of angels, and Usiel stopped cold. He knew those sounds. In a very real way, he *was* those sounds. Lucifer continued, and Usiel tried to lunge forward, to strike wildly, to silence the demon king before Usiel's True Name was completed, but it was too late. Lucifer Named him, and Usiel was trapped. The Name wasn't perfect—his term in Hell and his experiences on Earth had changed his nature slightly, and those changes were reflected in his Name—but it was more than enough. Knowing Usiel's True Name, the Adversary was free to imprison, destroy or command Usiel in any fashion he wished.

Lucifer's next words in the True Song almost sounded conversational. It was a minor and temporary edit to Usiel's

Name and self. The Adversary had disabled Usiel's voluntary muscle control.

The Reaper of Souls dropped in a heap to the desert floor.

"I asked you to join me in my fight against the greater demons," Lucifer said. "I retrieved this trinket for you, knowing you would use it against those freed from the Abyss." He tossed the scythe-ring into the dust by Usiel's face. "I even gave you advice—excellent advice—about strengthening your hand in Oswego with Glenda Fielding. Now you know that I could compel you if I wished—or devour you and add your small stock of power to my own depleted supply. But I'll do neither."

He turned to the door through which they'd entered. Usiel could now see that it was some sort of long-abandoned shack, apparently the only structure within miles.

He felt his muscles gradually returning to his control. "Why?" he asked with a thick tongue.

In the doorway, the Adversary paused and looked back. "Because I don't want to play God," he replied. Then he was gone.

Driving home, Gaviel was disgruntled, though he was careful not to let it show on his face. No one was there to see him, and he believed that expressions should only be used to communicate to others. Having facial expressions when no one was around to see them was a waste of effort and, worse, a sign of poor emotional discipline. It shocked him to learn that almost all humans did it.

The crack house he'd trashed was not under the influence of his Foe. (That was how he thought about the invisible and unknown malignity that had driven him out before.) He had identified three significant criminal structures operating in the area, and his unseen supernatural opponent was at the back of the strongest one.

Had the sofa-sitter taken his offer, his particular gang would have undercut the profits of the largest group, that is, the Foe's. Eventually, this would prompt reprisals, and the inevitable payback would embroil the Foe in a gang war it probably did not really want—especially with a third group around to play foolkiller.

Now, however, the weak group would see a terrible act against it with no clear-cut enemy to blame. If the Foe was smart (and Gaviel was confident it was), the other small group would soon be framed, prompting the two second-place contenders to savage one another instead of following their *real* interest and ganging up on the leader.

That was really okay with Gaviel as well. If the Foe could detect demonic influence (and Gaviel was pretty sure it could), it would scent the reek of his powers at the scene of the crime and—most likely—assume that he was covertly backing the third group against the second in hopes of strengthening it enough to challenge the first. In fact, Gaviel was planning to throw the entire balance of underworld power in East St. Louis out of whack in order to draw the Foe's attention and energies into schemes and manipulations of the two smaller groups— thereby allowing Gaviel to assess the Foe's powers. Gaviel wasn't particularly alarmed by the thought of the Foe succeeding in taking over East St. Louis: When the time came, he planned to strike straight at the Foe's heart. If anything, having the city's underworld united would only make it easier to usurp control once the Foe was vanquished.

Gaviel?

He heard the voice, not in his ear, but in his head. He recognized it instantly: Sabriel the Defiler.

He grimaced (involuntarily) and wondered whether he should respond or not. The two of them had worked together on a project—that low-level politician, Maryanne Prisco—and it had been a fiasco for everyone involved. Still, Sabriel was a demon, she had power, and if he was going to eventually charge in against the Foe, it might be nice to send her in first.

He had no doubt that her thoughts about him were similarly mercenary, but he was confident that he could out-scheme her. After all, in the rankings of angels, her house was four beneath his.

"Why Sabriel," he said out loud. "What brings you to grace my mind with your melodious voice?"

I just wanted to make sure you weren't mad about Prisco.

"In the long term, anger is a counter-productive emotion, so I try not to bear grudges or bottle it up. I just left three men to burn to death in a crack house, so I'm feeling quite upbeat and chipper."

It sounds like a lovely catharsis.

"It was, it really was. How are things with you?"

Exceptionally splendid.

"I'm *so* glad to hear it," Gaviel said, not believing it for a moment. "So wonderful, in fact, that you've decided to share your good fortune as an apology for our previous unpleasantness?"

Once again, you anticipate me adroitly. Gaviel got the impression that she was enjoying the exchange as much as he was. *I have, as you know, made my residence in Florida.*

"Are you sure I can't tempt you to join me in St. Louis?" he said, feeling certain that his encouragement would make her resist.

I wouldn't want to intrude.

"No intrusion. But if I can't tempt you…"

Of course you tempt me, but I'm quite content here. Recently I was graced by a visit from an old friend of yours.

"And who might that be?"

The Knight of the Hated Lash.

That gave Gaviel pause. "He's escaped then? How marvelous," he said, lest too long a silence alert Sabriel to how much the news affected him.

Didn't you know I was speaking to him a while back? I mentioned your name.

"I must have been distracted and ignored your invocation."

What a pity. He and I worked together on a fund-raising effort that went rather well.

"Do tell," Gaviel said, thinking of the messy heap of half-burned fives and tens in his singed briefcase. The gangster had, through luck or malice, torched the big bills first.

I'm surprised the two of you haven't gotten back together.

"Both quite busy, I'm sure, and I didn't even know he was out." Gaviel realized he was making excuses, and he grimaced. Then he realized that he'd grimaced without anyone to see it, and that annoyed him even more.

Hasmed—the Knight of the Hated Lash—had been his best friend and closest colleague during the war. Together they had battled mountains and murdered oceans; they'd raised up mortals into near gods and had turned cities into fine, dry dust. Yet, Gaviel found himself afraid to see his old battle-mate. Partly, he was ashamed of what he'd become. Partly, he was afraid what his friend might now be. He did not want them to meet as men, wearing human faces and talking as mortals, but he knew that might be the only way.

No doubt those are his reasons as well, Sabriel said.

"Now that you've informed me, I can remedy the situation. I am, of course, quite grateful for this valuable datum."

Then prepare for additional gratitude, as I have another valuable datum—this one a warning.

"I've braced myself to be chilled with dread."

Are you familiar with those demons called "Earthbound"?

"Powerful, crazy and tied into places or inanimate objects? I've had the displeasure."

One of your onetime allies has now become such a creature. She was one of the defenders when we slew Vejovis… I don't recall her title exactly, and I'm reluctant to speak her name…

"Understandably so. I believe you speak of the Keeper of the Twin Winds?"

That's it!

"I'm quite surprised to hear a warning about her. She was always so pleasant."

She's changed, Gaviel. I'm sure she couldn't fool you, but be on your guard nonetheless. She's attacked me, and I barely escaped intact.

"I see. I'll certainly take great care in dealing with the Keeper."

She now styles herself "The Tree of Ignorance."

"I'll remember that as well. Thank you for the warning. Is that all?"

The pair continued to chat and made vague noises about working together again.

When Sabriel disengaged her mind from his, Gaviel drove in silence for about five minutes, thinking hard but not using words to do it. Then he cleared his throat and spoke the name of the Tree of Ignorance.

"Avitu?"

A hole opened in reality.

On one side was the screaming mishmash of nightmare and dead memory and universal chaos that was the kingdom of shadows, the land of death.

On the other side was Oswego, Illinois. Specifically, the vault of Oswego's branch of Bank One.

Before being Bank One, it had been owned by Citibank, and before that it had been First Bank of Oswego. In the 1940s, a pair of men had robbed it, only to gun each other down during a disagreement over a woman.

One man got away. One died. The woman wound up with a good chunk of the money, and she settled down into a life of quiet prosperity.

Usiel had met one of the robbers, Tommy Jenks. The dead one.

After Lucifer left him, the Reaper of Souls took a long trip through the dead zone. He'd gotten into more than one fight. He was tired, he was hurt, and his grip on Clive Keene's body was becoming tenuously thin. He needed to rest and recover physically, but more than that, he needed to restore his spiritual strength. He'd cannibalized part of the demon Vassago, but that had been a long time ago. He'd expended a lot of effort since then.

He'd also realized that Clive Keene's bank account was nearly empty.

Usiel aimed for Oswego because of something Lucifer had said—he'd mentioned Glenda Fielding and promised that she would worship him. And Usiel knew without question that accepting the worship of humans was wrong—that was the sin of the demons, their dirtiest trick in a very dirty war. No way was Usiel going to fall into *that* trap.

Nevertheless, if this Fielding mortal was vulnerable to demonic influence, the decent thing to do was check on her and make sure no *real* monster was taking advantage.

It turned out that Glenda was a wealthy widow who'd recently moved back to the town of her birth... only to find that her past was imperfectly buried.

The haunter was (of course) Tommy Jenks and Glenda was (of course) the woman who'd provoked the lethal argument between Jenks and the other robber. You wouldn't think so to look at her. You'd think that she, like the millions of ordinary people in America, had never been involved with crime or murder or a haunting. But she was. She was haunted.

Jenks had hounded his killer for decades, finally tormenting the man into suicide. That done, he'd gone on to the next victim on his list—former gun moll Glenda.

Usiel had made the mistake of attacking Jenks head on, and had been shocked to learn that an old, experienced and crafty ghost could be a match for a battered, weakened and injured angel. Especially if the fight was on the ghost's home turf.

Jenks got away, Usiel decided to return to the material world… and, inspired by what he'd learned of Jenks's history, he decided to replenish his stores of cash while he did it.

The bank vault was dark inside, but that was nothing to the Reaper of Souls. Where he'd been was blacker than anywhere in the material world *could* be. The money he sought was behind a metal door, but his touch and a forceful word was enough to corrode it into a pile of rust and slag. He grabbed a sack of cash, then stepped away from the world of life again, traveling briefly through death and materializing behind a Holiday Inn.

Only then did he look inside and realize he'd grabbed a bag of one-dollar bills. With a sigh, he wiped his fingerprints off it and chucked it into a garbage dumpster. He didn't feel like taking the trip again, but he needed to pay his motel bill, so he went back. This time he got twenties, and this time he felt like he really understood the human concept of "exhaustion."

Gaviel couldn't find a parking space by his apartment, but as he was walking back, he saw a parked car with the engine running. A bag in the front seat held groceries, with a Kit-Kat bar poking out of the very top. A glance around revealed a woman across the street putting letters in a mailbox. With a nonchalant movement, Gaviel opened the passenger door, stole the candy bar, and closed the door again. When the woman drove past, he was eating it. She didn't notice it was gone until later.

It was a king-sized one, too.

Back in his apartment, Gaviel played an eager message on his answering machine, providing him information on when and where he could start his volunteer work with area high school students. There was a second, even more enthusiastic message about low-interest home loans, which he erased.

He sat on the sofa, watched a war on CNN, ate his stolen candy bar and counted his stolen money. If he'd had a friend there, he would have smiled.

When he pulled up in front of Glenda Fielding's house, the Reaper of Souls could feel the presence within: Jenks, he was sure. He strode forth with purpose, rubbing the ring on his finger. He'd slept well and woken up renewed—not back to his full strength, but certainly enough to deal with one dead uppity bank robber.

"Oh Jesus," he heard from within. "Oh lord, oh Christ, help me, help me!"

Clive Keene hadn't been a strong man, but Glenda didn't have a strong lock. Three hard kicks splintered the door, and he was in.

Glenda was praying on the floor in the living room. It was an overcast day, and the shadows were deeper than they should have been. To Usiel, the undead spirit was obvious, but Glenda peered through him unseeing. But she jumped, startled, when it whispered in her ear.

"*Bitch!*" he hissed. "*I'm burnin'! You're gonna burn too!*"

"Oh God, please help me, please God please…"

"He can't hear you, whore!"

"SILENCE!" Usiel had not cast off Clive's form, but he spoke with his own voice, the voice of an Angel of Death. "BLASPHEMOUS SPIRIT, BEGONE!"

As he shouted, the scythe came to his hand, and with one swing, the shadows cleared. Jenks tried to flee, but with another twist of the blade, his unseen form was caught, pinned.

"SUBMIT," said Usiel, changing scythe to ring, capturing the wraith within its circumference. "I BIND AND COMPEL YOU."

No mortal ear could hear the cry of terror and defiance that escaped the captured ghost, but Usiel heard, and it brought a smile to his lips. He raised the ring toward his mouth and, with a delicate sipping gesture, transferred the creature to a new cage within his body.

"Oh God bless you! God bless! You were sent from Heaven!"

Before he even knew what was happening, the old woman was clinging to his legs, sobbing, the way a frightened child clings to a parent.

"It's... it's okay," he said, reverting once more to Clive's voice. He desperately ransacked his host's memories for a way to deal with this, but Clive had always been rather reserved and formal. No help there.

Then he felt it.

He felt her gratitude and awe and reverence. It hit him like a wrecking ball, and suddenly *he* was the child. Like a newborn feeling its mother's arms after the trauma of delivery, he felt her faith. He reacted, as a baby does. It instinctively turns to the warmth, the embrace, something it has never known but wants and accepts and *needs* with every cell in its body.

He had not felt something like this since he was cast out of the Maker's regard, and it had been a long time.

"Do not worship me," he whispered. "Worship the Allmaker. Worship the one above." But part of him didn't want her to hear or understand.

"God sent you, didn't He?"

Usiel couldn't answer.

"The problem with greed is that it promises everything but delivers nothing! The problem with greed is that it blinds you! It takes the fast car and the Caribbean vacation... Jamaican vacation? Jamaican vacation. Jamaican vacation..." Matthew paused, picked up an ordinary PaperMate pen from a nearby table and made a notation on his 3x5 index card. He'd recopy it later and practice off the pristine one, memorizing for Sunday so it would all sound spontaneous.

He cleared his throat.

"It takes the fast car and the Jamaican vacation, and it makes you think that's all there is! It makes you think that spending your time on money to spend is the best deal you can get, and the more money you get for the time you give, the better *man* you are, the better *woman* you are! But..."

He flipped a card and looked at the next one. He always timed it that way. If you couldn't fit a meaningful thought on a 3x5 card, couldn't deliver it from that without a pause, it was too long and complicated for TV. People needed their pauses, needed a little silence to let things sink in.

"It's a lie."

This pause had a symbol on the card.

"It's a *lie*."

The second time, "lie" was underlined.

"It's a *lie* because the truth is *Christ*. The truth is we can get all we need, more than we could ever deserve, for *nothing*. Just for believing. Just for accepting it. Just for looking at good and saying, 'Hey! That's pretty good! That's a *good deal.*'" He frowned, crossed out *good* and changed it to *goodness* and then inked over the small G to turn it capital, so that the card read *Just for looking at Goodness and saying.*

He turned up the next card.

"Greed won't buy that. Greed won't believe it. Greed always tells you you need more." Another scratch out, changing *need* to *got to have.* He tried that. "Greed always tells you you got to have more; that too much is never enough. No matter what, you can never quit taking. You can never rest, never stop, keep pushing and grasping and *getting.* But the love of Christ is all encompassing. It's all give and no take. It's endless and bottomless and eternal, and once you have that, that's it! It's enough! Enough's enough, and when you have Christ, you have more than enough!"

He sighed. It still needed work.

Somewhere outside Las Vegas, the demon Avitu was growing strong.

Her High Priest, Theodore Mason, had arrived, so her ceremonies were finally being performed properly. Every man, every woman who volunteered to be purified brought her nearer to the surface of full wakefulness. Each fallen human redeemed into ignorance helped her shake off the slumber of centuries.

Most of the Tree was still dormant, but she was awake enough to consider her choices carefully.

There was the matter of Gaviel the Devil, for one thing. He had contacted her in a spirit of smarmy confidence, playing the lord who would choose between two bickering servants—in this case, her and Sabriel the Defiler. He had proposed a meeting but was unwilling to come see her. The question, then, became one of bearding him in his den.

Roused by her rituals and the presence of Teddy Mason, she had the strength to create a new automaton... but one such creature had already fallen to grief, a costly setback. In the last age, a man of stone had no vulnerabilities, but the clever hands of conscious humanity had forged great vessels and weapons capable of harming even such a being.

Alternatively, she could rouse her other servants, heal their wounds and use their regard to grow even stronger. But it would take time, and calling them from the sand would be a straining effort in her current weak state.

In the end, it came down to worship. She knew that Joellen O'Hanlon and Tim Grady would worship her beyond all reason. Indeed, their rejection of conventional thinking won them great love from her. If only Teddy had the same strength, or madness... if only Tim had Teddy's pure priestly bloodline... but there was no point in wishing.

TEDDY, she called. *COME TO MY BODY. I HAVE NEED OF YOU.*

Instantly, the priest woke in his sleeping bag and rose.

"Ted? Wha..."

"Go back to sleep, Birdie," Teddy told his wife. "I just gotta go out for a second."

Birdie rolled over, and had some concerns. Since starting this vacation, Teddy had been so peculiar, so taken with those ugly little hunched-up trees, so friendly with a number of odd other people who shared his fascination. She was worried and irritated, but she was also sleepy, so she convinced herself that Teddy was just taking a leak.

Teddy stood before the tree and said, "What should I do?"

CALL FORTH. YOUR FELLOW BELIEVERS SLUMBER IN THE SAND.

Before, in his old life in Montana, Teddy would have felt ridiculous. But here, in the desert of his dreams, it seemed the most sensible thing in the world to lift his arms and say, "Arise!"

Three figures came up from the sand. All three were battered and hurt, even through their coats of dust, but his eyes were drawn instantly to the woman. His jaw gaped and his eyes opened wide.

Her reaction was much the same.

"Black Hawk," she breathed. "That's him. That's the High Priest!"

Teddy's eyes flicked to the man she'd addressed. Both men swallowed nervously, neither spoke.

Joellen was staring with rapt adoration. She stepped forward with her arms open.

"It's him," she repeated. "Blackie, it's your father!"

Chapter Eight

G aviel didn't care for dreams, but nonetheless he dreamed. In his dream he saw his body from the outside and then realized, no, it wasn't him. It was Noah Wallace. He could tell from the way the body was held—its general confidence marred by a human shadow of self-doubt; its usual proud posture checked by just a dash of humility, uncertainty.

"I want my body back," Noah said.

"I'm afraid it's actually my body now," Gaviel responded.

"You? Who are you? You're nothing. You're nobody."

Gaviel realized that the young mortal was right. He had no body of light and glory to command, no burning wings and stunning visage. He was just another patch of darkness in the dark.

"If I'm nothing, what does that make you? You, who lost everything you had to me, to nothing?"

"You tricked me."

"I did no such thing. If I took your body, it was because you wanted it taken."

"That's a lie!" Noah cried.

"No, it's lies you *want*. You wanted the lie that you weren't what your father made you. You looked for the lie that all your thought and conjecture and hypothesizing *mattered*, and when you couldn't find that, you hoped for the lie that *no one* mattered."

"That's preposterous."

"Oh really? Name me one person you helped in the last four years."

"I... I helped Rick and Janice."

"I don't mean moving furniture or watching a cat! I mean someone whose life you enriched! Someone whose pain you eased, someone you comforted."

"Star," he said quietly. "After she got jumped. I helped her."

"I'll give you that. And did you help her with all your *knowledge*? Did you help her with all your *scholarship* and *intelligence* and *book-learning*?"

"I helped her! What does it matter how?"

"What matters is that you helped her by acting like your *dad*, but even *then* you couldn't own up to admiring him! I didn't have to trick you out of your body. Your grasp was so weak from fighting yourself that I pretty much just had to dust the damn thing off!"

"My sister," he said. "I helped Elizabeth. I helped her get free of Dad and Mom, and I helped her *be her own person*."

"Maybe you helped her, but did you help her more than you hurt her? More than you hurt Zola by not coming home for Christmas and Easter? More than you hurt your father?"

"He can take it."

"Which makes your cruelty okay, is that it? If Matthew only knew. I'm going to be a better son to him than you ever were."

"You're a *liar*!"

"How can you even judge? You had the truth. You were given the truth from the day you were born. Deep down in your heart, you knew it was the truth. Yet nevertheless, you ran away as far and as fast as you could the minute you could. I'm the liar? Yes I am, but at least I *know* my lies for what they are, and *that's* how I got your body. Because in your darkest hour, you *wanted* a liar. You wanted lies more than anything else in the world. And now, together, you and I are the biggest lie of all."

There was little left of Tim Grady's mind. Years of drugs and suffering and electroshock treatment had seen to that. But his spirit, while weakened, had never completely folded.

His body, too, was just a shadow of what it was. Worn joints grated against weakened bones impelled by withered muscles, all powered by a shaky heart. But the vessel, while cracked, still held. It didn't work well, but it worked. It held that spirit, nevertheless.

The spirit that believed. The spirit that acted. The spirit that had been willing to kill on behalf of its faith, even when the message from its goddess was weak and misunderstood. That spirit was worth more to Avitu than all the great minds at Stanford or all the strong bodies of the Green Bay Packers.

Avitu had been an Angel of Life, and the ills of age were nothing to her. Fueled by Grady's spirit, she turned his own belief inward. His bones became strong and firm, his sinews turned thick and supple, his muscles renewed themselves to the prime of his youth then became better still.

No one saw it. Joellen and Black Hawk were embroiled in a moment of family shock; they didn't even notice that their mangled, infected hands were healed. The old man could have flown away and they wouldn't have paid attention, so they easily missed it when his frame swelled with muscle, his skin flushed with renewed vigor, his eyes turned bright and sharp.

Tim Grady's mind was still damaged and dim, but he could hear Avitu and she could see through him. He felt alive. He felt more alive than he ever had.

"I go," he whispered, though no human ear was listening. Then he loped off over the sand toward the Masons' rented sport-ute.

"This is gonna be stupid," Renee DeVries predicted.

"Shoot girl, how you know?" This came from Renee's friend Monique.

They were the only two who'd shown up. They were in a classroom at their high school. Usually it was used for World Studies, but it was after school—the map was rolled up and the blackboard erased. They sat in desks with writing platforms bolted on one metal arm. Monique's had uneven legs, and she rocked it back and forth.

"This stuff's always stupid," Renee said. "'Mentor from the community.' Damn, how's it gonna *not* be stupid?"

"No, this could be okay. It's Noah Wallace."

"Who's Noah Wallace?"

"Don't you ever watch Matthew Wallace?"

"Who?"

Monique twisted on her chair, uncomfortable. "He's on the TV."

"He not that preacher, is he?" Renee sighed and rolled her eyes with the exquisite exasperation of a teenage girl. "You drag me here for some preacher's son?"

"He's smart," Monica said. "It could be all right."

The door opened and Gaviel entered. Renee blinked and opened her eyes wide.

"Dang," she whispered.

Gaviel smiled.

Birdie looked at her husband with cold fury. "So you just lent him our car?"

It was morning. Teddy was groggy and irritable: He hadn't slept well since running into Joellen for only the second time in his life.

The first time had been when he was sixteen and traveling through the Appalachians with his parents. He and Joellen hadn't said a single word to one another. They'd just gone off behind some bleachers and fucked. It had been the first time for each of them and, for Teddy at least, the best sex of his life. Then, silently, they'd gone their separate ways.

Now it turned out she'd gotten pregnant, and he had a grown man for a son. It was a lot to think about, and he hadn't fallen asleep very easily. He didn't know that the other man from the ground (and Teddy didn't know his name; the O'Hanlons had no idea who he was) had taken his car until Birdie woke him up this morning and said it was gone.

He'd calmed her down, said it wasn't a problem and that he'd explain after he had a chance to go to the bathroom and put on some pants. That had bought him a few minutes to think. For a moment, he'd thought about telling her that he'd left the keys in the ignition—who was going to steal it, out here?—but he worried that she would then bring up Avitu's other visitors... her other worshippers.

(The sacrifices.)

Instead he'd come back, started building a fire to cook breakfast, and told her he'd met a guy named Fred Allston. Fred's car broke down (Teddy said), and he needed to get back to town quick after a phone call about his sick daughter.

Birdie was far from mollified.

"You just met this man *last night*," she hissed "And you lent him our car? Which we *rented*? I mean, it's not like he was on the insurance agreement!"

"Honey, it's going to be okay."

"My purse was in there, Teddy! My purse with the traveler's checks in it!"

"What would we need them for? We've got enough food for days, and if we need a ride in to town, we can ask Gwynafra."

"You're awfully trusting of *her* all of a sudden. You're awfully trusting of *anyone* who comes out here and, and shows any interest in those horrible little trees."

"Birdie. Take it easy."

His voice actually made her pause. She wasn't used to hearing a warning tone from her husband—certainly not one that sounded like he was willing to back it up. She took a moment, wondering what had made him so mad... but then she rallied.

"That's not the point anyhow. The point is, how could you be so *gullible*? How could you naïvely trust some *stranger* with our *only transportation*?"

"Honey, if he was a con man, do you think he'd look for suckers way out here in the middle of nowhere? I saw him get the call. If he was faking it, he's just an incredible actor. He said he'd bring it back. I believed him. If that makes me a *bad person* for wanting to help a man with his sick daughter, well, I'm sorry."

"It just... It's just all so... It just *makes no sense!*"

"What makes no sense?"

"His car broke down on the highway, right? Then how'd he come way out here and find us? And how'd he find *you* anyway? I sure would have known it if he'd come to our tent. I've been sleeping light since all those... *people*... started coming out here." She said "people" as if she meant anything but.

"They're all right..."

"Fine, they're all right, whatever. That doesn't change anything."

"I don't know what you mean."

"I mean it *doesn't add up.*"

"Are you calling me a liar?" Teddy asked, and she knew.

He didn't ask it like he was offended or outraged. He asked it miserably, like he was trying to be defensive but knew he really had no defense. He said it like a liar.

"No," she replied, her voice uncertain. "Let's just... just forget it."

"I'd like to see Miriam Schirokauer, please."

The attendant gave the speaker a beady-eyed stare. She might as well have come out and said, "I'm memorizing your features to describe to the cops." The man was swarthy, tired and dressed too warm for Florida.

"Whom shall I say is calling?" she asked, her voice nasal.

"Her son, Harvey Ciullo."

The attendant called Miriam, gave him one last glare and let him in. When he asked which room, she sneered.

"First time visiting?"

"That's right, you smug fucking cunt," he replied.

She just gasped.

"The room number? I ain't getting any younger, and neither is my mam."

She told him. He went.

When Miriam Schirokauer opened the door, her eyes narrowed in suspicion.

"You're not my son," she said.

"No, I'm not," Sal Macellaio replied, "but I know him."

"One of his worthless buddies, huh? Go to hell."

"Please, Miss... lemme talk to you. It's important. It's about Harvey."

She looked him over. Good clothes, intent expression, a couple pieces of jewelry that were gaudy without being at all cheap… He was a cut above Harvey's usual no-good cronies.

"Fine," she said. She widened the door, and he came into her room. She went back to her chair by the window and did not hear the door close behind him.

"Harvey killed my boy," he said.

"What?"

"Yeah, that's right. Your sweet lil' son." He paused and realized that she wasn't incredulous, just deaf. She wasn't disbelieving, just confused.

"Never mind," he said. He raised his voice and asked, "Have you seen Harvey recently?"

"No, that ingrate never visits. My only granddaughter, and you know how many times I've seen her? Once. Once is all. One lousy four-day weekend."

"That's rough. Not being able to be around someone you love, I mean."

"What?"

"Fuggeddaboudit. Look, what about your daughter, Helena? You hear from her much?"

"She was a lot better than her brother—half brother—but she met some guy, and now she never calls anymore."

Sal's face shifted, just a little, hearing that. It was a mix of humor and nervousness and regret. "Yeah, well…" he said at last.

"Huh? You gotta speak up, I'm a little hard of hearing."

"Really? How 'bout that." He scratched his head. "You know, to be fair I really ought to torture an' kill you."

She shook her head again, impatient, and gestured to her ear. "What?"

"I said, I got a tape Harvey made. You wanna listen to it?"

She shrugged and pointed to an old gray boom box.

Sal put in the cassette and helped her into its clunky, can-style headphones. He hit PLAY and watched her face.

Harvey had, indeed, made the tape. It was him and a colleague murdering Sal's son, Scott. It wasn't quick.

Sal watched as understanding dawned on her face, then terror and a weird kind of despair. She started to cry, with a peculiar, drawn-out moaning underneath it.

Sal drew his gun but didn't fire it. He just watched as she clutched her left arm and sagged forward. He waited. Then he put the gun away, took off the headphones and ejected the tape.

"Hey!" he called out the door. "Hey! I think... I think she's in trouble, here!"

He slipped out while they were trying to resuscitate her.

For some reason, Sal felt bad about it.

"People think it's easy being seventeen, but it's not," Renee said, sucking hard on a straw and getting nothing. The straw's other end was embedded in a Concrete—a delicacy served by Ted Drew's Restaurant. The Concrete got its name because of its thickness. It was made with ice cream and custard and was incredibly rich and sweet.

"I remember," Noah said. The two of them were sitting inside Ted Drew's. He'd established a good rapport with Renee and Monique and picked Renee for special attention. Monique had the greater soul—larger and sweeter and less selfish—but that was a problem as much as a lure. Renee's weaker spirit was less likely to value itself and, therefore, would defend against seduction with decreased vigor. "I remember someone telling me that high school would be the best four years of my life."

Renee snorted. "Yeah, right." She gave up on the straw and started digging with a spoon.

"I found that statement so sad. Pathetic, really. Like the man—who was forty—had resigned himself to having the rest of his life slide down hill. What's life for if you aren't looking forward?"

"Testify," she said playfully, nervously. It was exhilarating, being out in public—almost like a date!—with this man who was so much older, and *smart*, with cool clothes, and really, *really* hot looking.

"When I was in school, it was mostly parental stuff with me. My mom said it was like trying to have two bulls in one field."

Renee shrugged. "Mine are alright, I guess. You know."

"Yeah? No big fights?"

"Oh, they get up on me about stupid stuff. Clothes, staying out late. But mostly they let me do what I want."

Noah nodded. "Soon you'll move out anyhow, right?"

"Yeah, I guess." Renee's Concrete had melted enough that she could use the straw, so she did.

"You got plans for after school?"

"I got a cousin here in the city. I thought maybe I'd move in with her for a while. Get some job. Make up some money. Maybe go back to school after a year or two. I don't know."

"Not planning to go straight to college?"

Renee almost got offended, but she didn't. It was the way he said it. When most people asked something like that, most *older* people, they said it like, "What, you're too dumb to go to college? Ain't that right, you dumb little nigger girl?" but Noah just said it as a plain old question. Like he was asking to really see what she meant, not as a way of pushing her toward the answer he thought she ought to want.

"I've had enough of school right now, an' I'm just a junior."

He nodded. "Sometimes I wish I'd taken a year or two off to work instead of going straight in. You know. Get a sense of how the real world works, what it's really all about, instead of going straight back for college."

They chatted some more, laughing and telling stories, then Noah asked if she had a boyfriend.

"Oh, kind of," she said. "It's not all that... naaah." She looked away.

"What?"

"You don't care about that kinda stuff."

He shrugged. "If you don't want to tell me, don't tell me. That's cool."

Her straw slurped up the thinnest dregs of her drink, and she decided impulsively to tell him about Leotis.

Birdie looked across the desert dust at an incredibly filthy car with an equally filthy woman sitting on the hood. Part of her was wondering who this creature was and what white trash lagoon she'd crawled up out of. Another part was wondering why so many people who were, frankly, goddamn scummy looking kept coming out here, to the middle of nowhere.

(She didn't think the word "pilgrimage." It wasn't a Birdie kind of word. And even if it was, she might have shied away from the concept of this being somewhere special, somewhere... holy.)

Parts of her were wondering about that, and her husband's connection, and the strange deference that he got. But mostly, she was looking at the Little Debbies.

Birdie, like a lot of women, was a little chubby and thought she was as big as a barn. She'd been unenthused when Teddy had proposed camping, but she'd decided to make the best of it by packing only healthy, low-fat foods. She'd fantasized about coming back from vacation ten pounds lighter with a deep, dark sensuous tan, so her cooler was packed full of Veggie Booty and rice cakes and low-fat yogurt. She was planning to "be good." (That was how she thought about healthy eating: In terms of moral action.)

And now she looked over at someone who looked like an extra from *The Grapes of Wrath*, and she was actually *salivating* because the woman was eating Little Debbie Nutty Bars. In her dietary enthusiasm, Birdie had not packed one single piece of chocolate.

She quickly averted her eyes and went back to scrubbing the breakfast dishes as the woman stood and started walking toward her.

Oh shit, she saw me staring, Birdie thought, convulsed by the particular, powerful guilt that grips the middle class when they think someone poorer might have caught them feeling pity.

"Mawnin'," the woman said. "Lovely day, isn't it?"

"Shaping up to be hot," Birdie replied, eyes down on her task. The woman didn't move, and Birdie eventually had to look up.

"I'm Joellen O'Hanlon." The woman was stick-scrawny, swarthy, with gray hair and veiny hands and blunt, flattened features. She stuck out a hand, and Birdie noticed that there was a touch of chocolate stuck on one fingertip.

"Birdie Mason," she said, standing, shaking the hand, irrationally irritated that she'd been made to stand up right after she'd squatted.

"Ah, you're Teddy's wife then?" The woman's dark, bulgy eyes seemed to glitter and tighten in the sun.

"Yes. You know Teddy?"

"We met."

"Ah."

Silence.

"Teddy and I are out here with our son, Lance."

"Lance, huh? Fine looking boy. Like his dad."

"Er, yes. And you're with…"

"My son, Black Hawk."

"That's an interesting name."

"We're native." There was a touch of smugness in her tone.

For a moment, Birdie felt an odd sort of relief—as if the woman's grubbiness made sense. Then she immediately asked herself why Indians—by which she meant Native Americans—should be exempt from good grooming?

"Are you going to be staying here long?"

"Oh yeah," Joellen said. "Like you, I s'pect."

"Well, we're really just camping for a little while. On vacation. My husband won a trip."

"Zat so?" The woman looked skeptical and amused, and Birdie felt another flash of annoyance. *I don't like this woman,* she decided.

"Yes. That's so." She turned back to her dishes.

"How'd you two meet?"

"In college."

"Nice. Been married long?"

"Seventeen years."

"That's great."

There was a silence, and Birdie swore to herself she wouldn't break it.

"So," Joellen said at last, "Whaddaya think about the tree down there?"

Birdie shrugged. "It's a tree."

"Ah." If she'd looked up, Birdie would have seen a calculating, almost cruel grin on Joellen's face. "I s'pect you're right about that."

Jerry Bogart gave a hard look at the woman sitting in front of his desk. She was a hottie. So what? For the kind of money Jerry was making running a major casino owned by a Disney subsidiary, he could hire a dozen as pretty or better. He could hire more hookers—legally!—than he could sodomize in a lifetime.

(Not that he did, of course. Disney employees did not frequent whorehouses.)

She was dressed in an expensive business suit that wasn't quite right. She was clearly trying, putting in lots of effort to look professional, and that was just wrong. Jerry knew real businesswomen—women like goddamn sharks, always moving, unblinking, bite your dick off soon as look at you—and they always looked professional without effort.

Maybe, he thought, *because they're professional. Whereas this woman is a professional.*

(That was how he thought of prostitutes—as "professionals.")

(And he never, ever went to them.)

In fact, the woman talking to Jerry was not a prostitute, although she'd applied for the job. The licensed brothels of Nevada required a blood test it seemed, but since she was not really human, she could not give one.

The woman was not a woman at all, she was animate dirt. She went by the name Gwynafra Doakes, and she was there to sell out her boyfriend.

That was what made Jerry horny for her. The boyfriend. Not just that she was big-boobed and leggy and pretty in the face; not just that she was a topless dancer and (he imagined) a wanton amoral creature who would do any bizarre sex thing a man could imagine, but because... because she... Hell, just *because.* All that stuff was pretty sexy, but having a *no shit gangster boyfriend*—wow. That put Jerry in the real hot seat, that place where a man doesn't know what to do with his hands but can't keep 'em still. The state of mind where at least 40% of the brain is trying to figure a subtle, dignified way to shift a stiffening penis.

"I'm not... sure, exactly... what it is you're asking."

"I want the sponsorship of your casino," she said.

"Sponsorship? You want a job?"

"A job, for starters, yes. You'll think of something." She said it cool and level and looking him straight in the eye, no double entendre, but he felt another surge in his pants, and his hands shifted off the Donald Duck statuette on his desk and started fiddling with a lovely onyx-inlaid pen—almost identical to the one Matthew Wallace used to write sermons, actually.

"I'm not sure I understand your motivation."

"Look, what I'm offering is, frankly, big picture stuff. You— and by 'you' I mean Disney and MGM and Hyatt and the other major corporations—want Las Vegas."

"Want it? Miss, I don't know if you closed your eyes on your way here but, we've arguably *got* it."

"You've got a piece of it, but you don't have all of it. There's still... an element. Yes?"

"An element."

"A criminal element. The people who did, in fact, found Las Vegas."

"Now, that's kind of a stretch."

"Bugsy Siegel and the Chicago Outfit made this town what it is," she said, in a severe and lecturing tone of voice. "The mob has had its hooks in here since day one, and you're trying to squeeze them out."

"Look, you should be talking to the cops, not me."

"Ah, the cops. Yes. *They'll* clean up Vegas. And after that, maybe the boxing commissioner will clean up boxing." She gave him a withering glance. "The cops are a tool that must be pried from the gangsters' fingers. I can do that, but not by myself. If I have someone with political juice... Say, a company that donated millions to everyone from the mayor up through the state senators..."

Jerry shifted in his seat. She went on.

142 / GREG STOLZE

"Someone with media clout. A company that owns a good share of the local TV stations and can pressure the others into coverage by playing on their fears of being scooped…"

"Go on."

"And someone who has the money to protect me and my interests. That's really what this all comes down to, right? Money, by which I mean power."

"Power."

"I need power. I'm the bullet that can bury a quarter of the mob action in Vegas, but I need a gun to shoot me and a strong hand to hold it. With you and Disney, I'm a priority to the cops, I'm an important blow against the mob to the newspapers, and I'm someone who survives to testify. Without?" Her eyes got flinty hard. "Without, I'm stuck sucking Sweet Pete's gruesome prick, taking his slaps and punches until I ugly out and get kicked to the curb. I try and get back at him, and I'm another page-three murder vic who washes up on the Jersey shore."

"Maybe you should be more careful picking boyfriends."

"Sweet Pete's better than nothing. Better than being poor, being a nobody, dancing my ass off until my tits sag."

"Then maybe you should just be happy with what you've got. It's what you want, isn't it?"

"Wanted. Past tense. You're a businessman, aren't you? Don't you understand the concept of goal-setting?"

He laughed.

"You start out driving a Ford Escort, and the Camaro looks pretty good. And then when you're driving the Camaro, the BMW looks pretty good. Is that it?" he asked.

"And pretty soon, I want a Lear jet." She nodded.

"Well, that's charming. It's lovely to meet someone with such naked ambition," he started, and he meant to finish with, "but I'm afraid I work for Disney and not Elliot Ness."

He got as far as "…but I'm… uh…" before trailing off. Gwynafra had stood up, and, in one flexible move, she'd whipped one high-heeled foot up onto his desk. The other remained on the ground, pulling her skirt up high and revealing the area where her panties would have been had she been wearing any.

"With respect, Mr. Bogart, I don't think you've seen naked ambition yet."

Sheriff Grant Dagley was having a bad day, the latest in a series of bad days. Joan Pratt, one of the state's Assistant Attorney Generals, had it in for him. It wasn't fair, but there it was. Grant had half a mind to drive up to Springfield and kack the bitch, but that plan only made sense when he was huffing fumes and he knew, in moments when his mind was better organized, that it was just plain stupid.

Besides, she was only concerned about him taking bribes and stealing. He'd felt out people in her camp, and she wasn't interested in getting a cut of his action. She seemed to be one of those people who wants to piss on everyone else's birthday cake and call it *integrity*.

(Grant thought he'd been pretty subtle about checking up on her people. In fact, his comments had only made them more certain he was dirty as a ditch-digger's shoe.)

The real bad news was that Joellen O'Hanlon and her son—whatsisname, Little Chief or whatever—had gotten away. That was no good for anyone, least of all him.

Still, he thought, *Coulda been worse. If I'd had her in the JAIL and she got out—damn, I'd really be up shit creek. And if I'd just dragged off some Jane Doe and she got away, she could go up to Springfield and accuse me to High Box District Bitch Pratt. But Joellen O'Hanlon, America's most wanted psychopath... nah. She ain't gonna bake her own buns just for a chance to frost my biscuit.*

He took another soothing sniff from the neck of the isopropyl bottle. Then he heard a knock.

Grant was standing in the supply closet in his office, and the knock had come on his exterior door. He put down the bottle and closed the closet door with undue haste—so much that he knocked the alcohol over and spilled it on his spare uniform, but he wouldn't find that out until quitting time. Then he took a moment to compose himself before opening the door.

It was his secretary.

"I'm sorry to bother you, Sheriff," she said, "but there's a man here. Says he'll only talk to you."

He looked over her shoulder and saw a very odd figure—a man in thrift-shop clothes, with long white hair, bronzed skin and the build of a weight lifter.

"I wouldn't have troubled you," she whispered, "but he said it's about Joellen O'Hanlon."

"Probably another nut," the sheriff said, "but I gotta be sure."

Sheriff Dagley had said—in public—that he'd been following leads about Joellen O'Hanlon in the region when the DA started what he called "her campaign of unfounded harassment." Naturally, the left-wing cynics in Springfield assumed that he was blowing smoke, which was just fine with Grant.

"Howdy," he said to the old bodybuilder. "I'm Sheriff Dagley. What can I do for you?"

"It's about Joellen O'Hanlon," the man said, without offering his name or shaking Dagley's hand.

"Well, I do suspect she's been moving around here 'bouts."

"You've seen her." The man tilted his head, as if listening to something. "Touched her," he said.

"Why don't you come into my office, and we'll talk this over," Dagley said, gesturing. The man went before him. Grant made a movement to his secretary, who sidled noiselessly near on her comfortable cop shoes.

"I think he's a nut," Dagley said, "but probably harmless."

"I dunno. Those eyes... I think he's a tweaker," she replied.

"Nah, nah. Guy his age? It's all the young punks. I'll handle him. If I hit the intercom though, bring in Luke and Dean." They were two of his deputies, his favorites, the two with the optimum mix of loyalty, stupidity and brute strength.

She nodded, and he went into the office. He'd half expected the man to be pawing through the stuff on his desk or playing with the mounted fish and ducks he had on the wall, but the man just stood there. Perfectly still. He wasn't at attention—he had kind of a limp, stooped, caveman posture. But he wasn't *doing* anything but looking slack.

Like a sock puppet when you take your hand out, Grant thought, then shook his head and dismissed the notion as leftover fume-think. He closed the door and surreptitiously checked his stun gun.

"So. You've seen Joellen O'Hanlon?"

"You chained her up. Then you put your baton handle in her vagina."

Grant stood stock still. The man hadn't even turned to look at him. He'd said it as calmly as he might say "I take cream in my coffee" or "It's very windy today."

"That's a mighty serious accusation," Grant said, staying well back from the man, going around him to his desk. "Just who are you, anyhow?"

"I am..." the man paused, like he was trying to remember. Again, he cocked his head. "I'm not important," he finally said. "I'm a messenger."

"A messenger from who?" Dagley asked, wondering if this was going to turn into some kind of blackmail shakedown. He'd dealt with the like before. Two blackmailers were buried near the barn.

"I'm a messenger from a goddess."

"Uh huh." Dagley relaxed. The guy knew something, but he was clearly a wacko. "Which goddess, then? Hm?"

"Avitu."

There was something.

Maybe it was the way the man said it. He didn't say it defiantly or worshipfully or like he was trying to convince anyone. He said it with perfect faith—a faith so rare that Grant had never before heard the like, only its wan shadows in churches and prayers and the screams of Christian junkies as they dried out in jail.

Maybe it was the word itself—like the word had extra echoes, extra tones and resonance, something ordinary words lacked.

Something.

Something that made the idea a lot less silly.

"Avitu," Grant said, and licked his lips. "Just what's she the goddess of, exactly?"

"Ignorance. You have molested one of her prophets."

"Beg yer pardon?"

"Joellen O'Hanlon. She is a prophet of Avitu. As am I. Joellen wishes you punished."

Dagley was getting nervous. He puckered his lips and ran his tongue over his teeth and then he felt something. This time it wasn't something subtle or abstract. He felt a sharp, painful sore on the roof of his mouth. As he probed it with his tongue, he felt a similar pain take hold there. The sores deepened and multiplied with unnatural speed. He could *feel* them spreading, as if they were crawling in his mouth, his tongue swelling behind sore teeth as a thin condensation of blood and spit and pus began to form in the back of his throat. Suddenly panicky, he leaned forward over his wastepaper basket and spat out the foul-smelling mixture.

"Wha' you doi'g?" he asked, through lips that were beginning to crack and drip.

"That is the power of Avitu," the man said calmly. "Were Joellen here, that illness would consume you, until your whole body was as riddled with rot as your spirit and your mind."

"Oh... oh ghawd..." The sheriff had pressed his hands to his face, but he could feel the sores spreading under his palms, seeping and needling, moving down his throat toward his lungs, creeping up his cheeks toward his *eyes*... "Pleesh, no!"

The man stood and walked over to him. With hands like steel, he grabbed Dagley's wrists, pulled up and out. The strength of it hoisted Grant out of his crouch and revealed his rapidly decaying face.

The man kissed him full on the lips, and suddenly the sores were gone. All of them, gone, as if they'd never been.

"They can come back," the man said, "Or you can pledge yourself to the goddess."

Unseen, the ghost of Rosemary Nevins watched this with a great deal of interest.

"Did I tell you yet how nice you look?" Gaviel asked.

"Yes," May said. Her voice was very quiet. She blushed; he blushed back.

They were in Noah's apartment. Soft music played from a tape deck. (He'd told her he'd borrowed it after his own stereo equipment had been stolen during his move home from Bowling Green University.)

"So... mm, what do you think of the soup?"

"It's really good," she said. "I've never had anything like it before, what did you say it was called?"

"Thom kai gai. It's Thai."

"I heard about Thai food, but this is the first time I've tried it."

"I'm glad you like it. I was walking down the street one day here and I smelled it coming out of the restaurant."

The conversation paused again, and May knew it was more than the spices that were making her tingle and sweat.

"So how are your classes going?" she asked at last.

"I've really only got my thesis to do," he replied. "It was kind of unusual, transferring colleges when I was almost finished, and they had some questions about whether my credits would transfer or if I'd have to take some classes here…" He trailed off, as if he'd realized he was rambling. The devil within rummaged ruthlessly through Noah's memories and experiences and pulled out a good, shy, "I'm babbling and I'm sorry, but it's because I'm nervous" smile.

"It, uh, it all got straightened out though."

"That's good."

"How's work with you?"

"Oh, good, good…"

Another long pause. Gaviel let the tension grow, linger… It was delicious.

"So, did I tell you about Renee?" he said.

Boom.

He saw concern and self-distrust and fear waver over May's face. It was brief, just a ripple, but she might as well have held up a sign that read *Oh God, he's married or he has a girlfriend or a daughter*.

"Uh… no. No, I…" She cleared her throat. "I don't think you did." She waved a hand in front of her neck, fanning herself. "Whew! Those spices kind of sneak up on you, huh?"

"Mm, yeah, stealth seasonings." He took another bite. "I told you about volunteering to be a mentor, right? Renee's one of my… what would you call it? A mentor-ee, I guess."

Now the sign changed to *I am so relieved*.

"Ooooh. I get it. No, you didn't tell me."

Gaviel could tell she was interested—not just selfishly interested because it meant she didn't have a romantic rival, but *really* interested, because she cared about helping kids. Wow.

"Well, Renee's your typical teenage girl, I guess. Young, and bright enough, got her whole future ahead of her and no idea just how much potential she's sitting on. Know what I mean? Spends most of her time and attention mooning over some guy."

"Oh, I know what that's like," May said softly.

Gaviel did an absolutely flawless job of pretending the comment went right over his head, even when she leaned in a little and let her eyes go soft.

"Some football player named Leotis, and of course he's got a girlfriend already. Renee's totally jealous..."

"Of course."

"...but you know, what's interesting is how much time Renee spent talking about the *girlfriend*. I mean, talking about the guy she sighs and blushes and looks away, thirty seconds or twenty, that's it. But the girl—her name's Jewel—Renee just goes *on* and *on*, half trashing her and half talking about how pretty she is and how popular and smart and this and that and the other thing."

"Uh huh?"

Gaviel could tell that he wasn't losing her attention, but that it wasn't as intense. Still, he was going somewhere with this. "In fact, I think she talked more about Jewel than about herself. Why is that?"

"Why is what?" May seemed taken aback—he'd been monopolizing the conversation, and then suddenly he'd jerked her back into it.

"Why can she talk so much about the good the other girl has and so little about her own? I don't even mean the boyfriend, I mean... stuff like 'she's so cute' and 'she always knows the answer in class' and so forth. Why is that?"

"She's probably... you know, she probably has low self-esteem." May shrugged, uncomfortable.

Probably thinking about herself at that age, Gaviel thought with great satisfaction.

May lobbed the ball back into his court. "So. What did you tell her?"

"I told her to go for it."

"What?"

"I told her that if she really wanted this Leotis fellow, she could probably get him. If she believed in herself enough and was willing to put in the effort instead of crying and moping about what might have or should have or could have been."

May just stared, confused. "But... I mean, you told her to break him up with his girlfriend?"

"It's not like they're married. There's no commitment before God or society. Surely you're not going to argue that everyone who, uh... shifts romantic allegiance from one person to another is doing something *wrong* are you?"

"I don't know."

"Relationships change, right?"

"Well, yes, certainly..."

"Especially in high school."

She nodded.

"So should I have told Renee her best bet was to do nothing and hope that he breaks up with Jewel on his own?"

"You should have told her that you can't always get what you want in life!" As soon as she said it, May half raised a hand to her mouth—perhaps afraid of her boldness in contradicting him.

He smiled and raised his glass like a salute. "I'm glad you respect me enough to disagree openly. I'll return the favor by...

disagreeing with you." He said 'disagreeing' as if it was some voluptuous and exotic sex position, and took a sip of wine.

She swallowed too, although her mouth was empty.

"I think Renee, and girls like her, already know that you can't always get what you want in life. I think that's a lesson they learn pretty early. And then they go on and think that they shouldn't even bother trying, and *that's* what I just can't stand. Should I have told her, in effect, she can't *ever* get what she wants in life? Maybe she'll get her heart broken. And probably she'll learn, like I did, that getting what you want isn't always what makes you happy. But I want her to have the courage to try, and if she fails, to try again until she succeeds."

Suddenly, he dropped his head.

"Maybe..."

"What?"

"Nothing. I should go get the chicken. It's in the oven, it's going to dry out."

He stood, and then she stood too, right in front of the doorway between him and the kitchen.

"What were you going to say?" she asked.

He could *see* her nervousness, *smell* it, and it was good.

"M... maybe I'm just setting her up to fail," he said, his voice soft.

Their bodies were uncomfortably close. The nearness wasn't unpleasant, not at all, but it was far from comfortable.

"Maybe that's the only way to learn courage," May said.

Gaviel waited just half a beat, and then kissed her—a gentle kiss, tentative and hesitant and not (in fact) the way Noah would have kissed her at all. It was the way she had always *dreamed* Noah would kiss her.

He got the chicken, and they ate it and sat on the couch and held hands and talked and listened to music. They did not have intercourse. He walked her to her car and they kissed again, through the window, and then she drove off.

If she'd made the first move, he would have moved on to stage three of his plan, but since she waited for him to kiss her, he knew he needed to put in more effort before completing stage two.

Chapter Nine

Hasmed, Knight of the Hated Lash—known variously as Zoth-Tocatil and Harvey Ciullo and Mr. Fortune—sat in a New Jersey McDonald's nursing a cup of coffee and waiting.

Down the block was a nondescript apartment building, and in the basement was a man named Joey Maddox. It would surprise no one that Joey's nickname was "Mad Dog." No one, that is, who knew that Joey was mobbed up.

Mad Dog was part of Rock's crew, which was part of Jonathan "Johnny Bronco" Vuoto's crime family. Except, Johnny Bronco was dead, and Rock was dead, and Joey Maddox was taking orders from Steel Pete Petrucci.

Steel Pete was running Vuoto's mob pretty much by default. The only other crew chief who might have challenged him was Sal Macellaio, but he'd bailed, and even Sal's own *soldati* didn't know where he'd gone. Half of them had beat feet themselves. The others had grudgingly signed up with Pete, even though he treated them like goddamn pissboys and had about as much brainpower as Macellaio kept in his jock. (At least, that was what they muttered to each other as Pete sent them on the most dangerous jobs. They whispered that Pete was dumb, and Sal was smart, and Pete had stayed, and Sal had run, and what did *that* tell ya?)

Steel Pete was at war with Rico from Atlantic City, and Hasmed/ Harvey/ Mr. Fortune was taking Pete's army apart piece by piece.

Today's piece was Mad Dog.

Hasmed and Maddox had jobbed together one time—shooting up some of Rico's people in a cemetery, ironically enough. They'd met just that once, but it was enough for Hasmed. They'd exchanged names and shaken hands, and now Hasmed could find Maddox anywhere in the universe, anywhere between Heaven and Hell.

Hasmed was waiting for Joey to nod off. When he knew Maddox was asleep, he paid up and went down the street. He loitered in front of the apartment and waited for someone to go in or come out. Eventually, someone did, and that someone didn't notice Hasmed because he didn't want to be noticed.

Inside, he went to Maddox's door and opened it with a lockpick gun, thoughtfully provided by Rico Pudoto.

Hasmed woke Maddox with a jolt from a stun gun (also a Pudoto gift) and then, while Joey's muscles were unresponsive, he tied him to the bed and gagged him and explained things to him. When Joey understood that Hasmed was a demon, that he'd come from Hell and that his intentions were purely malevolent, the bedclothes got soiled with Joey's sweat and urine. Hasmed took that as a good sign and soiled them again over the next half-hour, this time with blood.

Hasmed dedicated the murder to his lord, Vodantu.

When he was finished, he changed back into human form and left, making sure to leave no fingerprints.

For some reason, he had a headache.

The Reaper of Souls sat in a borrowed car, frowning and watching.

He was on the campus of a community college in Oswego, Illinois. It was a windy, snowy day, so anyone outside was walking with a purpose. No one was paying attention to a bald black man watching a squat brick building.

She was in there.

Usiel didn't know her name, but he knew what she was. What she'd done. He hadn't been in Oswego long before he felt her. He was at a grocery store, in the cereal aisle, and she was one over in bread, and he knew she'd touched a demon. When he came around the corner, he could scent it on her, like the tang of ozone after lightning strikes. She was a plain woman, beat down by life, but vivid and clear at the same time. Her master had remade her in a shadow of its own image, and even as she double-checked that her rye bread had no caraway seeds, she had some tiny whiff of celestial glory.

At least, she did to Usiel.

His first impulse was to take her right there—call the scythe, kill her, bind her ghost and be gone. Who would see him? And if anyone did, what could they say?

But he waited and followed and thought, and now he was parked outside her place of business.

Do I have the right to condemn her? he asked himself. *If she's a sinner, doesn't that make Glenda one too?*

Glenda.

He had saved her, answered her prayer, and she was a faithful woman, a Godly woman. Wasn't it only fair that he receive good from doing good?

Was it like this for the fallen? He'd always imagined their first use of humans—their first blasphemy, their first usurpation of the worship that was rightfully due the Allmaker—as a cheat, a trick, a fraud perpetrated on mankind with deliberate, cynical forethought. But what if...

What if they just... fell into it? Slipped in, comfortable, natural, not really understanding what they were doing until it was done?

As I did?

He frowned. Told himself that there was a difference, a *big* difference. That difference was that he was still loyal to God, and they were rebels. No matter that God had punished him... he looked down at his hand. The mark there, incised by angel fire, was still visible, sore and charged with foreboding. It had faded somewhat—enough that he could grow back fingers—but he suspected it would be some time before it vanished completely.

He felt a surge of frustration. *Why now? I did wrong in the War of Wrath and I paid, and now I'm trying to follow Him still. I resisted the wiles of Lucifer... didn't I?* He picked at the mark on his hand, fruitlessly. *Lucifer wanted me here. He wanted me to... to form a relationship with Glenda. And I did it. Did he trick me again? Or is he sincere about wanting to stop the others, the fallen and the damned?*

At the back of his mind was the terrifying knowledge that the Adversary could, at any time, summon and bind and compel him. Any act, any betrayal, any atrocity... he could be the Devil's puppet and dance helplessly to Lucifer's tune.

Why didn't he enslave me? He said he didn't want to play God, but what did he mean?

Thinking back on that defeat brought a frown to Usiel's lips, and his hands switched to fondling the ring.

He wants me to join him willingly. He wants to take me away from God. He knows that if he commands me, the sin is his and not mine, and he wants his evil to spread.

He could feel the itch in his sixth sense as the woman, the devil's thrall, came near.

Lucifer's trick is to try to convince me my mission is his own. He tells me what I ought to do—recover my scythe, save faithful Glenda—hoping I'll resist and not do it. Perhaps it's the same with telling me he wishes me to fight the fallen. He hopes the encouragement of my enemy will discourage me.

She came out the door of the building, and he pulled his door latch.

There is a difference between this woman and Glenda. Glenda worships God through me, and I am loyal to Him. This other, willing or not, follows a creature of the Abyss.

They aren't the same at all.

I'm not the same as them.

His decision was made.

"Y'hear about Pete?"

"Ah fuck," Sal Macellaio said. "What now? Pudoto's goons finally find him?"

"Huh? Pudoto gots nothing against Sweet Pete." Sal's host folded his paper and gave the gangster a sharp look. "Not unless you know something I don't."

"Sweet Pete? I thought you were talkin' about *Steel* Pete. Fuggeddaboudit."

"*Steel* Pete, oh, yeah, no. No, this is Sweet Pete. The Vegas guy. You know him?"

"A little. What's his beef?"

The two men were poolside, Sal trim and muscular but pasty around the midriff, the other fat and bronzed and covered with hair. He was a specialty film producer, and Sal was staying with him for a while—not long.

"His beef is, he's in fuckin' jail."

"Yeah, well." Sal shrugged.

"His beef is, it's his goddamn girlfriend put him there."

Sal made a *tsk* sound in his throat. "See, what I've always said is, keep your woman happy. You give her some deep dick often, some flowers and diamonds and candy, and you ain't got this problem. That or you can beat the fuck out of her alla time, but who needs it?"

"C'mon, you ain't tellin' me you kiss your wife's ass, are ya?"

"Nah, but shit, it doesn't take much. Good fucking and some diamonds and she's *happy*. Like a happy dog. You keep your dog happy, and he doesn't leave the yard, y'know?" He shrugged. "Now, you got a, what, a little prick or somethin' — y're *inadequate* — and then you gotta alla time be beating on your wife, and what? What's that get you? A tired arm and a wife who ain't pretty no more."

"So you think it's Sweet Pete's fault he got done up by this bitch?"

"Fault? I don't know from fault, I just now heard about it." Sal was tired. He'd been running for a while. He was sick of being a gangster.

"Listen, Sweet said he sent some guys to whack her out, y'know, 'fore she could testify? She'd fuckin' hired bodyguards and everything but, get this, one of them was actually the *nephew* of a guy that worked for one of Pete's *soldati*. Ain't that perfect?"

"Yeah?" Sal got a little interested despite himself. "This nephew do it or just let 'em in?"

"Better'n that. He tells 'em where she's hiding and everything, they're gonna come in with tasers and beat on both guards, right? Only what he doesn't know is that they have *guns*. They kill the other guard and wing him."

"No kidding?"

"Yeah, they get him in the hip, I guess he pissed himself and squealed like a pig and everything, but it's perfect, ain't it? No one's gonna suspect the guy who got shot, right?"

"Probably not."

"I mean, yeah, the guard's not happy about it but, hey, who's he gonna complain to, am I right? Fuggeddaboudit."

"Fuggeddaboudit," Sal echoed. "So, they kill the girlfriend then?"

"Nah, here's where it all turned to crap. Though it's kinda funny, actually. They weren't just gonna, you know, cowboy her up. Nah, Sweet Pete wants an *example* made, so he's going to have them haul her off and, y'know, take some time."

The film producer paused, then looked over at his guest. Sal was looking off into space, a cold, dead look on his face.

"Sal? You listenin'?"

"So torture," Sal said, in a voice like he was chewing rocks.

"Yeah. He asked me if I wanted to *film* it." He paused, but Sal's silence and demeanor made him nervous, and he started to speak faster. "Y'know, like a snuff movie? I tol' 'im it was easier to fake that shit, less trouble, special effects are so good nowadays... Though, I tell ya, ever since that *8mm* movie came out, there's demand. What's 'at tell ya, huh?"

"So the girl..."

"Oh yeah. Here's the funny part. They're gonna grab her, tie her up, stick her in the trunk, but one of the triggermen gets *sick*. I mean, maybe he'd had this germ or whatever for a while, but right then he starts to puke and cough and I don't know what all. He's useless, so he can't get the cuffs on her or anything. The other soldier, he's trying to do it himself, but he's distracted. His pal's puking all over his shoes, he's thinking about the forensic shit they can get outta puke, and the gal whacks him across the chops with a phone or something!"

"This guy couldn't handle one stoolie bitch?"

"He was sick too. She clobbered him and went out the window or into the bathroom or somethin', and he tried to get his buddy out but crashed his car leaving the parking lot! I tell ya, that sorry SOB lucked out, getting put in quarantine. The two of 'em, they got East Nile or that Bangladeshi crap—some sickness, I dunno what. One of 'em died already, and the other's going down to that, what, that thing for Disease Control."

"Sick, huh?" Sal turned and suddenly, he wasn't a million miles away. Suddenly he was locked on. The producer licked his lips.

"That's what I said, ain't it?"

Sal was thinking about a steel mill, about Harvey Ciullo turning into a shadow and Sal's best gunmen coughing, unable to fight.

"And this was in Vegas, huh?"

"Yeah. Yeah, Sal. How come?"

"No reason." Sal chewed his lip. "So your man, your sound guy. He's comin' back in town soon, right?"

"Yeah, Sal." He didn't know why, but he was glad to change topics. "Yeah, Duke's gonna be back tomorrow."

Gaviel woke up from a night of hot, sticky sex and realized that one of his thralls was dead.

He'd been dreaming about Noah again, so he was already cranky. Realizing that he'd lost one of the nourishing worshippers whose praise sustained him took his mood from blue to vengeful black.

He took a deep breath and felt outward, wondering which one it was. Lynn? Or Renee?

Little leaks of it were still seeping into him from outside—a sweet trickle of that irrational human power, the one thing angels couldn't make for themselves—and the flow tasted headstrong and wild and bare. Probably Renee then. Lynn's belief had been more like relief, gratitude that there was someone to look out for her, someone in control, while Renee was thankful for someone who could help her see herself the way she wanted.

Poor Lynn. Poor confused, self-destructive, firebug Lynn. Probably dead. At least Gaviel hoped so. He didn't want to contemplate a force that could sunder the connection between a living servant and her demonic master. Certainly there was no human way she could have renounced the pact... was there?

"Noah? You okay?"

He glanced down at the woman beside him—a nurse he'd met visiting Lynn in the hospital. She thought he was a no-fooling hero, a man who'd run into a burning building to rescue a trapped woman. Which was close enough, except for the "man" part. He'd been curious about banging someone who thought he was noble and selfless and brave. It had been nice.

"I'm fine," he said. "Go back to sleep." He rose and went into the bathroom. She sat up behind him.

"Uhhh, I should get going."

Gaviel brushed his teeth and thought about the quickest way to get her out the door.

Ten minutes later he said, "You're sure I can't tempt you to breakfast?" and she shook her head—regretfully, it seemed—and said, "Work won't wait. Call me?"

"Sure," he said, lying. It had been nice, but it wasn't worth a follow-up. If May found out... no. That was an unacceptable risk.

He was gloomily wondering if it had been a tactical error to send Lynn so far when his buzzer sounded. He was in the shower and decided to let whoever it was wait, but they were still buzzing when he emerged.

"Who is it?" he asked on the intercom.

"We're from Avitu," came the reply.

He sighed. Then he berated himself for, once more, communicating with no one but himself.

Get a grip, he thought.

For a moment, he let himself think things through without words. He put his emotions in order. He reached out with extra senses and realized there were two of them, thralls—like Lynn had been.

He buzzed them up.

"Wow, that was quick!" he said as he let them in. "I didn't expect Avitu to get around to speaking with me for some time. Really, it's flattering. You guys want coffee or anything?" He gestured them to the table and added "You can call me Noah."

"Noah," said the first, who was dressed in a brown police uniform. "That coffee sounds peachy. I take it black."

"One black, coming up. You are?"

"Grant Dagley. This here's Tim." He gave Gaviel a squint. "Haven't I seen you on TV?"

"*The Hour of Jesus' Power*, yes. I could ask you the same thing."

The sheriff shook his head. "That damn DA bitch has it in for me."

The second man—a muscle-bound giant in mismatched clothes—shuffled to a chair but said nothing.

"So," Gaviel said brightly. "What can I do for you—and for Avitu?"

"She wants you to come to Nevada," the giant said.

"Well, that's sudden. Shouldn't we have dinner and a few drinks before she tries to sweep me away on a weekend vacation?"

Grant chuckled, but Tim's gaze was like stone. "Your charms won't work on us," he said flatly. "You can't make us like you."

Narrowing his eyes, Gaviel realized it was true.

So that was one thing you bargained for from your mistress, he thought. *Freedom of mind. Always a good choice.*

"All right," he replied. "I'll consider going to Nevada, but not right away."

"Now, you're starting to sound what I'd call recalcitrant," the sheriff said.

"Why, because I won't drop everything I'm doing? Avitu's been stuck out there for centuries. She can wait a while to see me."

"She sees you now," Tim said.

"Then I'll put on my very most charming smile." He did. Then it fell off his face like a dropping curtain. "That does raise the question of why she wants me out there at all."

"Some things are best done face to face," Grant said.

"Like what?"

"Oh, conversation. So you can look the other fellah in the eye."

"Maybe that cornball shit—pardon my language—works for humans, but I think I'm beyond it, and I think Avitu doesn't have eyes. You're almost making me suspect that what she really wants isn't a heart to heart but a knife to the back."

"If she wished you ill," Tim said, "We wouldn't be speaking. You know you're vulnerable. You must know that."

Gaviel gave him a hard look and thought about Lynn.

Did Avitu send some fucker to kill my worshipper?

If they'd been open to his powers, he'd quickly have known she didn't, but unable to compel the truth from them, he was suspicious.

They did. They killed Lynn to soften me up.

"My my, how long did this conversation last before the threats were made? Back in the day, Avitu was ever so much sweeter."

"Welcome to the twenty-first century," Grant said. Gaviel could tell, just from simply reading the man's expression, that Dagley was at sea but trying to keep up with the game.

Tim's in charge here... and it looks like Avitu really fired him up. I wonder how long Dagley's been a thrall? Not long, I'd guess. I wonder how much she could improve him? I don't think it was a lot.

"It's a new age for all of us, and I think there's plenty of room to share. Why don't Avitu and I just go our separate ways for a little while—say a decade?"

"A *decade?*"

"Come on, Sheriff, that's like a half-hour in demon years," Gaviel replied. "We'll take stock then and see if we can have contact that doesn't involve threats and insinuations."

"That's not acceptable," Tim said. "Instead, why don't you come with us?"

"Clearly we disagree on what's acceptable. Do you really think you can compel me?"

Without even glancing at one another, the pair leaped up and seized him, one on each arm.

"You're a paper tiger," Tim rasped. "And the Tree of Ignorance knows it."

Gaviel didn't answer. He was busy changing.

When the light and beauty burst from his skin, the sheriff instinctively leaped back. Tim's hands, strong like a vise, remained clamped on Gaviel's arm, but now the demon had three free limbs—an arm and two wings—with which to wrestle. A clap of his pinions and he was free, flying backward, and the crash of the window sounded like an organ note as he shot through it...

...with his glory already fading, fading... It was as a man that he plummeted from his second-story apartment, crashing hard to the pavement below.

"Help me!" he shouted—in a human voice, but laced with subtle command. It was more than words and tone, it was perfumed to draw compassion and concern from all who heard. "Help!"

He was genuinely hurt, breathing was painful, but he did anyway to whisper, "Avitu, call off your thralls or I tell the world that Grant Dagley just threw me out of a window. I may not be able to move your toy soldiers, but you can't enthrall every judge and juror in Missouri."

There was a pause, and he heard people running toward him, cries of, "Oh my God!" "Did you see that?" "Someone call an ambulance!" Then, behind that, he heard Avitu's reply.

YOU'VE MADE AN ENEMY, GAVIEL OF THE SUMMER SUN.

"As have you, Avitu of the Twin Winds."

Lance Mason wandered among the low dunes, hot and bothered in more ways than one.

Most obviously, he was hot because it was *hot*. He was in the middle of the desert with those stumpy weird trees and all those stumpy weird people. He could still see his folks' tent a half-mile away, and being out here was—Dad's increasingly weak speeches about natural beauty aside—*really, really boring*. Privately, he'd kind of hoped to see Las Vegas, if only so he could tell his pals at home how lame it was. Or at least Lake Mead and Hoover Dam—those would be cool. But no, it was all just desert and those dumb shrubs.

Plus, there was nowhere to jerk off, which was Lance's real purpose on this walk. He'd done it several days ago in the hotel, but he was fourteen, and once a week was *not* enough. It had gone beyond something he'd like and was now something that was pretty damn uncomfortable. Besides, if he waited much longer, he might have a wet dream—in the tent he was sharing with his parents. Yeah. No thanks. He didn't want to be going to a shrink like his dad when he got that old.

(Normally, he would have felt a little guilty about looking down on his dad's psychiatrist, but screw it. The desert sucked, and he had a sore boner.)

And then there was Gwynafra. Dang. When he told his buddies about her, they wouldn't believe it. He thought about taking a picture, but he knew what his mom would say when she got them developed, and he didn't have a camera of his own. He figured he'd think about her while spanking the monkey.

He was carrying a canteen of water and a small tube of Vaseline (supposedly to keep his lips from chapping) and he wished they were in the woods. If they were in the woods, he'd be *done* by now, not still trying to find somewhere out of sight. His mom had (of course) picked the spot with the most privacy for their latrine area, and horny or not he didn't think he could pull it off (so to speak) around that smell. So now he was looking for another spot behind some tall dunes, preferably with shade.

He found a spot hidden away, but someone was already there.

"Oh. Hey," Lance said. It was that big guy with the long hair.

"Hi. How's it going?"

"Okay, I guess. How 'bout with you?"

"Hot."

"Yeah, no kidding."

"But at least it's a dry heat." The big guy laughed a little. Lance didn't.

Then Lance noticed that the guy had an open bag of 3-D Doritos—half full!—sitting on the sand next to him.

"So, what's your name?"

"Black Hawk O'Hanlon."

"Black Hawk?"

"Yeah, it was my mom's idea," he said, in a resigned voice. Like he'd said it a thousand times. "I usually go by Blackie. You?"

"I'm Lance Mason." He rolled his eyes a little. "It was my mom's idea."

Blackie laughed. Then he blinked. "Wait, so you're... you're Teddy Mason's son?"

He said it weird. He said it like the word "wow" would be next. Like Teddy's dad was Tom Brokaw or Ozzy Osborne... someone important.

"Yeah," Lance said, suddenly a little uncomfortable. Blackie, perhaps sensing his discomfort, composed himself and held out the bag of chips. Lance took a few.

"I grabbed the low-fat ones by mistake, but they're still pretty good," Blackie said.

"They don't have that stuff in 'em do they? That Olean, Olestra crap?"

Blackie looked at the bag. "Shit, I hope not." He glanced up. "No pun intended."

Lance chuckled and decided this guy was probably okay. As okay as anyone out here, anyway. He sat and had some water.

"What you reading?" Lance asked. The man had a slim paperback in his hands—not mass-market sized, but looking kind of cheap and poorly produced. It looked like the kind of regional interest book you find in Wisconsin or Alabama, something with typos and bad layout explaining local history or wildlife or tall tales.

"It's a book about bristlecone pines."

"Huh."

"Those trees back there? Those are bristlecones."

Another tree-hugger, Lance thought. *Great.*

"What's so special about 'em?" Lance asked.

"Your dad didn't... I mean, you don't know?"

Lance shrugged. "It's no big deal."

"Uh... well they're..." Blackie coughed. "They're really old, for one thing. I mean, *really* old. There's this one they call the

Methuselah Tree, they think it's the oldest living thing in the world."

"Yeah?"

"It's ancient. Older than the pyramids. I mean, there are trees out here that were alive when Christ was walking around in Israel, you know?"

"Okay." Lance shrugged. "So they're old. So what?"

"Well it's... they're interesting, is all." Blackie shrugged. "There was this one guy in the '60s, this scientist, he thought they held the key to immortality."

"Yeah? You mean, like, living forever?"

"Uh huh."

"What happened to him?"

"He died."

There was a pause.

"So I guess that immortality thing didn't really work out," Lance said.

Blackie chuckled. "Yeah, well, it was just a theory. They buried him in a grove of bristlecones, though. An' I think he was the same guy who'd cut down one of the oldest ones. But maybe I'm mixed up." He shrugged. "I mean, don't you just... just get a feeling off them? A feeling like they're... Ah, I don't know. Like those Easter Island statues or Stonehenge or something. And they're probably *older* than those things."

"I'm not all that interested in old stuff," Lance said, taking some more chips.

"Maybe when you're older," Blackie said. He gave Lance one more hard, odd look. "I think I'm gonna head back, see how my mom's doing."

"Okay," Lance took a swig of water. "See you 'round, I guess. Nice meeting you."

"Yeah, nice meeting you, bro."

That last word sounded odd to Lance, but he didn't think about it much. He thought more about waiting until Blackie was gone, and the Vaseline... and Gwynafra.

"So, um, what is it you need?"

The sound guy's name was Duke, and he looked (to Sal) like a goddamn hippie. He had long hair and jeans and those brown hippie sandals on his brown, dirty feet. He even had an earring like a girl or a fairy, for Christ's sake.

"I got this tape," Sal said. "There's some stuff, like, in the background. I wanna hear it."

"That's, okay, no problem. I mean, it's *probably* no problem I can... uh, it's a cassette tape?"

"Yeah. Ordinary size. Like for an album or something."

"Okay." Duke rummaged around his black boxes of stereo components and his gray boxes of computer equipment. "Lay it on me."

Duke didn't know anything about this guy Sal except that his boss had said that whatever Sal wanted done, Duke should make sure it got done and don't fuck it up, 'kay?

He put the tape in and hit PLAY.

"*—didn't even know he was your dad?*"

"Salvatore Macellaio is my uncle. You... you guys are all turned around."

Duke cocked an ear and said, "Yeah, this is a crap recording. Probably just a built-in mic from a boom box or something. Real cheap; no depth."

"Doesn't matter," Sal said. "There's just a couple parts I'm wondering about."

They continued to listen. Duke's expression slowly got more and more intent as the tape's content became clear.

"Physical pain. Physical pain."

"Ah… ah… Ahhhiiiiieeee!"

"Pretty bad, huh kid?"

Duke looked at his guest and licked his lips. "This isn't…? Um…" He coughed. "What is this?"

"It's what it sounds like."

"It's not a… It's not from, like, a movie?"

"My dad… my uncle… he's, he imports specialty foods! He sells olives and cheeses! He never killed anyone!"

"Do you ever read the goddamn newspapers? Never heard of Sal Macellaio, the alleged hijacker and robber, suspected member of the Vuoto crime family? No? Stuck to the comics pages, eh?"

"It's not a movie," Sal said.

"Look, I… I don't know what you want me to, do or… find. I… I mean, I'm just, I'm just a technician. I'm just a sound geek."

"See, we're not gangsters. We're not some petty crooks, breaking human laws. Should we show him, Has—"

"There!" Sal said. "Y'hear that?"

Duke frowned. "Yeah, I did."

Duke was surprised, and rather pleased, to find that he could do his job even when he was scared shitless. He rewound the tape and listened again.

A voice said *"Should we show him, Has—"* and then there was a pop on the tape, a hissing sound for a few seconds, before it started again.

"What is that?" Sal asked quietly.

"I *think* what happened there is that… that one guy, the speaker, he said something and… and whoever sent you this tape, he didn't want you to hear it. So he probably took the tape, listened to that part, and taped over it. But he didn't do a real good job."

"Yeah?"

"Yeah, hold on a minute," Duke said brusquely, instinctively, then secretly thrilled inside to realize he'd just told a murdering robber and thug to wait—and the guy was *waiting*. "I'm going to sample that and use the sample so we don't degrade the source tape any more."

"We'll be able to hear what they covered up?"

"If he just hit the RECORD button on his cheap shitty boom box... mm, probably yeah. I can probably tune it in right *here*." He shook his head. "Guy should have degaussed the tape there, or taped a discrete signal over it, or better yet, digitized the whole thing and blanked that part before burning it to disc..."

"I guess this guy ain't a sound technician," Sal said. "How long's this gonna take?"

"It's one o'clock now? How about I call you at four?"

"How 'bout *I* call *you*?"

"Where is our truck?"

"Birdie..." Teddy Mason sighed.

"No, Teddy. Look. Look, Teddy, *where* is the *Bronco*?"

"I guess—"

"You guess what? 'Cause you lent it to that *weirdo* four *days* ago, and he hasn't come back with it, now has he?"

"I guess I made a mistake."

"Made a mistake? No Teddy, a mistake is, 'Oh, I think we should have turned back there.' A mistake is, 'Oops, I locked myself out.' 'I think I'll lend my car with all our traveler's checks and my wife's ID in it to some stranger who shows up in the middle of nowhere in the middle of the night'—that's not a mistake. That's... that's fucking *idiocy*!"

"Language, hon..."

"Fuck language! I'm less worried about Lance hearing the f-word than I am about Fred Allston—if that is his real name—tooling around the country in a car *we rented* with all of *our money*. I'm more worried about being stuck out in this godforsaken sandbox relying on some big-tit bimbo whore to bring us water."

"Now, that's not fair to Gwyn, she's been very—"

"But most of all I'm worried about *you*! Jesus Christ, ever since we've gotten out here it's, it's like you've been in a fucking *trance*!"

"I feel I belong here."

That stopped her cold.

She opened her mouth once, shut it, then just stared at him for a moment.

"*What*?"

"I feel like I belong here." There was a flat sincerity to his words, unmixed with any rhetoric, any manipulative inflection, that put a hard brake on the argument's momentum. He didn't say it defensively or aggressively or apologetically. He said it the way he'd say water was wet. He said it like a fact.

But Birdie had built up a serious head of steam. She wasn't about to let a good squabble die without at least attempting resuscitation.

"You must be *joking*," she said. "You? Belong *here*? There's barely any here *here*! It's just, just piles of dust and those little scrubby dwarf trees, it's just scorpions and cactus and rock. No, you don't belong here. You belong back on your psychiatrist's couch!"

"Is there a problem?"

Birdie spun to see Joellen standing behind her. She hadn't heard the other woman approach (which was not, perhaps, surprising).

"I couldn't help but overhear," Joellen said in her southern purr.

"And I guess you couldn't help but stick your goddamn oar in, either," Birdie replied, turning and taking a step back so she could face both her husband and the interloper at the same time. "Yeah, there's a *problem*. The problem is my husband is either stupid or insane, and the problem is he gave our car away, and the *problem* is there's some mangy Okie bitch sniffing around with her scrawny snout in our business."

Joellen's fists clenched.

"It's okay," Teddy said. "There's no trouble. Really."

"If you say so, Teddy."

"It's all right."

"Aw right. If you *need* anything," she said, looking only at him, "y'all come by."

"I'll do that," he said as she walked off. She spared one look of pure venom for Birdie, but the glare Mason's wife fired back was just as vicious.

"We're leaving," Birdie said flatly.

"Look... honey..."

"I'm taking the tents down and packing up. You get us a car—if you can find someone as *stupid* as you were to lend us one. Otherwise I'll call us a cab."

"Don't drop the tents."

"No Teddy!" Her voice was close to hysteria. "We're going! Now!"

He sighed.

"I'll borrow Blackie's car," he said, "And I'll drive you into Vegas."

There was a pause.

"You're staying." Her voice was incredulous but, nevertheless, she didn't say it as a question.

He nodded.

"Lance is coming with me," she said.

There was a long pause before he sighed and nodded again.

Chapter Ten

Gina Parris had big, slack breasts, and if she lay on her back with her bra off, they'd roll down either side of her rib cage like fat drops of water heading toward her arms. At least, they would have if Reverend Matthew Wallace hadn't been kneeling between her spread legs, pushing her tits together with his hands while his mouth danced voraciously from one nipple to the other.

Gina giggled, as if he was tickling her — for all he knew, he was — but there was a breathy, throaty, *sexy* side to her laughter that made his cock even harder. He felt like it was straining toward her like a dog at the end of a leash. Like it wanted to jump right off his body and bury itself inside.

He ran his hands down her sides, feeling her soft flesh shift under his hands, and his mouth raced them, nuzzling her stomach and down, lower, until his hands were under her rump, pushing her pelvis up into his face.

Her giggles turned to moans. "Uh huh... oh. Ohhh my man. OOOhhh my maaaan..."

She was ready, really ready, and so was he, but he was thinking about the demon.

What would Gaviel say about this?

He tried to push the thought aside, but he knew that part of him didn't want to push it aside. Part of him wanted it front and center. Part of him wanted his guilt and fear overlaid on the sex, deepening and broadening it.

"Matthew, baby, you keep on that clam diggin' and I'm gonna go crazy," Gina said. When he lapped at her sex, she called it "clam digging." Now he had a separate, secret smile he wore whenever he ate clams.

He rose up and crawled forward, getting ready to plunge into her, plumb her depths, plunder the pleasures, and in his mind he saw Gaviel's smirking face—his son's smirking face.

How do I know he's not behind all this? That thought was almost enough to soften him, but he couldn't believe it. He'd been screwing his church choir leader for years—hell, even before Noah left for college. The demon hadn't been around then, this was all Matthew's doing. His sin. His fault.

Or what if? What if… this… is what let him find my boy?

"Sugar, what's wrong?" Gina had sensed it when his rhythm flagged, and she reached down to give the join of his thighs a gentle, tickling caress. "Your knee hurtin' you again?"

"Yeah," he muttered. "I'll be fine."

"Now you're lying to your whore," he imagined Gaviel saying. *"Which is, I suppose, pretty trivial. Like worrying about the calories in the cherry when you're about to eat an eight-pound sundae."*

Matthew worked to banish that carping, sarcastic voice. He focused on the woman, on the wrongness, on the deliciousness of his failure—a minister! A married man! Father of three!

Gina smiled, lazy, as she felt his return. Before anything else could happen, she guided him forward, working him into an opening that was more than ready.

Matthew plowed in deep and heard her gasp. She pulled him to her hard, and he could hear sticky slapping sounds as their bellies came apart and went together. Like every time, he wondered why he was betraying a wife he truly loved, a religion he truly believed, commandments he valued more than life itself.

You love to do good, said one part of his brain—some logical part, unstirred by the biological rampage affecting every other cell in his system. *You also love to do wrong. So maybe what you really love is freedom.*

He thought that thought, and he came like a detonation.

"You know, I'm still pissed that you didn't invite me to your party."

Thomas Ramone jumped and almost shrieked. He'd been out at the bars with some buddies of his, and his apartment was completely dark when he let himself in. So hearing a voice come out of that darkness when he thought he was alone freaked him right out.

He turned on the light.

The woman sitting on his couch had an unfamiliar face, a big tattoo on her arm and a petulant expression. The voice, however, was one he knew well.

"Don't you ever knock?" he asked.

"This is Christina," the demon on the sofa replied.

Thomas recognized her, of course. Her real name was Sabriel, and she'd tortured him into becoming her worshipper. On the plus side, she'd gotten him a better job.

At least she never pretends she's going to be nice to me, he thought. She scared the shit out of him, but at the same time, he felt a weird sort of sympathy for her. She'd once told him about Stockholm Syndrome—maybe it was that. Or maybe it was because she almost always looked like some variety of gorgeous woman.

Still, she'd never asked him to feel sorry for her, and when she kept breaking into his apartment and doing menacing stuff, it definitely cramped their relationship.

"Christina?" Thomas's beer-buzz was rapidly evaporating, but he was still not at his brightest.

"Christina! You remember me telling you about her, don't you? The stupid slut who tried to kill herself and wound up getting me instead?"

"Yeah, I guess. Jeez, you don't need to yell."

"Can you believe this dumb tattoo? Soooo 1999."

"Then why not get rid of it?"

"Christina's real attached. So to speak." Sabriel stood up and started pacing. "You want coffee? I want coffee."

"I'm fine."

She stopped and looked at him, waiting.

He sighed, went to the kitchen, and started making coffee. "Cream and sugar, right?"

"Yes," she called from his living room, where she was pacing again. "Not too much sugar though, not like last time."

When he came back in, she was looking through his CDs. "I can't believe you listen to Foghat," she said, and tossed the disc out the window. He heard a clatter in the parking lot below.

"Not anymore, I guess." He set her coffee down. "So what's bothering you?"

"You didn't invite me to your party," she accused.

He sat on the couch and gave her a hard look. "You ever hear the phrase 'that dog won't hunt'?"

"Is that a Foghat lyric?"

"Did you really think I'd invite you to… I mean, y'know, a special occasion? Getting done with parole? All my friends an' everything? You've made it crystal clear that you're not my friend. The only time I see you is when you need something or want something or you're pissed about something and need someone to roll your shit downhill on." He shrugged. "Y'know, I figure you're about to mess my head one way or another, but that doesn't mean I have to accept that it's my fault."

Sabriel grunted. "Christina used to hate you. Now she just feels sorry for you."

He looked to the left, then to the right. Finally, he said, "Huh. I have no idea how to respond to that."

"She seems stronger when I'm in her shape."

"So why take that shape?"

"I don't know. I don't even like her pretentious *faux*-primitive piercings."

He shrugged again.

Sabriel turned to look out his window and said, "I'm thinking of going to St. Louis,"

"Yeah? So go. See the, what, the Gateway Arch an' shit."

"There's a colleague of mine there."

"Like that guy from Jersey?"

"Sort of like, sort of not. If 'Mr. Fortune' was a designated driver, this guy's the good-looking asshole who knows the bouncer at the bar. He's a demon of the First House, which is kind of like going to an Ivy League school. You think you're better than everyone else, and half the people secretly agree, either loving or hating you for it."

"Doesn't sound like you like him much."

"He was all right during the war. Fought with honor and distinction, all that crap. But all of us were all right back then."

It was stuff like that—the raw, sad way she said "all of us were all right back then"—that was what made him forget that she was a demon, she'd tricked him, enslaved him, could kill or betray him at any moment.

"What's he want?"

"He's probably in trouble." She frowned, turned to pick up her coffee. "*Probably*. But it could be a trick, to lure me in so he can sell *me* out."

There was a pause. Thomas felt like she was expecting something, so he said, "Okay. Sounds like you shouldn't go."

"Yeah, but if I don't go and he's in trouble, it could make worse trouble for me down the road. If I do go and he's got problems, I can help him and then he owes me, and I can use him later on to get my back against *my* problems. Especially since I strongly suspect we've really got the *same* problem. It's like Don Henley and Glenn Frey getting together again. If they weren't hard up for money…" She set down her coffee and started pacing again.

"Who?"

"Another crappy rock band that Christina secretly liked. The Eagles? The 'Hell Freezes Over' reunion tour?"

"Oh yeah, the 'Hotel California' guys, right?"

She rolled her eyes and sighed.

"Maybe you should go," he said.

"But what if that's just what he wants? He's been acting like he wants me to keep away, which probably means he wants me to come, because he's smart enough to know that I'll suspect him of double-dealing. On the other hand, if he really *does* want me to stay away, I probably should go because it means he's either planning to backstab me *or* he's got something good he wants to keep to himself. But maybe that's just what he *wants* me to think…"

"Sabriel? You're not gonna be mad if I speak honestly, are you?"

She stopped, turned toward him and narrowed her eyes.

"I don't know, Thomas," she said, her voice like ice. "I suppose that depends on what you say."

"Never mind then."

"Oh no, Thomas, I'm interested." She took a step closer. "I'd *love* your clever insights on demonic power politics."

He slouched deeper into the sofa. "It's not that, it's… Look, never mind."

"Please, speak."

"No, you're right, what the hell do I know? I'm just some stoner who works in a bookstore. Listens to Foghat, who cares what I think?"

"I care what you think, Thomas."

"Yeah, but if I make you mad by talking, you could really F me up."

"True, but you're *definitely* making me mad by staying silent."

"Okay, okay… It's not really that big a deal anyhow. I was, y'know, just going to say we've got a phrase for the kind of thinking you were doing."

"We?"

He shifted, uncomfortable. "We call it 'cocaine logic.' You know? When you just go into all those connections and 'if then, but, but then, but if, unless'… it just ties you in knots."

She leaned in, hands on hips. "Unlike your daily grind of drugs and drudgery, I have *complex* things to think about."

"Fine. But… look. You can't figure this guy from way out here. So either decide *you* want to go and go, or decide *you* want to stay and screw him in the ear. Forget about me, forget about him and his games, forget about what Christina wants or thinks." He paused. "Or am I being over-simplistic?"

She straightened. "Once again, you sell yourself short. This is why I use you as a sounding board, Thomas."

"Great. Glad I could help."

She pursed her lips, then nodded.

"I'm going."

"That's terrific."

There was a pause while she looked at him, an expectant expression on her face.

"What?" he asked.

"Shouldn't you start packing?"

He groaned.

"That's great," Gaviel said, speaking into his hospital phone. He glanced up and smiled at Matthew as the door opened. "I'm really looking forward to it. Do you mind if I let you go, though? I've got a visitor. Okay. Thanks. Goodbye."

There was no one on the other end of the line, just Time and Temperature with the volume turned low. Gaviel had actually been speaking to Sabriel.

"Good morning," Gaviel said to Matthew.

"What happened this time?" Matthew asked.

"Two men broke into my apartment and threw me out a window."

"Really."

"What do you think? That I jumped out myself?"

Matthew frowned and looked at the foot of the bed. "Why didn't you stop them?"

"I couldn't."

"You *couldn't*? C'mon now, I've… I've seen you do… I mean, I've seen *you*. The real you."

"So did they. They weren't impressed."

"How's that even possible?"

"I don't know. Maybe they were on drugs. Maybe they were *expecting* what they saw. Maybe their own hearts were so hardened and closed that no hint of the numinous could enter, even when it's crammed down their throats." He sighed. "I haven't wanted to burden you with my fears and weaknesses, but there's a lot I don't understand about my freedom, my… situation. The world I find myself in."

Matthew gave him a long, hard look.

"You haven't wanted to *burden* me. Fearing that I might turn against you had nothing to do with it?"

"What do you want? You've hounded me about your dead son like it was *my fault* since the first moment we met! I'm sorry your boy died in such a stupid, senseless way, but if he'd been an organ donor and I was a human who lived because of his heart, would you be so angry at me, so suspicious, so accusing?"

"But you're not a human."

"Funny thing. Back in the seventies, George Lasalle and his Klansman buddies would have agreed with you."

"That's not the same thing at all!"

"No? How is their judging you by the color of your skin different from you judging me by my immortal nature?"

"Because you're a..." Matthew paused and lowered his voice, aware that he'd been about to shout. "You're a demon," he said. "You rebelled against God and were cast into Hell."

"Yes! I'm a sinner! I've never denied my sins. But you're a sinner too, Matthew. To quote an old Greek playwright, 'There is guilt enough to be shared by all.'"

Matthew opened his mouth then shut it, turning his face away with an aggrieved expression.

"So, how are you feeling?" he asked at last.

"I'll be fine. I'll be out of here this afternoon, they say."

"You know, Zola wanted to come down. I asked her not to."

"Thanks. I'll see her when I get out."

"Is that a promise or a threat?"

"Oh give it a rest."

"Noah Wallace?"

A bald, black head poked itself around the edge of his door, and squinty, suspicious eyes peered in.

Gaviel's own gaze hardened.

"Just who might you be?"

"You can call me Clive," the stranger said, entering.

"I'd rather call you by your real name," Gaviel said. "Matthew, this is another demon."

"Think again," Clive replied. He stepped closer to the bed.

Matthew stepped into his path.

Although Matthew was taller and broader, there was something about the little man that bespoke power and violence. Nonetheless, the minister interposed himself.

"Why don't you tell me why you're here?" he asked—his resonant voice a perfect mix of stern and reasonable.

The shorter man looked at him and sniffed.

"I have no quarrel with you," he said. "You're untainted… so far. But he," he said, gesturing at Gaviel, "is a rebel against God. A betrayer and blasphemer."

"Can that be Forguel?" Gaviel asked, and for the first time since the demon took over, Matthew heard surprise in Noah's voice. "No, that doesn't sound like Forguel, nor the Angel of Pain either. But you've got the shadow of Hell on your features, no matter how much you speak reverence for the Allmaker. So you must be Usiel, the Reaper of Souls."

The small man gave three short, sarcastic claps. "I'd say you have the advantage of me, but really, you don't. Which miscreant are you? From your stench of vanity and indolence, I'd guess you a traitor from the First House."

"Impressive. Yes, I'm Gaviel, Lord of the Summer Sun."

Usiel laughed, one short bark, but there was no humor in it. "You're lord of *nothing*, Namaru, devil, unclean spirit! You're nothing but an escaped slave of God's contempt, and I'm here to put you back where you belong."

"I think it's time you left," Matthew said, his voice ringing with command. Yet his posture was less certain. It was subtle, but he was almost cringing.

"Step aside, mortal," the Reaper said, and emphasized his point by putting his left hand on the side of Matthew's face and shoving him out of the way. The minister stumbled back. Usiel's lip curled as the deadly scythe materialized in his hand…

"Merciful Jesus, stop."

…and the Reaper of Souls stopped.

Matthew swallowed and his voice rose a notch in volume. "The power of Christ compels you!"

Usiel flinched as if stung.

"By the power of God the Father, Christ the Son and the Holy Spirit, I command you! Get out of this place! Return to, from... return to where you came from!"

"That's it!" Gaviel said—and Usiel could sense the inspiration behind the devil's words, the encouragement that rallied a million men to their doom in the War of Wrath.

"HE'S USING YOU," Usiel grated at the minister. "DON'T BE HIS PAWN!"

The monstrous tones of the Reaper only steeled Matthew's faith. He had a small gold cross holding his tie in place, and he held up the tiny symbol between thumb and forefinger. "I cast you out! I demand that you flee! In the name of Christ Almighty, I command it!"

Usiel snarled, and the grotesque scar on his hand seemed to glint for a moment, as if its lines had cracked open and bled. He turned toward the minister and raised his scythe.

"Yes," Gaviel cried, his voice mocking. "Show your true stripes at last! Strike down a faithful man, a Godly man, again! You hypocrite—you were condemned with the worst of us, and you are as unrepentant!"

"The power of Christ compels you! The power of Christ compels you!"

"I'LL RETURN FOR YOU, DEVIL—WHEN YOU DON'T HAVE YOUR HOLY FOOL TO HIDE BEHIND!" The Reaper swung his scythe, and there was a sudden, ghastly wind, a banshee howl like a dying child, the charnel stink of a mass grave. Usiel stepped into that stench and gust and vanished.

The two who remained were silent for a moment.

"I think maybe I should stick around for a while," Matthew said.

"I'd really appreciate that," Gaviel replied.

Teddy Mason did a sloppy job parking the O'Hanlons' car, but everyone was parked sloppy out in the desert.

When he opened the door and emerged, his shoulders were slumped and his head hung low. As he'd pulled in, he'd seen Gwyn's truck and a few other cars, a few SUVs he didn't recognize. He didn't really care. He started trudging toward his empty tent.

"Teddy?"

He turned.

Joellen stood before him, though he barely recognized her.

"Hey," he said. He blinked, trying to get up the motivation to talk. "Nice haircut," he said.

"Thanks. Gwynafra took me to her apartment, had a woman come in, someone she knew from doing her shows. I got a cut, shampoo, highlights... a facial too. Manicure, pedicure, it took all afternoon. I would have been happy with just a shower." She gave a short, awkward laugh.

"Has she found a plastic surgeon for you and Blackie?"

"Soon, she says." Joellen turned toward the hills, the dunes that hid the Tree, their Goddess. "She's showing the contractors around now. She says she'll have the land purchased by tomorrow afternoon."

"That's good. Who owned it again?"

"Some real estate speculator."

He nodded. "Where'd she get the money?" He said it like he wasn't really interested, like he was just being polite.

"Oh, I don't know. Her job at the casino, I guess. Maybe she can win at cards easily, I... I guess I don't know. She's got plenty of money though."

"That's good."

"Teddy? Are you all right?"

He sighed.

"I just drove away the mother of my child, a woman I've been married to for nineteen years. She told me she's asked that our joint account be frozen until we can agree to split it down the middle into two separate accounts." He took a deep breath, a raggedy, uneven breath. "She thinks I'm crazy," he said. "She... she can't even look at me, anymore. Or when she does, it's... that's worse, seeing how she sees me now. Crazy."

"Teddy..." Joellen stepped up, hesitant, and put her arms around him. He didn't move closer, but he didn't move away.

"You know," she said, "She's not the only mother of your child."

"Oh, no, look..."

"Teddy, *please!*" She took his face in her hands and turned it to her, and he could see tears streaming down her cheeks. "She had you for years, and I only had you for minutes, but you were the only man for me. The only one! I've never..." She bit her lip, took a breath as shaky as his. "I've always known that the Goddess wanted us together," she whispered. "From the first moment. You knew it too, I know you did. All this time, I've been faithful to you. There has never been anyone else."

He just stared into her eyes.

"You feel it too, don't you?" she asked.

Mute, he nodded.

"I don't know what I... deserve," she whispered. "I know what I want. I want you. More, I know that Avitu wants us to be together. You do recognize that?"

"This is... it's too soon." But he didn't pull away, and she could feel the tension between them growing. Not a painful tension, but an electric one—an energy that made every inch of skin tingle like a lover's caress. "Please," he said. "It's too much."

"It's too strong to fight," she said, and kissed him.

He shivered, delicious, and she did too, their bodies quaking for each other. The kiss went on and on, Joellen pouring in her years, her decades of longing. She started to pull his shirt free of his pants...

And he backed off.

"No, *please*," he said. "It's... it's just too... please don't ask me. Don't ask again, yet. It's too soon. I... I couldn't say no." He held his hands up as if to ward off a blow.

Joellen almost nodded, almost stepped away. But she wanted it. Avitu wanted it. She respected the High Priest, but...

SHOW HIM HIS TRUE WILL. The voice of the Goddess echoed in Joellen's soul, and she could not disobey.

Slowly, but with a new confidence, she unbuttoned her shirt.

"Walk away, Teddy," she said. The edges of her shirt slipped over her shoulders. In the harsh daylight, her dusky skin looked vulnerable, as if it might blow away in the next breeze or shrivel into nothing. "If you feel that strongly, walk away." The shirt dropped to the desert dust, and her hands moved to the buckle of her belt.

With a moan, Teddy stepped forward into her embrace.

"I think we've got a deal, dawg," Gaviel said into his cell phone. For once, he was actually using it. "You sure it's clean? I don't want any hassles... uh huh. Solid. How soon can I pick it up?"

That transaction complete, Gaviel hung up. He was driving to the high school, and he tried to think wordlessly, to calm himself. Instead, he felt Noah stirring within him.

Why don't you give up? the mortal wanted to know.

Giving up was your tactic. It's not mine, the demon thought in reply. He made an effort to subdue the rebellious human parasite—Noah shouldn't be able to address him like that, not during the day. It was because he was tired. Transforming, healing himself, persuading the cops, bolstering Matthew against Usiel… all of it was effort, the hard labor of bending and twisting and wrestling Reality. He was plumb tuckered out, and Noah was taking advantage of his laxity by nagging him.

There's this Avitu with a dirty cop who runs his county like it's a feudal kingdom. Then there's that thing, whatever, your "Foe" in East Saint Louis. Just when you get done antagonizing it, you run into this Reaper of Souls. He scared you, didn't he? He scared you shitless.

Don't you worry, Gaviel thought in response. *I'm far from played out.*

Oh yeah, you're bringing in your ally who did such a good job with Maryanne Whatsername the politician. Did anyone come out of that on top? Maryanne's dead, you wasted a bunch of your time, and that Sabriel creature got her left arm burned to a crisp!

Sabriel's not the type to let a little thing like a burned arm get in her way, Gaviel responded. *That's what you human spirits fail to comprehend. We're not like you. We're not plagued by doubt and regret; not shackled by fears about what we can or can't do. We know what we can do, and we know our limitations without making up imaginary ones. If you had our unity of spirit, if you could truly marshal your potential, you could do wonders. Instead, you—and here I mean you personally, Noah—you squandered it, pissed it all away, wasted your time in pointless intellectual onanism.*

That's not fair. Noah's voice whined across Gaviel's psyche, but he could tell Noah was weakening. Only human, after all.

Admit it, Noah. You loved it when I was fucking with those drug dealers. You loved it when I was stealing shit in California. You even got a secret thrill watching me betray and manipulate other demons—no secrets here, not between us, right? And let's not get started on that lady cop. You envy me. You always wanted to be effective, to make a difference, but you always knew you were just another neurasthenic dilettante who'd rather write a small check and a large letter to the editor than actually go out and take action. So rather than give up—and let you get back to frittering away your life, only with the bonus of having the money I got and the reputation I earned—I think I'll ride this thing out to the end, thank you very much. After all, what are they gonna do to me? Send me back to Hell?

Gaviel paused, and there was no reply from Noah. He was happy, but he didn't smile, there was no one to see it, his face was perfectly blank.

Privately, he intended to never again be weak enough that Noah could insult him by daylight. This mentoring trip would, he hoped, provide him a reservoir of strength.

"Hi, Monique," he said, nodding as he entered the classroom, "Leotis. Chasney, Emmaline. How y'all doing?"

The four teenagers looked up at him sullenly, but he knew it was an act. They were there, they were listening, they were hungry for a touch of his glory.

"Where's Renee?" he said, looking at Monique. She looked away and slid her eyes over at Leotis. Gaviel turned to him and raised an eyebrow.

"She not coming," Leotis said.

(Leotis Grant's parents were both college educated. His mother was an insurance adjuster and his father a manager at a sewage treatment plant. It made both of them absolutely crazy that their son insisted on speaking in the street patois he'd picked up from TV and rap records.)

"Oh?"

Leotis shrugged. "Say she don't need no mentor no more." He sounded surly.

"Well, I guess that's her choice." Gaviel feigned surprise, but he knew very well that—thanks to her wishes and his fulfillment—his only surviving thrall was busy living life on her own terms. She'd persuaded Leotis to come two weeks ago, and they'd sat with two desks pushed awkwardly together, her clinging to his arm, him looking lazy and cocky and satisfied.

Last week they'd come together again, but this time it was Leotis who was pestering her for attention—Leotis who sulked and pouted when she brushed him off.

The demon was pleased.

They spent an hour talking about goal-setting and priorities and self-confidence and remaining true to their true selves—the kind of encouraging platitudes that Gaviel could mouth in his sleep while bickering with Noah's ghost. They had smiles— weak smiles, shy teenage smiles, but smiles—when they left. He'd used one of the faded reflections of his old power, a power that had once sent men screaming into battle against animals and trees and even rivers infused with celestial might—sent them screaming and led them victorious. These sad, confused adolescents would use that little drop of inhuman encouragement on their next Physics test or track meet, and they would remember him.

Except for Leotis.

Leotis didn't smile, and he didn't leave.

"Mr. Wallace?" he asked, as the others shuffled out.

"Mr. Grant," Gaviel said, mock-formal but expressing a core of care that wasn't really present. He sat on the edge of the teacher's desk and gave the teen a frank look. "What's up?"

"Renee." He looked down at his shoes.

"You two not getting along?"

Leotis shrugged. Gaviel waited. Getting a teenage boy to talk was like pulling teeth, but fallen angels were used to waiting.

"She... at first it was great, she was all... y'know. She was into me, really into me! Now... she ain't got no time for me. I dunno. It's all fucked up." He looked up suddenly, realizing he'd let an F-word slip out, but Gaviel let it slide.

"Well, easy come, easy go. I mean, you two were only together for a couple weeks... right?"

"Naw, it ain't... I mean, yeah, it wasn't long but *dang*... I mean, I thought it was, y'know, f'real. Know what I'm sayin'?"

"Are you talking about *love*?"

Leotis shrugged... nodded.

"Well, what about Jewell?"

The teen shook his head, made a *tsk* sound in his throat, made a gesture like he was brushing away dust.

"Naw, it ain't... She's not, y'know, not in the picture no more."

"Do you think maybe *she* was hurt when you dropped her for Renee, just as you're feeling hurt now?"

Leotis gave him a look of pure, uncomplicated confusion. "Huh?"

It never even crossed his mind, Gaviel marveled. "Never mind," he said. "Renee is the one you want, and why not? She loved you once, why not again?" The boy shrugged and shifted his posture, uneasy. Gaviel didn't let him off the hook. "I guess I don't see where I 'enter the picture' as you might say."

"Well it was just... it was just that it was, you know, after you started... you know. That was when she got all... you know."

"She got..."

"She... I dunno. She seemed different."

"That she started to interest you?"

The boy couldn't look at him, just the floor. "Aw..." he muttered. "Aw, f'get it."

"Leotis, look. I don't want to diminish your feelings. I can tell they're strong. But unless you tell me what you want, I can't help you get it. And until you tell me what you think I can do, I can't tell you whether you're right or not. Dig?"

"It's like... Monique said that after meeting you, Renee got all... she was... Monique's like, 'It's like a miracle.' That's what she said, like a miracle or somethin'."

"So you want a miracle. Or something."

"Never mind." He turned to the door, but Gaviel spoke his name. The boy froze as if he'd been nailed to the floor.

"Leotis, what if it's not a miracle?"

The boy turned—almost as if he was moving against resistance.

"What do you mean?"

"I can't make Renee love you, and I wouldn't if I could. But what if I could make you the kind of man you want to be? The kind of man she'd love? The kind of man *any* woman would love? Would you like that?"

"Well… sure. I mean, why not?"

"What if it wasn't a *miracle*? What if there was a cost? A *high* cost?"

"I dunno… it, uh, I guess. I mean, it would depend on what that was. Y'know."

Gaviel nodded. "Leotis, is any price too high to get everything you want in the world?"

"Huh?"

"Don't you understand the question?"

"I… I…" He looked down, then looked up, and his eyes were hooded and cool, his chin high and arrogant. He'd slipped on the street 'tude of his TV heroes with the ease of sliding into favorite jacket. "*Everything* I want? Shit, ain't no price can *be* too high."

"Then I think we can do some business."

"Hello?"

"Yeah, Duke?"

The sound technician swallowed. He knew the voice, pronouncing his name "Dook." It was Sal Macellaio.

"Mr. Ma… um, uh, hi. I got that… that thing. Your…"

"That thing we talked about."

"Uh huh."

"Terrif'. I'll be over presently."

When Sal walked in, Duke had cleared off a spot on his table and neatly set out three objects.

"The first is, that's your source tape of course, the, the original," he said. Sal nodded. The tape had a label on it that said "Scott" and had become a frequent element of his dreams and nightmares. "And when I cleaned it up I, uh, I burned it onto a CD. It's on there as a wave file, an MP3 and in a standard mix format. If you want to label that or, um, the case, I got a marker around here somewhere."

"That won't be necessary. And you put it on cassette too?"

"Uh huh. I didn't know if you had, um, I mean..."

"It's the little touches like that which lend class to any enterprise," Sal said gravely, and Duke gave him a weak little smile.

"I'm going to take it as read," Sal continued, "that you did not make any copies of this thing for yourself, in any way, shape or form."

"Oh no. No, I, I didn't. No tapes, I nuked the samples on the computer, I... in fact, why don't I defrag that hard drive just to make sure they're gone, okay?"

"You do that," Sal said, picking up the two tapes and the CD. Without asking permission, he slipped on a pair of headphones and plugged them into one of the many CD players present.

As the machine whirred, he noticed that there were different tracks. A Post-It note on the back of the case listed them.

1. *Intro.*

2. *Erasure 1*

3. *Erasure 2*

Very tidy, he thought, licking his lips. He pushed PLAY, then SKIP.

"...Alakazam, you poor bastard." It was Ciullo's voice. Sal had heard this part. In the background, his son was screaming. But this time, instead of a rumbling hiss, the sound levels dropped and then got hollow and scratchy—like he was listening through a tin can.

He could hear a voice—Ciullo's voice, presumably—saying something, but the words made no sense. It wasn't English or Italian or any other language Sal could name... it had a hissing, cracking, caressing sound. It was like the pop of a fire and the moan of wind and the whispers of waves on a shore. It gave him the creeps.

Is that fuckin' Greek? Shit, I didn't even notice anything missing, before.

Erasure 2 was only seconds after Erasure 1, and Sal almost missed it musing over Harvey Ciullo's strange phrase. He hit a button to rewind it, and this time Ciullo's companion, the unfamiliar voice, was speaking.

"Should we show him, Has*med*? *Should we show mm mph beautiful truth?"*

The break off in that section was in the middle of "Hasmed," and some words were still too obscure to hear. But what was a Hasmed? Why would they want to show it to Scott? Was it a word in that weird other language?

Erasure 3 was a third voice—an unearthly voice like the sound of a saw cutting metal—and it started with, "INTO THE MAW OF THE DEMON DUKE VO*dantu, where your soul's torment will leaven the pain of his durance, even as you howl and* SUFFER IN ETERNITY FOR YOUR FATHER'S BOLDNESS!"

The distortion of the recovered sound was a relief with that voice, and its volume ensured that the words were loud and clear—and (Sal privately thought) weird as could be.

He kept listening through Erasure 4.

"IF YOU WOULD PRAY, PRAY TO YOUR NEW MASTER, *Vodantu! Unlike the Allmaker, he will hear and respond! Perhaps you can bargain away your life and soul in return for mitigated torment!*"

The hollowness of the recording faded, and he was once again hearing the sounds of his son being tortured to death. He pushed the STOP button.

"What the hell is a Hasmed?" Sal muttered.

Who calls?

Sal jumped, and his head whipped around. There was no one behind him, just Duke puttering around with an elaborate coffee-maker. For a second Sal thought the voice came from the CD, but he looked and it was stopped.

Who is it that calls me?

The voice wasn't in his ears. It was in his head.

"Who the fuck are you?" he muttered, stealing a glance at Duke.

You invoke my name but don't know me? Name yourself!

"I'm Carl Booker," Sal said, voice low, using the name on his Florida driver's license. *What the fuck?* he thought. *If he's asking my name, he doesn't know, and if he doesn't know, how'll he know I'm lying?*

Where did you learn my name?

"Oh, wouldn't you like to know?"

Don't toy with me, pal! Hasmed of the Hated Lash is not to be invoked lightly! I spent eons with my name unspoken, and now you call? This better be good.

"What are you? What's your connection to Harvey Ciullo?"

Sal?

Oh shit, Sal thought.

The voice in his mind chuckled, and there wasn't an ounce of humor in it.

Sal Macellaio, you sad sack of shit. You found out who I really am, huh? Well good for you. Nice job with Ciullo's mom, by the way. Did you put an air bubble in her arm for that heart attack or just scare her to death?

"I played her the Scott tape."

There was a pause. Sal had time to think that maybe he'd scored a point, and he had time to notice that Duke was starting to look at him funny before the voice in his mind came roaring back.

Very clever, fuck-pole, but it ain't gonna do you no good! You think I give a shit about that old bag? You think I care about Harvey's fuckin' sister or anyone else? The guy I care about is you, Macellaio, 'cause you've made yourself a big enough pain in the ass! I'm gonna find you, shit-stink, and I'm gonna eat your soul like a motherfuckin' donut. And every time you speak my name, you're gonna be easier to find. Like right now—who's the fucko with the beard and the coffee cup? Where you at? Looks like somewhere sunny... still down in Florida? Didn't flee the state when you killed my... Harvey's mom? That's an ugly suit, by the way. Navy blue, fuggeddaboudit. Looks like ass on you.

Sal felt a chill as he realized that whatever Hasmed was, it could *see* him.

No snappy comeback, Sal? Didn't think so. I enjoyed this chat. Call me again, any fuckin' time you like. Day or night.

Sal stumbled to his feet and ran out the door.

"Sorry. My insurance won't cover it if I sleep with someone old enough to be my grandfather."

"Whoo, you're a lil' spitfire! I jus' wanted to buy you a drink."

Sabriel had seen a cute yellow chiffon dress on sale at Kohl's and had crafted a sultry, black-haired body to fill it. She'd started with Christina but had upped her buxomness by 10% or so, made the face a little more worldly, but a little less tired. She'd had to be Christina for the flight, which was irritating — the dress didn't look as good on her — but she'd changed in the bathroom after landing.

It was a good look, but it had caught the eye of some octogenarian Lothario. He had food stains on his shirt and hideous false teeth. She turned her back with a dismissive gesture, tapped her fingers impatiently and then saw Thomas and Gaviel approaching. Gaviel was carrying half the luggage Sabriel had sent Tom to fetch, and the two were gabbing like old friends. She smiled a sour smile, which turned sugary sweet when he was close enough to see it.

"Noah!" she said, popping off the barstool and giving him a hug. "It's so great to see you."

"I feel just like you do."

She pulled a light satchel off his arm and slung it over her own, taking advantage of the movement to glance at the old man. He had a stricken look, as if he'd just seen her embracing a rabid dog.

"I can't wait until your big black cock is pumping me full of jizz," she said, just loud enough for the old man to overhear. Then she hooked one arm around Thomas and the other around Gaviel, steering them toward the metal detectors.

"My my, that's a warmer welcome than I expected."

"Don't get any ideas. I just wanted to give the old lecher in the bar an aneurysm. Is he twitching and frothing?"

"Afraid not. He does look like someone just slipped dog shit in his daiquiri though."

"Ah well. Maybe I can give him a heart attack on the return trip."

"He'd probably prefer it if you gave him a stroke."

She rewarded his feeble wordplay with a brief smirk. "One stroke from me and he'd probably have a coronary *and* an aneurysm."

"I was serious when I thanked you for coming out here."

Looking at him—and more, using celestial senses of realness that humans could only approximate in moments of perfect clarity and total intimacy—she almost believed him. But if anyone could fool an angel, it was a devil.

"What's your situation?" she asked.

"Things were going just fine for a while. Something's infected a crime structure in East St. Louis, and I was picking at it to see what it would do—stealing some money, killing some pawns, nothing too ambitious."

"When you say 'something'…"

"Not one of us. Not one of those 'Earthbound' either. Something young, something I haven't seen before. Clever though. Certainly not human, but nothing I couldn't handle."

"I see."

"Then I ran into a pair of ugly thralls to your old friend the Keeper of the Twin Winds. They threw me out a window."

"Thralls? You're sure they were human and not… anything else?"

"As human as this one," Gaviel said, jerking his thumb at Tom. He turned to the mortal with a smile. "Is your name *really* Tommy Ramone?"

"I prefer Tom or Thomas," he said, gritting his teeth.

"Really? She told me Tommy." Sabriel giggled and blew Tom a kiss as Gaviel continued. "Then, while I was in the hospital, guess who showed up? The Reaper of Souls."

"Who?"

"The Reaper of Souls. Formerly Throne of the Sundered."

Sabriel stopped in her tracks.

"That's right," Gaviel said, curious about her reaction. "Didn't you know he was out of the Abyss?"

"The Abyss? But Usi—"

"Shh!"

"But... the Throne of the Sundered never rebelled! I mean, he was a loyalist!"

Gaviel gave her an incredulous stare. "When did you get cast down?"

"Fourth siege of Genhinnom."

"Hm, midway through then. You never heard about the Mountains of the Morning?"

"No."

They reached the metal detectors, so their conversation paused as they made their way out of the airport. When they were leaving the terminal, Thomas spoke up.

"Sorry but... what are you guys talking about?"

"Old times," Gaviel said, flashing a smile. "Old war stories. The *oldest* war stories." He turned to Sabriel and said, "Short version, the Reaper and his army were approaching from the south, and our commander—you remember her?—she wanted to retreat to the north, through the mountains. Only our followers... they couldn't keep up."

His eyes seemed to go distant. The three of them wandered down corridors of Fords and Hondas, but he seemed to be a million miles away... or a million years.

"All our believers were crowded into the pass. A lot of us were First and Second House, so we had pretty good control of the sky but... we couldn't get our people out in time. The Reaper had told a human tribe, loyal Abelites, about us, and they were coming into the valley from the west, all the forces converging on that one gorge... The Abelite tribes attacked our followers—it was late enough that even the humans were fighting—and then the Reaper killed them all." He opened the trunk, looking away from her as he and Thomas loaded up the suitcases.

"All of your followers?" Sabriel couldn't keep a note of sympathy out of her voice, and she wanted to… but the Gaviel she'd known in the war had been a kind master to his humans, generous with his gifts and quick to defend them.

He looked up and met her eyes with a cool, neutral gaze. "All our followers, and all of the Abelites. He killed all the mortals. You see? He couldn't wait for the loyal humans to retreat and let his celestials mop up. By the time the Abelites disengaged, we 'demons' would be long gone. So he killed his friends in order to kill his enemies."

"I don't believe it. I knew him before, Gaviel. I knew… I knew him with Haniel."

"The war changed him a lot. It changed all of us, loyalist and rebel alike."

"But… but if he was willing to slaughter the faithful to fight us, how could he ever join us?"

"He never *joined*. He never *rebelled*. But when the war was over, the Ancient of Days rewarded his… his zealous loyalty… with the same punishment given to the most black-hearted demon. For committing atrocities in the name of God, he was flung from Heaven with the rest of us."

Gaviel slammed down the trunk and unlocked the doors of his Lexus.

"From the way he spoke, he's still fighting the war, still loyally assaulting every demon he meets." He slid in behind the wheel and put his key in the ignition.

"One more interesting trivia fact," he said. "The Reaper has acquired a releasing tool. Maybe even the same one he used in the war."

Sal came back to Duke's studio two hours later, but the sound man wasn't there. A couple phone calls located him, though, and soon Sal was meeting him at a local Burger King for a final chat.

"You didn't see nothin', and you didn't hear nothin'," Sal said. No hello or anything, this time.

Duke's eyes were wide and frightened. "Okay," he said.

"Here." Sal held out an envelope. "Take it!"

Duke did, gingerly.

There was a pause.

"Ain'tcha gonna open it?"

Duke peeked inside. There were fifties held together with a paper clip.

"Uh, thanks. I mean… thanks. Um."

"You don't even count it. Nice. That's classy." The tension between them eased down a notch. "First time I saw you, Duke, I thought, 'Here's some hippie faggot asshole,' but you're okay. You do things right."

"Uh. Well. Thanks."

"You did a good job. I value and respect people who do their work right." He drummed his fingers on the plastic table top and frowned. "Now, about me leaving your establishment."

"Oh, uh, hey, it's… it's no big deal."

"That's what I like to hear. Nobody needs to hear about that, you got me? Nobody needs to know that. *You* don't need to know that. Fuggeddaboudit."

"Sure, it's… I mean I'm… Yeah."

"And when I say fuggeddaboudit, I mean forget… about… it. It did not happen. You did not see me do nothin', you did not hear anything, 'cause there was nothing to hear or see. I want to be very, very clear on this subject."

"You're clear. I've, it's forgotten."

"What's forgotten?"

"Uh… everything?"

"That's right." Sal leaned in, and his gaze was intense—not merely menacing, something Duke had been steeling himself against, but also haunted and somehow desperate. "The stuff you heard on the tape you got to *especially* forget. Those words are not ever to be spoken. Never. Not ever. Not. Fuckin'. Ever. Is *that* clear?"

"Sure."

"'Cause if I find out you said those words... well shit." He leaned back, and the pleading element of his look grew stronger. "If you say those words, you'll be in such trouble I won't need to do nothin' to you. If you say those words, it'll be too late."

"I won't say 'em."

"Don't."

"I won't."

"Don't. Because I'll just kill you. But those words... they'll damn you."

They sat in silence for a while before Duke asked permission to leave and, when it was granted, left as fast as he politely could.

Sal had come from Duke's studio and, before that, from a Catholic church. He wanted to go back to the church, talk some sense to that priest, see if he could get a serious exorcist. But he knew the smarter play was to go straight to the airport.

Sabriel sat in her hotel room, chewing the ends of her hair. It was one of Christina's old habits, and sometimes it crept up on her when she was unprepared.

She'd seen and done some wicked things since returning. Even before, in Hell, before that, during the war, she'd seen horrors untold. But Usiel... Usiel, who rejected Lucifer to his face, who never wavered in his faith... if even *he* could earn the wrath of Heaven, who could ever be safe?

She remembered, before the Fall and the ugliness, Usiel had been sorrowful when he had to pluck the life from a daisy, somber when he had to even take a blade of grass... he'd always approached his duties with grave solemnity.

And Haniel... she'd been like Sabriel's sister, formed by the Allmaker on the same day in the same house. She'd seemed to have a nearly unique ability to draw Usiel from his shell. The few times Sabriel had heard the Throne of the Sundered laugh, he had been with Haniel.

It was hard to remember now, to think back through all those eons to when the world was whole, but she remembered how Usiel had cherished Haniel. She remembered them twined together in the ebb and flow of an ocean wave stroking the shore, remembered them taking form through the movements of the currents and titans of the deep, remembered them on more refined levels of reality, meshing together as functions of time and direction and pattern change.

She remembered Haniel's fate and she sighed.

How to do it? she thought. She'd told Gaviel she could take care of Usiel, if Gaviel saw to Avitu and her minions.

A thousand stratagems flitted through her mind, each dismissed instantly. Such ploys might be fit for humans, but an angel of the Lord deserved better.

In the end, she simply invoked him.

"Usiel," she said, then moistened her lips. "Usiel. It's Sabriel."

He didn't respond. She felt the connection falter and fail, but she tried again.

"Usiel, I'm in Saint Louis," she said. "I know you're here too. Where?"

This time, the connection remained open. But he didn't reply.

"Usiel, I didn't know you'd… you'd been imprisoned with us. I wish I'd known." She stood and paced, then peered aimlessly out the window. "It must have been even worse for you," she said, realizing it only as she spoke. "At least we had each other. Or we did at first, before the infighting, before the hatred ate us up. But you were all alone from the first. Weren't you?"

Still no answer, but that sense of listening. She began to feel uneasy. She narrowed her eyes, looked at the sleet that was falling outside. The patterns it made snaking down the glass looked familiar, almost as if they were animated by someone she knew, someone she'd worked with… but that was impossible. The angels were all gone.

"Getting out must have been hard too," she said, opening the window and idly running her finger down the icy screen, watching the snowmelt form films on the tiny squares, the pattern of water following her gesture. "Finding out that the loyalists were gone, that the world was just a device now, ticking along… no room for wonderful things, only horrors like us. Like me, I guess."

She paused, feeling the small grinding crunches between her teeth as she chewed Christina's hair. There was a chill to her connection with Usiel, an underlying movement, like the static when she contacted other demons in Hell. Had he gone back? Been sent back? This felt different.

Then, suddenly, a bitter wind flooded the room. She spun and saw a thin sliver of the world wither and die before her eyes, a slit gaping open and a figure emerging from that strange cold space, the realm of the Slayers.

Usiel emerged as a smoldering skeleton with scythe in hand, and for a moment she was frozen, seeing how he'd been twisted and perverted by war and punishment.

"IT'S TOO LATE FOR YOUR PITY, DEFILER."

Once, his voice had been soft as fog and gentle as sleep. Now it grated and howled, the edge of sound between the growl of a cat and the scream of a hare.

The scythe lashed out, Sabriel leaned back against the screen and then she was water, drizzling down the front of the hotel. Her pretty yellow dress fell to the floor, slashed into two pieces.

Splashing to the ground, Sabriel began slithering between patches of ice and snow, still liquid, trying to put as much distance between herself and the Reaper as she could.

He tried to kill me, she marveled. *Gaviel was right about him still fighting the war, that's for sure. Shit.*

She reached out with her spirit, feeling for him. She could sense him, still on an upper floor of the hotel, not moving. What was he waiting for? She couldn't get that firm a sense of his location, despite the strength that rolled off him like a chilly breeze.

I guess it makes sense. He didn't get the crap kicked out of him before being imprisoned. He's probably as strong as any of the fallen.

A man was splashing along the sidewalk, and Sabriel oozed along with him. The presence of a mortal, an unbeliever, might inhibit the Reaper. Or at least make him hesitate.

He got a lock on me when I invoked him, then went into that dead world of theirs to get to me... just so he could take me by surprise. Bastard!

Was he drifting downward... floating down the stairways like a bad dream? Or just taking the elevator? No matter, he'd be on the ground soon.

The man she'd been following opened a door, and Sabriel heard the sounds of dining and celebration coming from within. With an effort of will, she changed from water to mist and drifted along beside him.

Once, she'd been able to switch between shapes effortlessly, and being water or flesh was natural to her—as natural as being

206 / GREG STOLZE

pattern or flow or only potential. But now her only true form was bone and blood, and being anything else was a labor. She coalesced in the cloakroom, slipping into a woman's coat and casually adjusting her height until it fit properly.

Peeking through the door, she got a better look at the party. At the front of the hall, a long table facing the guests. In the center, a man in a black tuxedo and a woman in a long white gown. On her side of the table, more women, each dressed in violet velvet. On his side, men in tuxes.

A wedding.

Naked beneath the coat, Sabriel cinched her belt tighter and started wondering how she could get some shoes.

Usiel took the hotel elevator, and he did it in Clive Keene's form. His other shape was too heavy a burden, in a building full of sleeping mortals. He'd had his chance with it, and he'd failed.

Compulsively pushing the button in and out, he gritted his teeth.

She wouldn't be a problem. She could run, but not fight—not him, anyhow.

When the elevator door opened, there was a man inside. The man—a comptroller at a dental supply firm—felt a sudden tingle in his left arm. That was the arm that had gone numb when he'd had a heart attack five years ago, and for a moment, the comptroller almost panicked, thinking about his family, thinking about almost dying.

It was not a comfortable ride.

Usiel left the building, sniffing the rainy air, seeking... He turned and stalked through the slush, sensing her.

There was a twinge of discomfort from the real Clive Keene—the soul he'd pushed aside to return to the mortal world. Clive was a weak spirit, timid, and his complaint wasn't even conscious enough to be verbal. But Usiel found himself feeling that it was a shame, that she was so young, a pretty little slip of a thing.

Yeah, about the age your daughter would be — if she'd lived, Usiel thought, bitterness rising. *Someone of my house had to claim your daughter's soul, because creatures like that thing broke ranks and defied Heaven. If not for Sabriel, and the demons like her, your daughter would be alive, and your mother, and your wife too.*

Keene's resignation was part fear and part despair. Whatever. He backed off, and the Reaper remained in full control.

"Excuse me sir, this is a private party."

A strong hand took his arm. Usiel reached over so that his ring touched that hand... then stopped. For some reason, instead of releasing the doorman's soul, he coughed up a ghost, instead.

"Remove him," Usiel said, but it wasn't really necessary. The slave ghost — one of the demon vassals he'd killed down in Florida — flowed out of Usiel's mouth and up the guard's nose like secondhand smoke.

The mortal's eyes grew wide with panic, and he fled out into the cold.

Usiel glared around the room, impatient for his mortal eyes to adjust. Everyone was clinking their glasses with their silverware, a bride and groom blushed and kissed... and everyone was distracted from the demon in their midst. Everyone but him.

She was standing next to the front table, far off to one side, bending down. He couldn't see what she was doing until he took several steps to his right.

Despite the cold outside, the crowded dining hall was hot. One of the bridesmaids had kicked off her shoes, and the demon was taking them.

"Sabriel," he said, smirking, "Can't you stop stealing? Even to run away?"

She looked up, and her expression was scared. It gave him a pang, another taste of life from Clive Keene. Other men might like the look of a frightened woman, but it only made Clive sad.

The Reaper was by the hall's right wall, and he started making his way along it toward her. He was ready to finish things once and for all.

He was so intent on her that the bright burst of light took him totally by surprise. He flinched, turned, almost called his weapon. He was halfway convinced it was a demon of fire or lightning materializing to aid a fellow... then he realized it was the wedding photographer, taking flash pictures of the guests. He grimaced and looked for her... but she was gone.

Or not gone, but changed.

Usiel, you don't have to do this.

The voice was as close as a lover's kiss, but he couldn't feel the direction. He was close, too close, it was like she was everywhere around him.

Don't you remember me? Remember the joy you gave Haniel and myself, the smiles you brought to the Singer of the Western Waves? How can you strike at one who was your hostess once, and once your guest?

"If you're looking for mercy, don't remind me of the paradise you ruined," he muttered. There! She'd gotten shorter, stouter, darkened her skin to match the olive tones of the husband's family, but the coat was still the same. She was on the opposite side of the room. He reversed his course, intending to skirt the dance floor and get her...

"Okay everybody! It's time for the bride and groom to have their first dance!"

Again he blinked and cursed Keene's dim eyesight as the lights went down in the room and brightened only above the dance floor. He'd lost her again, and she would almost certainly change form to confuse him.

What will killing me accomplish? Will it salve your wounded pride? Restore the fallen world? Make God love you again?

"It will shield your future victims from the pain of your attention."

How do you know I haven't learned my lesson?

"Don't make me laugh. Your kind doesn't change."

Don't you mean our kind? Weren't you damned, just as I was?

"That's different." He knew she was baiting him, distracting him from the hunt, but...

Did you learn your lesson?

As she asked it, he froze in place. For just a moment—hearing the voice of his onetime friend, a voice so close to his lost lover Haniel—he wondered if he truly had.

He blinked, and it was as if he could see the faces of those he'd killed since returning.

Gordy Hines, a murderer as remorseless as any denizen of the pit... who died wailing with the baffled terror of an infant in pain.

John Bow, demon slave, who died surprised and defiant.

Max Hirniesen, a man who had usurped part of a dead angel's spirit. He'd struggled to the last.

The nameless others he'd fought—some who died, some who survived, some with faces showing rage or pain or mortal fear, some whose expressions were only confused as they tried to comprehend the power they battled.

Lynn Culver, whose feelings had rattled back and forth between helpless fright, and an anger that was close to madness. Neither mood had saved her. She had died afraid and still feared him after death.

Have I learned my lesson?

Then he shook his head, seeing her, now a redhead, again slipping behind the main table. She was trying to keep the dance floor between herself and him, hoping he wouldn't plunge straight across it and draw everyone's attention. Or perhaps she hoped he *would* make a scene, hoped that the gaze of mortals would keep his true majesty contained, keep him trapped in the body of Clive Keene.

He turned around, going back to the right. There was a door nearby, he'd get her out of the crowded hall , maybe even drag her into the realm of the dead. She'd have nowhere to flee him there.

The bride and groom were dancing, the music was booming, drowning out even normal conversation, let alone his hushed debate with Sabriel. Now other couples rose, blocking Clive's sight. (Keene was a short man, and suddenly he was lost in a forest of taller guests.) He pushed and dodged, but he knew she'd be gone by the time he got to the front of the room. Sure enough, she was.

Still close though. Still close enough to feel; still too close to get a direction.

Aren't you tired?

"Weariness is a human luxury."

Even God rested on the seventh day.

He just snorted derisively in reply.

You fought the war. Did you get much rest before being condemned? And I know the struggles I faced in Hell. One lone angel surrounded by demons... yours must have been far worse. And now that you're back in the material world, have you even paused in your wrath to take stock? To ask who you're really mad at, and why?

"My anger is toward your vile ilk, because you destroyed a world I loved."

From what I hear about the Mountains of Morning, you did your share of destroying, and more. Do you think getting revenge will fix anything?

"When all is lost, all that remains is to share your loss with others."

Did you think that up yourself? Or are you quoting the Stone of Despair, or the Lady of Dust, or one of the other demons who wants to burn down the world?

He saw her again. She wasn't far, just a few tables down, blonde and slender with her back to him, moving away, threading her way between children and chairs.

Would you be so angry if you still had Haniel?

"She has nothing to do with it!"

Would you have slaughtered all those humans if she'd been by your side?

"It doesn't matter!"

She was changing again, hair turning dark alongside her skin. She was moving quicker because she was taller, had longer legs. He started to push people aside, no longer caring what they noticed.

Were you ever angry at her for picking God over you?

"Never! If she'd done otherwise, she'd be as bad as Lucifer. As bad as you!"

Were you angry at God for taking her away?

He closed in, grabbed her shoulder and spun her around.

Then he froze.

The woman who faced him looked somewhere between twenty and forty. She had cedar-brown skin, loose frizzy hair, a solemn face. She was pretty; the lines of her face were clean and pure and a little sad. Her neck was slender, graceful, vulnerable.

She looked a lot like Clive Keene's dead daughter.

She looked a lot like Keene's dead wife, too—like she had when Clive was young.

Usiel had never realized how much Keene's beloved dead looked like his own lost love. Dear Haniel, angel of the tides, who had asked God why humanity had to suffer and strive. Haniel, who longed as much as Usiel to be near the humans, to comfort and protect them and be loved in return, but who obeyed God's sternest commandment to remain distant, aloof, unseen by mankind. Haniel, who laughed and danced with Usiel and, in secret grottoes and hidden stretches of beach, played at being human, as did he, a private game they never let others see. Two angels in mortal form, trying to live as humans lived. Trying to understand.

Haniel, who asked God why. Who was told, "To know what I know, you must see as I see." Who accepted those terms and was lost to the world forever.

"How?" He swallowed, his voice suddenly dry and cracked and humanly weak. "How did you know? How do you know that face?"

"Oh Usiel," she said. He was close enough to hear her whisper, but the echo of his name put her voice in his head as well. "I can see it in you. This is the shape of the hole in your heart. Hers is the face of your loneliness."

He stepped forward and put his hands on her shoulders. He trembled, he was weak and confused and full of a surging energy he couldn't understand or release. In his games with Haniel, they had never imagined this, never imagined what it truly was to be a woman or a man.

"Will you kill me now?" she asked. It wasn't a challenge. It wasn't a plea. There was nothing to the question but its most obvious meaning. He could destroy her, and they both knew it.

Instead, they danced.

Chapter Eleven

"So you're meeting Boyer downtown?" Roscoe Paum asked. Hasmed grunted an affirmative. He was busy adjusting the dimple in his new silk tie.

"You think I'm gonna let that guy know where Tina's at?"

Roscoe shrugged. "Man, you wouldn't believe what he told me the last time I saw 'im," he said.

He waited for Hasmed to express interest. When no interest was forthcoming, he went on anyhow. "He said he read that pro athletes are all drinkin' breast milk now. You believe that?"

"In this stupid, crap-hole world, I believe anything."

There was a pause.

"Hey, Hawvey, you mind me sayin' somethin'?" Roscoe didn't know the demon's name, referring to him as Harvey.

"I guess it's a free country."

"Shouldn' you be happier?"

Hasmed swore, jerked the tie out of its knot and started retying it. "Who says I ain't happy?"

"I stand corrected."

"I been *made*," Hasmed said, stubby fingers fumbling the silk. "I got a crew of my own, and we just kicked the holy hell outta Bronco's mob. I'm Rico's fuckin' fair-haired boy."

"Are you, now?"

"I got a beautiful *daughter*," he said, jerking the knot tight. "She's in a good school, has a good nanny, the best motherfuckin' *child psychologist* money can buy…"

"Yeah, that Dr. Anders, she's really something, I guess."

"So why wouldn' I be *happy*?"

"Sorry I said anything," Roscoe muttered. "Fuggeddaboudit, sheesh."

HASMED. I CRAVE AUDIENCE.

The voice was only in the demon's head, and he winced. Leaving his tie sloppy, he reached in his pocket and pulled out a pager.

"Damn," he said. "I gotta take this."

"Who is it?"

WHAT?

"Never mind," Hasmed told Paum, heading toward his bedroom. "Gimme some privacy, y'mind?"

PRIVACY? YOU PRESUME MUCH, SCOURGE! YOU MAY HAVE THE FREEDOM OF THE WORLD OF MEN, BUT YOU ARE NOT FREE OF ME AND NEVER WILL BE.

"Forgive me master. I was not addressing you, but rather a mortal in my presence."

There was a pause, during which Hasmed thought *Y'know, for an infernal archduke who sees the future, Vodantu can be pretty damn dense.* He had a moment to be surprised at himself before his invoker spoke again. This time, the superior demon's voice had a mollified tone.

I SEE. ONCE AGAIN, YOU RESORT TO A RUSE TO CONCEAL YOUR NATURE.

"Only when I have to. You have *no idea* how tired I am of putting on the fake and pretending to be human."

AND YET YOU MIMIC THEIR LAZY SPEECH, EVEN WHEN ADDRESSING YOUR SUPERIORS.

Hasmed opened his mouth, shut it and then realized that, dense or no, Vodantu had a point. "Forgive me. Months in this frame have made me careless. I will guard myself against such shameful lapses in the future."

SEE THAT YOU DO. NOW I HAVE A TASK FOR YOU.

Hasmed's stomach clenched as he wondered what it would be. "I am yours to command."

RABBADÜN HAS NEED OF YOUR ASSISTANCE. HE HAS FALLEN AFOUL OF HUMANS IN SOME PLACE CALLED "ALABAMA" AND IS IMPRISONED.

Hasmed felt an uncomfortable prickling sensation in his neck. "But Rabbadün is a master of portals. What human could keep him restrained?"

THAT IS WHY THIS IS A MATTER OF SUCH CONCERN. APPARENTLY THESE HUMANS WERE AN UNEXPECTED CHALLENGE, AND RABBADÜN EXHAUSTED HIS POWERS FIGHTING THEM.

"So you want me to rescue him."

IMMEDIATELY.

Hasmed gritted his teeth. *Wow, this timing just could not be worse,* he thought. *Just as I'm getting everything squared away here, finally getting a little respite, some well-earned rest—fuck, the very night Rico's having his celebration dinner—I'm supposed to drop everything and go out to Shitty Butt, Alabama to save a stupid fucker I can't stand?*

On the other hand, what are my options?

"Do you know anything else about these mortals? The ones who can exhaust and imprison our brother?"

NO. MY PERCEPTIONS ARE STRAINED BY MY CONFINEMENT.

Better and better.

"I beg your indulgence, master. Give me three days here to attend to matters, and I will be able to go forth in strength."

THREE DAYS? NO. IT PUTS MY SERVANT IN TOO MUCH PERIL.

Fuck, I think Vodantu likes Rabbadün better'n me, Hasmed thought. *No big surprise, I guess, being from the same house and all. Crap.*

"If it's your will, I'll dispatch one of my servants immediately to scout the situation. I know you are a wise master who will not squander the lives of your agents. Let me look before I leap."

There was a long pause.

VERY WELL. I WORRY ABOUT YOU, HASMED. YOU HAVE PLEASED ME GREATLY IN RECENT DAYS, OFFERING MUCH FIT TRIBUTE TO ME. BUT I HAVE NOT FORGOTTEN MY FEARS THAT YOU ARE BECOMING LOST IN THE MORTAL WORLD—BECOMING TOO AFFECTIONATE. NEVER LOSE SIGHT OF OUR MISSION.

"Your fears are groundless. One day we will kill them all. One day we will desolate this world, completing the destruction the Allmaker began with his punishment of us." Even as he mouthed the vengeful platitudes, Hasmed experienced another surprising emotion: Boredom. *Crap, how many times do we have to swear we're gonna destroy the world?*

When his master was done ordering him around, Hasmed sat for a while, taking stock. Then he invoked Rabbadün, but the imprisoned demon was barely comprehensible. After ten torturous minutes, Hasmed had gathered that there were six humans holding Rabbadün captive, they were in Eufaula, and they'd cut out the demon's tongue. It was a painful guessing game to get even vague hints and descriptions, but by the time he brusquely cut off Rabbadün's pleas for help, he had some leads.

Serves that wacko right. The thought of Rabbadün's fear and helplessness brought the day's first smile to Hasmed's face. *Maybe this is a good thing after all. I pull that asswipe out of the fire, get him when he's helpless… maybe it's time to even the score.*

He called Lee Boyer Jr. on the phone and told him to go to Eufaula. When Lee got done complaining, Hasmed explained how to invoke Rabbadün and warned Lee not to do anything crazy until he was sure he knew what was going on. Lee said he figured he could handle a pack of crazy Crimson Tide fans.

"Don't underestimate these guys. They've caged a *demon.* They may working for some other demon, or… or it could be something else. It's a weird world. Remember, I can't get down there for a couple days. You'll be on your own."

"I been on my own my whole life."

"Until you met me."

"Yeah, boss." There was something in Boyer's voice—a gleeful adoration, an eager abasement—that made Hasmed's stolen skin crawl. "Until you."

Hasmed told Roscoe about the trip. Roscoe made some comment about how Harvey never saw his daughter anymore. Hasmed took it personally. There was yelling and Hasmed stormed out, slamming the door. But he couldn't hold it against Ros because he knew Paum was right.

Fuck, Tina's gonna have something new to tell her head-shrinker, he thought, driving toward Rico's dinner.

He could see in his rearview mirror that his tie was still askew. At a red light he started to fuss with it when he heard another voice in his head—another demon invoking his attention.

Hasmed?

He rolled his eyes and thought, *Aw hell, who is it now? What's the deal here? Did someone announce that the hundredth demon to invoke me wins tickets to Christina Aguilera?*

"Who is it?"

It's Gaviel.

Hasmed swallowed and bit his lip.

"Gaviel. Wow... You're, uh, you're out?"

Yeah. I'm in St. Louis.

"New Jersey for me."

I know. Sabriel told me.

"You're working with her?"

Yes.

"A'right. You know your business, I guess. Just..."

What?

"I wouldn't trust her."

I don't trust my deodorant for more than twelve hours, but I still use it every day.

218 / GREG STOLZE

Hasmed chuckled and found himself relaxing. "What are you doing?"

Still trying to get settled, really. I've got a few challenges.

"I hear ya."

Have you heard about the Reaper of Souls?

"Uh oh."

He's out. He tried to kill me the other day.

A car behind Hasmed honked. His middle finger shot up, but he took his foot off the brake and drove through the now-green light.

"Since you're callin' from St. Louis and not Hell, I'll assume he failed."

Quite. How are things going with you?

"Been busy but... eh, maybe calming down. Getting under control, a little. Why?"

I'd like you to join me here.

"I'm flattered, but I can't."

There was a pause.

I see.

"Nothing personal—I mean, shit, you're my... It's just that I been working hard, and now it's finally paying off."

I wouldn't ask you to abandon your work, certainly. I just thought...

"Hey, I mean... how stuck are you in St. Louis?"

I have commitments.

"Ah. That's... that's too bad. I mean... well, it woulda been good to see... to work with you again. You know."

We were a good team.

"We were." Hasmed frowned. "Gaviel are you in... you ain't in some kinda trouble are you?"

There was a pause.

I could use a friend, right about now.

Ouch, Hasmed thought. *Admitting that must have hurt. A lot.*

"Well I'd... I'd like to... It's just that I'm really swamped."

I understand, completely. You're under no obligation. I just... hoped...

"Look, in... in a little while, maybe but right now, when everything's so crazy. I... I mean, I just can't."

Hasmed. It's okay. Really.

"Well... I mean, stay in touch."

I'll do that.

"Take care of yourself."

Goodbye.

Hasmed felt the connection fade. He drove two more blocks in silence. Then he clenched his fist and hammered the steering wheel, hard.

"Damn it!"

I get as far as writing "isolation" on the wall.

I change my mind

Tell everyone I cut my finger slicing ham.

Gaviel's eyebrow quirked up as he read the rest of the poem. It was dreadful. He loved it, but no expression showed on his face. He was terribly upset that Hasmed wouldn't help him, but he was under control.

He'd given a description to the police that fit the sheriff, but which wasn't definitive. He'd hidden the coffee cup with Dagley's fingerprints, so that was a lever he could use. The situation wasn't good, but it was stable.

The Foe didn't seem to have an eye on him, so that was stable too.

As for Sabriel and Usiel—well, who knew? He'd invoked her a couple of times since she'd gone off to see the Reaper, but she was being very cagey about what was going on. Not a good sign, that. But on the other hand, Gaviel didn't have a releasing tool jammed up his ass. So that was something.

All in all, a complicated situation. Best to fall back, strengthen his position and see what developed. And to that end...

Gaviel smiled as the teens entered the room. This week, both Renee and Leotis were missing, but that was fine. Gaviel knew they were okay. He could feel the trickles of faith and strength, dripping from them into him. Still weak stuff, but two was better than one.

And three would be better than two.

It was more standard mentor bullshit, rah-rah, you can do it, I believe in you... but he had a darker edge to his words this week. Where his bait for Leotis had been all promise and ambition, this time he used the flavors of sorrow and despair. He talked about the challenges teens face, about drugs, depression, self-destruction. He spoke of the need for vigilance and strength and commitment, sending them out on a high note, a ray of hope to see them through.

They left with thoughtful expressions, and Gaviel said, "Chasney? May I speak with you?"

Chasney Shaw was thin—thin with a sunken chest, shoulders hunched forward and a little bit of a curve to his spine. His dress was (to Gaviel's careful eye) calculatedly average. Here was a boy who wanted nothing more than invisibility—but, at the same time, who wanted someone to notice him despite his attempts to hide.

"I read your poem in the literary magazine," Gaviel said.

Chasney smiled weakly. "Did you like it?"

Gaviel just nodded. "It's touching. It's sad. Do you feel like that often?"

"Oh well, y'know... Teenagers an' depressing poetry, 's like chocolate 'n' peanut butter, right? Two great tastes..."

"I remember how hard it was."

Gaviel waited, but Chasney said nothing. He seemed twitchy and uncomfortable.

"I remember feeling that it was unfair. Like I had to put the brakes on my mind to fit in. You ever get that feeling?"

"Oh, I dunno," Chasney said, while his face lit up with agreement.

"Would you like to go get a burger or something? My treat?"

Gaviel was ready to entrance the boy, but he didn't even have to. Chasney decided to trust him freely, and Gaviel was pleased to have guessed right. Chas was desperate for someone to confide in.

It took an hour of small talk, and then another hour of heart-to-heart, before Chasney admitted he was homosexual.

"An' it's not like that's easy," he said, glancing over his shoulder. "I mean, 'round here, 'burning gaze' isn't a description, it's a socially accepted hobby."

Gaviel snickered appreciatively. "Very clever."

"You like that? I got another one. 'In my neighborhood, when you say you shot a swish, people don't assume you were playing basketball.'"

"Black, gay and an intellectual. Isn't there some kind of three-strikes law in this state?"

Chasney hung his head and shrugged.

"You know I'm not just a mentor," Gaviel said.

"No, you're a famous and handsome mentor."

"I'm not that famous. I'm better than famous. I'm something else entirely. BELIEVE ME."

Gaviel pushed the kid with the last phrase—pushed hard and saw Chasney's eyes widen.

"What was that?" he whispered.

"Just a taste. Would you like to be able to do that?"

"I..." Chas licked his lips. "Renee. You..."

"Helped her." Gaviel nodded. "Among others."

"Why me?"

"Why not you? If you believe... why not anything?"

"But... Why would you help me? I mean, you could... with, with what you did to my head, you... You could have anything you wanted."

"You'd think so, wouldn't you? But what I want, is you."

Chas smiled a sickly, self-hating grin. "And here you slipped right under my gaydar."

"This is no time for jokes. I don't want your flesh, and you know it. I want something unique. Something more precious and far more valuable. I want your faith."

"Faith?"

"Believe in me, and all things are possible. What do you want? Physical beauty? Strength? The power to enthrall with a word—you seemed pretty impressed with that." He leaned in and spoke each word clear, slow and distinct. "What... do you... want?"

Chas swallowed and asked, "Can you make me straight?"

Gaviel leaned back and narrowed his eyes.

In his mind, the conversation was like a chessboard. Each move he made opened possibilities for Chasney, leading the boy in a variety of directions. Each path ended with the boy pledging his soul to the demon, but Gaviel knew that for all his power, Chas might still drift off course if not carefully led.

The most dangerous possibility was that Chas would ask for something that Gaviel could not (for all his insinuation) provide, and the question of "becoming straight" was definitely a gray area for the fallen angel. He could persuade, he could encourage, he had some power over the shape of the boy's self... but could he change the boy's essential nature? He didn't think so. Was his orientation that critical to the boy's identity? Gaviel didn't know. It had never come up before.

So in that momentary pause as he changed expression and position, he recalculated the many paths he was preparing and opened a different gate. "Why don't you ask to be white, while you're at it?"

"What?"

Gaviel himself couldn't change the boy's skin, but for Sabriel it would be almost effortless. Of course, then Gaviel would owe her—owe her even more—but a new thrall would be worth it.

"I could make you white. I could turn you into a woman, if you're feeling trapped in a man's body. I could make you a beautiful, blonde goddess—if that's what you desire."

"No!"

Gaviel laughed. "Okay, you don't want to give up the gadget—can't say I blame you one bit."

"I don't want to be white!"

"No? Even though it's sooo much easier?" Gaviel leaned in and let a sneer twist his lips. "If you believe that black skin is going to help you into college instead of holding you back, then some Republican PR flack in Washington deserves a big bonus this year. If you think a future of racial profiling and bad service in restaurants and suspicious glances if you decide to have lunch with a white woman... if that's what you want, walk away."

"You think I should give up just because it's hard?"

"Well, you did suggest the easy out with..." Gaviel trailed off but made a limp-wristed, effeminate gesture with his left hand.

"There's more to being black than being a victim."

"Oh, that's nice. You paid attention in one of your Civics classes. If you're not interested in the Michael Jackson plan, we can take that off the table."

"Fine."

"Three... two..."

He saw Chasney swallow and squint his eyes shut.

"One. Right." Gaviel shrugged, smiled, straightened his jacket. "I'm surprised, I have to say. Can I ask why you weren't interested?"

"Well, I mean… yeah, it's… there's a temptation. Sure. But to be that different. I mean, I… I don't know how to be white." He tilted his head back and squinted off into the distance. "I'd be an alien to myself," he said.

"Interesting."

"Not to mention my family. I mean, I'd have to leave them, right? I'd have to leave my mom and my sisters and everyone."

"Presumably. But don't you think they'll notice a difference if you completely rewrite your personality?"

"Huh?"

"The other thing. Goodbye RuPaul, hello Mike Tyson."

"Well, that's different. I mean, being gay isn't like… I mean, it's just like… like having a phobia or something, right? I mean, it's just a, a little… a little kink in…" He gestured to his head, a little hesitant.

"Oh, you're buying the 'homosexuality is a disease' theory? No wonder you're looking for the easy cure." He leaned in and said "You've been gay as long as you can remember, right?"

Chas looked down at his lap, nodded.

"Has it influenced your feelings?"

"Well, yeah."

"Changed how you see things? How you understand things?"

"I dunno. I guess."

"Do you speak German?"

"Huh? No."

"If I suddenly made you forget all the English you know and replaced it with German, do you think you'd be confused?"

"Of… of course."

"Yet you think your lifelong lexicon of gender perspectives can be fundamentally altered without it changing anything else about you?"

Chas opened his mouth, then shut it without speaking.

"Look, I could have just done this as a handshake deal and let you run into the unanticipated consequences later. If you've read 'The Monkey's Paw,' you might think that's how Faustian pacts usually go down. But I have no interest in selling you a false bill of goods." He gave a small smile. "My business grows by referrals from satisfied customers, know what I mean? I can do this thing for you, but go into it with your eyes open."

"But... I mean..."

Gaviel could feel him teetering, and the perfect way would have been to fall back, take his time, let the kid sell himself on the idea. But Gaviel didn't have time for the perfect way. That was why he'd called Chasney out. He felt the need for the blunt way.

Of course, Gaviel's blunt way was still very smooth.

"Or..." Gaviel's voice was silky as the note of a clarinet, sliding through the hubbub and clatter of the restaurant's background noise. "Or, instead of making you less yourself, I can make you more. I can give you the strength to believe in yourself. I can teach you the courage of character to accept what you are and not give a shit what anyone else thinks. I can give you the will to be an individual. Unique. A man standing above and beyond the rest." He raised his hands, palm up. "Or, if you prefer, I can help you shrink into the crowd, fit in, and never—ever—be noticed.

"You pick."

The Reaper of Souls walked down the sidewalk with an atypically hesitant step. He was frowning, but it wasn't his usual frown of righteous, vindictive wrath. It was a puzzled frown, uncertain and unhappy.

A large part of his confusion stemmed from an existential dilemma: If he stopped persecuting the demons and their dupes, what purpose did he have?

When he was with Sabriel, things seemed to make sense. The idea that the fallen—like himself—might crave the Allmaker's forgiveness... it was a seductive idea. It explained some things. And yet...

He sighed and looked at the wood and brass doors before him.

At least now I have time for this, he thought, and pushed his way into the concert hall. The Boston Pops were touring, and Sabriel had gotten him tickets.

His inhuman senses sprang alert as he passed through the door, but it was too late to halt. He stepped forward and felt himself wrenched out of space, taken away...

He emerged in darkness, ready to fight. He saw no one.

But he felt it. He turned slightly to the right, and the scythe sprang to his hand. He was outraged but also, somehow, relieved. This, at least, wasn't complicated.

Then the syllables of his True Name rang out in the darkness, and he knew that this would be complicated as well.

"Who summons Usiel?" he demanded.

A match flared, revealing a squat and hairy man sitting at a table. The stranger lit a candle, and as Usiel's tired mortal eyes adjusted, he saw that he was in a tiny bar—long and deep but barely more than ten feet wide. The man had a bottle and two glasses.

"Care for ouzo?" he asked. "I'm going to have some."

"Who are you?"

"Don't recognize me without red hair, green eyes and desert sand?"

Usiel sighed. "Lucifer." He meant it to sound bitter and defiant, but it was just tired.

"Pull up a chair."

Usiel drew breath to refuse, but then wondered what good it would do. He sat.

"Where are we?"

"Kalamáta." Seeing Usiel's blank look, Lucifer added, "It's in Greece."

Usiel blinked. "Why did you bring me to Greece?"

"Why not Greece? And the ouzo here is really top-flight. It's local, doesn't even have nationwide distribution. Maybe I'm selfish, but I kind of hope it stays obscure and special." The Prince of Pride pushed a glass across the table.

"I'm not thirsty." Usiel sighed. "I thought you were done with me?"

"Did I say that?"

"You said you wouldn't play God."

"And I won't. But I will play devil's advocate." He cleared his throat. "As your attorney, I'm advising you to sell your soul for immortality and superlative guitar skill."

Usiel gave a short, sarcastic laugh. "Did you call me here to practice your standup routine?"

"No, no... I called you here to find out what the *hell* you think you're doing."

"I'm not sure."

"You're not sure. I'm not sure. I guess the only one who's sure, is your new friend Sabriel."

"You mean my old friend Sabriel." He said it hoping she'd hear, hoping the invocation would open a channel... but nothing happened.

How does Lucifer do that? His unease was back and multiplied. Both sides in the war had assumed that invocations were private, inviolate. If the Morningstar knew enough to block them... what else could he do? Pose as a different demon, or even as an angel? Listen in? What were the limits to his power?

It was the Morningstar's voice that called Usiel back from his worries.

"There may be a continuity of experience between the Sabriel you knew then and the one you know now, but that doesn't mean much. The tiny drip that welled up in a Wisconsin forest a billion years ago is, technically speaking, the same Mississippi river that churns through St. Louis and dumps a hundred towns' toxic waste in the Gulf of Mexico. That doesn't mean the water from each tastes the same."

"So you pulled me here to tell me she's changed?" Usiel shook his head. "I never claimed to be the smartest angel in Heaven, but even I knew that. She's changed. I've changed. You've changed. I think you've got something else on your mind."

"I'd love to know how she talked you out of killing her."

"Why didn't you just spy on us?"

"I've been distracted. Since last we spoke, I've been destroyed twice."

Usiel wondered exactly what Lucifer meant by that, but didn't ask. "You think Sabriel is deceiving me? Manipulating me?"

"I'd bet my spear on it."

"If I trusted you not to welsh, I'd take that bet. If I told her about you, I'm sure she'd accuse you of the same thing."

"Interesting point." Lucifer stroked his chin, tilted his head, and then Enochian syllables rolled off his tongue once more.

Usiel felt something in him shifting and changing, but he couldn't have said what it was. "What did you do?"

"I apologize, but I decided I didn't want you telling tales out of class. Now you can't speak about me. Invocations are okay, but no gossip."

Usiel gritted his teeth. "I remember all your rhetoric about equality and merit during the war. I'm so glad to confirm that it was all bullshit. You're more of a tyrant than the Most High ever was."

"Don't presume to insult your betters." He leaned in. "Tell you what. I did screw you a little, just now. I violated your free will. Sorry. But I'll give you a gift to make up for it."

"What, a bottle of your lousy ouzo?"

"Oh, much better. I'm going to attune the phrase 'Reaper of Souls' to the name 'Usiel.' Now you'll hear it whenever people discuss you by your title, instead of just your celestial name."

"I don't want your gifts."

"You didn't want my command of silence, either. Sorry. I guess I've outgrown my democratic phase."

Usiel drew breath to argue, but the chatter in his mind had doubled. He was used to ignoring continuous, low-grade invocations. Like demonic crank calls, he simply disconnected them. But now he was aware of a lesser susurration, the mutter of demons and ghosts and thralls, all over the Earth and in Hell and the limbo of the dead, all talking about him.

"...Reaper of Souls in Washington, and I was surprised John survived the encounter. If he comes for you..."

"...Reaper of Souls, mighty angel, Slaver of the Spirits, hear our plea! Reaper of Souls, come to us, bless us with your power!"

"...Reaper of Souls is loosed from the Abyss, and he walks up and down in the Earth, taking..."

But one voice caught his attention over the rest. Sabriel's voice.

"...Reaper of Souls to me. It's under control."

A third vein of belief—even the thin, faltering trust of an insecure teen—was nourishing, but Gaviel didn't allow himself to savor it. He had an uneasy sensation—a feeling of being watched, niggling and nagging at his small sense of the fate around him. He tried to turn his astral eyes upon it, but it danced back, away, subtle, always in the corner of his perceptions. It bothered him the entire time he went downtown to meet a man in a car park and hand over a sack of money in return for an item wrapped in oilcloth and cardboard.

A situation as active as his own demanded constant vigilance, and as he parked a block away from his apartment, his alertness was rewarded. He felt a demon waiting for him.

"Sabriel? Are you in my home?"

Indeed I am.

"You know, the humans consider it polite to ask permission before entering." He slammed his car door and started down the street.

I know that humans also consider it polite to defer gratification and respect one another's rights and personal sovereignty.

"Touché. Nevertheless, I think their concept of privacy has some merit. Is anyone with you?"

No one important, just Thomas.

When he entered, he found the two of them on his sofa, playing with Noah's PlayStation.

"Yeah, who's no one important now, huh?" Thomas crowed. An annoying burst of tinny electronic music burbled from the TV, and Sabriel dropped her controller with a moue of distaste.

"Thomas, why don't you go out and get us some coffee and snacks?"

"There's coffee in the kitchen."

"Then why don't you just go out?"

"Oh." He sighed. "I guess the grown-ups have to talk, huh?"

"Stay close. Watch for anything weird on the street."

"Like a couple of shape-shifting demons turning into water?" Thomas muttered, but he left.

"I thought I had the music disabled on *Madden 2003*," Gaviel said, switching off the TV.

"Thomas turned it back on. He can be a clever little monkey." She raised an eyebrow. "So?"

"So?"

"How goes it with the Tree? Have you made any progress?"

"I believe the Tree is in check, but not checkmate. The good news is, East St. Louis is under control, and our power base here is growing."

"By which you mean, *your* power base here is growing."

"You should rein in your suspicion. You'll get wrinkles." Gaviel went to the kitchen for a bottle of cream soda. "What about you? I notice that you're conspicuously un-reaped."

She shrugged and gave him a cool smile.

"Have you spoken to him? Seen him?"

"Oh yes. Who do you think I've been with the past few days?"

Gaviel tilted his head and gave her a curious look. "How'd you manage that?"

"Call it feminine wiles, if you wish."

"Playing it close to the vest, are we?"

"Wouldn't you?"

"I trust you," he said carelessly, sipping his pop, "so if you say he's no longer a threat, I'll take him off my threat list. But I must confess, I'm wildly interested in how you managed it. You don't know his True Name or something, do you?"

"Nothing like that. But I know him. It's okay. Leave the Reaper of Souls to me. It's under control."

"The situation's under control, or he's under control?"

"He's no threat to me, and I'm pretty sure I can steer him away from you. Gaviel, you can't imagine how... how lost and alone he was. Confused, really."

"You make him sound like a stray puppy."

"A puppy with dangerous fangs. I haven't plucked them— yet—but he's wagging his tail, for now." She stood and stretched, cracking her neck bones and fingers. "And why disarm him? He could be an asset against our real problems."

"From where I sit, he is a real problem."

"He's not. Not anymore. Not with me. Now perhaps you should describe your brilliant strategy for ridding us of the Keeper of Twin Winds?"

In Greece, Usiel slumped in his chair. Absentmindedly, he picked up and drained the glass of ouzo. It tasted awful, which was fine. It matched his mood.

"You see?" Lucifer said.

"I only heard her half," Usiel muttered. "It could mean anything. There could... I mean..."

"Oh, you're getting as bad as the humans. You don't want to believe it, so you'll cover your eyes and bite your tongue and stick your fingers in your ears. Exactly what interpretation would you put on 'a puppy with dangerous fangs'?"

"How do I know this isn't a trick?" Usiel asked, even as he realized his fears were justified, that Lucifer could somehow spy on invocations.

"It could be. Either I'm tricking you or she is. Frankly, as long as you wake up to the fact that someone's got you bamboozled, I'll be satisfied. For now."

"And what would you have me do?"

"If you think you're up to it, play along. But honestly, she was an angel of inspiration before, making her a demon of confusion now. When it comes to mind games, she's playing grandmaster chess while you're still back on Snakes and Ladders. No, it might be best if you just stayed away from her for a while. Ignore her invocations. Don't try to explain. Don't try to find the truth. Just stay far enough that she can't scratch your belly and throw you a bone."

In the guttering candle light, the only sound was Usiel's teeth grinding back and forth. Lucifer gave him a sympathetic pat and continued.

"Look, it's not the easy way, but it's the right way. Remember this: You'll hear it when she talks about you. And now she doesn't know that. You play it cool for a while, and you might find out that she was honest."

"You don't think that's likely."

"I don't think she could be honest, even if she swore she was lying."

Gaviel had a strange sensation and realized it was a headache. He did not frown—he was much better now when it came to controlling his expressions—but it bothered him.

Why now? I'm not sick, I'm not injured...

A thought occurred.

Oh no. This isn't a stress-induced headache, is it? That's all I need.

The idea that he might have such a human weakness filled Gaviel with revulsion and undirected anger, and his head throbbed sharply in response. He attempted to heal the damage, but there was no damage. This was simply pain, meaningless pain, resisting all his attempts to dispel it.

While he was washing a Nuprin down with brandy, the phone rang.

"Hello?" His voice betrayed no trace of his irritation.

"It's me."

"Matthew! I'm delighted," Gaviel lied, thinking, *What now?*

"I think I..." There was a pause, a muffled sound of Matthew clearing his throat. "I think I maybe owe you an apology."

"An apology? For what?"

"For... well, I... I kind of spied on you."

"Really?" Gaviel felt a prickly sensation on his spine, and the brain-bruising pain of his headache seemed to boil on top of it.

"I..." Another muffled cough. "Well, I found out that you were mentoring at the high school. And I feared the worst."

Gaviel also feared the worst. He felt his nipples harden as a chill apprehension rippled through him. *Remember, he's apologizing. He's not accusing you. He must not know.*

"May told me about it," Matthew continued. "She just... she was at the church, dropping something off, and she mentioned it in passing. And I assumed... like I've always done, I guess, I... I wondered why you didn't tell me."

"Matthew," Gaviel said. He wondered if the minister had been drinking.

"No, let me finish! I thought there was, you know, something fishy going on, and I didn't ask you to your face I just... I went and, and... and I talked to them."

A sigh came across the line.

"You've got good kids there, No— Gaviel. They think the world of you, they... it was just so clear from the way they spoke of you, the respect and... I've seen that look before, y'know? That look is the reward I get for helping people. It's the reward God gives me, and I... all this time I was assuming that you were hurting them."

"There's no need for, uh, all this…"

"Please, I… I really want to say this. I've misjudged you so much, and it's time I made that right. I misjudged you at the fire, when you were a genuine hero. I misjudged you when you wanted to go to Los Angeles, and I've heard about the great things, the uplifting things, you did and said to the congregation there. Now I misjudged you again on this, and… I'm sorry. I truly, deeply apologize."

Gaviel felt an unaccustomed bitter taste in his throat, dry and grainy. He swallowed and said, "Well, knowing what you know… Knowing what I am, who would blame you?"

"Let him without sin cast the first stone. I should have paid attention to John 8:7, but my pride, it blinded me. I'm sorry for that."

"Look, if I say 'apology accepted' can we drop it?"

"All right. I just wanted to get it off my chest."

"Apology accepted." Gaviel swallowed again. "I have to go, okay?"

"Okay. See you Sunday?"

"Wouldn't miss it."

Gaviel hung up and picked up his coat. He didn't have anywhere to go, but he wanted to leave.

Just be glad Sabriel wasn't there when he called. He stalked down the street, face carefully neutral.

This is what Noah did, isn't it? He'd get upset and confused, and he'd take a long walk. One of his many impotent gestures.

That thought didn't cheer him one bit. He turned and started walking along the green, grassy sward of Wash U's campus, heading toward Forest Park.

He considered, and discarded, several plans. He couldn't strike against Avitu—he wasn't strong enough. It was too soon to move against the Foe, and doing so would invalidate all of his recent efforts at concealment. As for Sabriel, betraying her was unthinkable as long as she was his shield against Usiel.

He tried to think wordlessly as he walked, but he couldn't seem to calm the monkey-chattering of his human brain.

All right, let's try logic. Reason. Your tools, Noah, however clumsy you were with them.

A half hour ago, I was happy that things were stable, happy that there was nothing I urgently needed to do. Now I'm antsy and agitated and absolutely miserable.

A frown escaped him, and he didn't even realize it.

Clearly it was the call. Even Noah would figure that out. But what was it about the call? The call was good news. I've suckered Matthew more firmly than ever. Although, I guess it wasn't me that fooled him. Is that it? That's it. I'm upset that I made a mistake. Matthew could easily have discovered my true intentions and ruined everything. Dumb luck saved me, and I resent that.

His frown deepened. He actually felt the tightness in his face and realized that he was frowning. It took effort to banish the expression.

But it wasn't even dumb luck, was it? Matthew was fooled because… because why? Because he wanted to be fooled, most likely. Is this such a surprise? He fought the good fight against me for months. I suppose he just got tired.

Matthew Wallace, the most faithful man I've found, has given up. He willingly deceives himself, rather than face my cupidity. He's beaten. I've won.

He felt an unfamiliar burning sensation in his eyes and nose, a hot closeness that blurred his vision. Instinct raised a hand to his face to find tears, tears of bitter disappointment.

Angels could weep, and Gaviel had, but it wasn't like this. Angel tears were pure and graceful and beautiful. Human weeping was ugly and embarrassing, hitching sobs and dripping snot, and the more he tried to restrain it, the stronger it became. He couldn't control it, couldn't control himself, and that was the gravest insult of all.

He drew in a deep breath and screamed out words of power.

Across the street, the gas in a parked Toyota pickup truck heard his words, and the latent flame it held sprang to eager attention.

Watching the debris fall, Gaviel wiped his nose and felt a little better.

There was a cabin in the desert, now. There was a cabin and a generator and a composting toilet. A truck had hauled out a brand-new, stainless steel water tank, the ground was still uneven where it had been buried to stay cool. The foundation was poured for a larger building, four times the size of the cabin, and twenty acres had been fenced in by barbed wire — seemingly overnight.

Lying in bed in the cabin, Teddy Mason stared at the ceiling while Joellen told him about the progress.

"The next big thing will be electricity," she said. "We've got months' worth of gas for the generator, long as all we're running is the stove and fans and, you know, the air conditioner here and the water pump. I s'pect we'll use more and more juice as the compound grows, but it shouldn't be a problem."

Teddy grunted.

"Are you comfortable?" Joellen asked. "I can kick that AC up a notch."

"It's fine."

She frowned, looking at him, bit her lip and felt like she might burst into tears.

"Money's good, real good," she said. "Gwyn said that I — we — whatever we need, it's... We can just have all we want. I don't have a bank account, of course. But soon. She said I'll get one. She's met people, they... they're gonna get me a whole new life, new past, new identity. It'll be just like that movie *The Thomas Crown Affair*. You see that one?"

He shook his head.

Silence.

"You never told me how you like my new face," she said.

"It's fine."

"I look younger, don't you think? Maybe kind of Anglo, but I guess plastic surgeons don't get a lot of people asking for Indian noses."

"It's fine."

His voice was so dead, so flat.

"Blackie got his done, too. And of course, usually we'd be all bruised for weeks, even a month or two, but not with Avitu, just one little touch... we came back from that doctor looking like we'd boxed ten rounds, black eyes and noses all swollen and then that... that sweet breeze, that healing breath, and now we're fine. It's a shame Black Hawk had to cut his hair, he was so proud of it, but if the Tree says it's okay..."

She trailed off. No answer. She tried again.

"You ought to tell Blackie his new face is nice. It would mean a lot to him."

Nothing.

"He really looks up to you, y'know. Maybe you don't think so, but he does. He's never had a daddy, so... well, he's shy. It wouldn't be so hard for you to reach out to him, would it? To reach out to your own son?"

"My son."

Teddy sat up in bed, and his voice had more passion than she'd heard in weeks. Looking at the desolation in his face, she wasn't sure it was an improvement.

"My son is in Montana. My son is named Lance. Black Hawk is your son. Birdie has mine."

"Teddy..." she put a hand on his chest, but he pushed it aside.

"Are there new sacrifices?" he asked. "I'm going to go check."

He stood and left without looking back.

Joellen sat, very still. She worried that if she moved, she'd fall to pieces.

He'd been like this since his wife left. She'd hoped making love with him would help, would fix things, but it just got worse. He still touched her—the Tree could fill him with lust, he couldn't resist that, and Joellen prayed for it almost every night—but afterward, lately, he'd cry. It was horrible.

Joellen sat and bit her lip and tried to think of what she could do.

Eventually, she thought of something.

Gaviel made a few calls, checked his watch and went to the St. Louis Zoo. Admission was free, and it wasn't far from his apartment. In fact, as he walked there, he could see the police tape where he'd detonated the truck. It would have brought a smile to his face, if he let his face reflect his feelings.

He went to the zoo and visited the new hippopotamus habitat. It was a nice one. There were thick glass panels along one side of the hippos' pond, like a shark tank in an aquarium. The hippos spent most of their time in the water. Out of it, they were ungainly, awkward and slow, but they moved like graceful blimps when submerged, seemingly tiny hoof-taps sending them floating along, the bulk transformed to buoyancy.

The water line was at the level of Gaviel's eyes. Looking above the surface, he saw their eyes and noses, just a little hint of the mass beneath. The water served as a lens, so that what was underneath looked closer, even bigger.

He stood for a moment and thought of huge things, things that needed the right environment to use their power, things you couldn't guess about from just seeing the surface. He saw that one hippo, the male, had a small school of fish clustered around it, eating debris off his belly and flanks. Gaviel thought about parasite feeding, too.

He unfolded his cell phone and said "Avitu."

GAVIEL.

"Why are we fighting?"

An eavesdropper might have thought he was speaking to a lover.

WHY WOULD YOU NOT COME TO ME?

"I was afraid you'd betray me."

EVEN THOUGH WE FOUGHT SIDE BY SIDE IN THE WAR?

"You fought alongside Sabriel, as well." He felt a flicker of attention from the other demon as he spoke her name, but he wasn't saying anything he didn't want her to hear.

THE DEFILER IS DIFFERENT. SHE HAS RETURNED FOR LOW AND UNWORTHY REASONS. SHE IS PETTY AND VENGEFUL. I KNOW THIS. SHE CAME TO ME, AND I SAW THE ROT IN HER HEART.

"So you want to inspect me now?"

YES. I CAN ONLY DO THAT AT MY HOME.

"And if you don't like what you find?"

THEN I MUST DESTROY YOU OR MAKE YOU MY SERVANT.

"Now, that's interesting. Most of us, in your situation, would sugarcoat it at least. Leave the threat implied. Or most likely, try to piss on my leg and tell me it was raining."

I DO NOT FOLLOW YOUR METAPHOR.

"Why not lie to me?"

THAT WOULD BE DISHONORABLE.

"Ah." He switched the phone from his left ear to his right. "What are your plans?"

WHY SHOULD I TELL YOU?

"Well, you condemned Sabriel because you didn't like her 'purpose.' It seems only right that you let me know yours."

There was a pause. A long one.

VERY WELL. MY PURPOSE IS TO SAVE HUMANITY FROM LUCIFER'S CURSE.

"That sounds manageable. What exactly do you mean by 'Lucifer's curse'?"

YOU KNOW WHAT I MEAN. YOU SHOULD, OR YOU'VE FORGOTTEN FAR TOO MUCH WHILE YOU WERE IN HELL AND I WAS ON EARTH. I REFER TO THE PLAGUE OF UNDERSTANDING. THE KNOWLEDGE OF EVIL AND GOOD. I SPEAK OF THEIR NEED TO CHOOSE BETWEEN RIGHT AND WRONG, WHEN THEY ARE CLEARLY NOT EQUIPPED WITH THE DISCERNMENT TO DO SO.

Gaviel fought an impulse to smile, simply at the scope of her ambition.

"You would remove a gift from the Morningstar himself? Wash them clean? Return them to ignorance?"

RETURN THEM TO PURITY. RETURN THEM TO THEIR TRUE SELVES.

"Uh huh. How's that working out for you?"

YOU MOCK ME, DEVIL. BUT EVERY DAY, MY AGENTS FIND THOSE WHO HAVE REALIZED THE HOPELESSNESS OF THEIR CONDITION. EVERY DAY, EAGER MEN AND WOMEN COME TO SACRIFICE THEIR KNOWLEDGE, THEIR THOUGHTS, THEIR EVERY CHOICE TO ME. THEY HAVE TRIED AMBITION, AND THEY HAVE TRIED DRUGS, AND THEY HAVE TRIED EVERY VICE AND EVERY VIRTUE TO BLOT OUT THE CURSE OF SELF, BUT ONLY I CAN GIVE THEM THE FULL ABSOLUTION THEY CRAVE.

"Mmm. Well, give the people what they want, and so forth. I've nothing against the fulfillment trade. I'm dabbling in it myself."

DO YOU GIVE THEM WHAT THEY WANT OR WHAT THEY NEED?

"I give them what they ask for."

THEN YOU ARE AS BLIND AND FALLEN AS THE HUMANS THEMSELVES.

"Oh dear. This sounds like a breakdown in negotiations." His tone was light, but inside he felt his guts clutch.

IN THE END, EVEN YOUR THRALLS WILL CRAVE MY OBLIVION. THEY WILL DRINK DEEP FROM YOUR POISONED CUP AND WONDER WHY THEY ARE ILL, AND IF THEY KNEW OF ME, THEY WOULD CRY OUT FOR MY RELEASE. YOU SELL THEM NOTHING BUT THEIR OWN MISERY. YOU GIVE THEM NOTHING BUT THE MEANS WITH WHICH TO DESTROY THEMSELVES.

"In what way is man who has lost—oh, I'm sorry, a man who has 'relinquished'—his thoughts and will still 'himself'?"

THAT DOESN'T MATTER. WHAT MATTERS IS THAT WHEN THEY COME TO ME, I REMOVE A BURDEN. WHEN THEY GO TO YOU, YOU DOUBLE THEIR BURDEN WHILE CLAIMING TO EASE IT.

"How sad for you that my clients—should they ever despair, as you claim they must—will have no sweet faith left to offer you when they come crawling for deliverance."

THAT ISN'T IMPORTANT.

"Oh really? You don't feel the expression of belief they need to put themselves under your knife? I find that hard to believe."

THEIR BELIEF IS MY REWARD FOR DOING RIGHT, BUT I WOULD DO THIS THING EVEN UNREWARDED.

Gaviel wondered if she might actually be telling the truth. He hoped not. Idealists were, in his experience, much harder to deal with.

Although, he mused, *they're also much easier to trick.*

"Tell you what," he said. "I'll call your bluff. I'll freely tell my vassals about you. I'll even ask them to invoke you. I'll let them know that you offer them the ultimate anesthetic, the final escape clause from the angst of knowing they're human. If they opt to take your 'last exit' package, tomorrow or in seventy years, I'll release them from their pacts so that you get the benefit of their self-sacrifice."

There was a pause.

WHY SO GENEROUS?

"I don't think any of them will take it."

AND IN RETURN?

"You go your way, I go mine. You call off your toy soldiers; I don't get them arrested. You agree not to harass me, I agree not to harass you, and we call it square."

A NON-AGGRESSION PACT.

"Indeed. There's only one sticking point. I'll need part of your True Name."

OUT OF THE QUESTION.

"Come now. You're much stronger than me. It galls me to confess it, but, there it is. You've proved that you can strike my people and I cannot protect them. I, therefore, need some assurance that you won't simply shake hands and betray me when I'm no longer convenient. A syllable or two would go a long way toward squaring things."

AND WHAT ASSURANCE WOULD I HAVE OF YOUR RELIABILITY?

"You can trust a man with broken arms not to pick your pocket. Come on Avitu. You've seen what I am. What I've been forced to become. I can't seriously threaten you. I can only annoy you, slow you down. I don't want to do that, you don't want me to, but if you're going to destroy me anyway... why wouldn't I bite your hand as I fall?"

There was a pause.

YOU'RE ASKING ME TO TRUST IN YOUR VINDICTIVENESS AS MUCH AS YOUR HONOR.

"Look, how about I sweeten the pot?"

AN INCENTIVE?

He explained what he had in mind. After thinking it over, Avitu agreed.

Gaviel closed his phone and walked home, checking his wristwatch again as he did.

May was late.

"I'm sorry," she said, coming in the door. "It was traffic, all up and down the highway it was terrible, and you know what parking is like around here."

"Don't worry about it," he said. He led her to the sofa, sat and patted the cushion beside him. Two glasses of white zinfandel were on the coffee table, and they each took a sip.

"So," she asked, "Why did you want me to come down here?" Her tone was a little too bright.

Gaviel didn't answer the question directly. He put on a sober face, looked deep in to her eyes and said, "Do you know why I came back?"

May swallowed.

"Because... because of faith," she said.

"That's right. I know now that without faith, I am nothing. I need that faith. Like Matthew's faith. Like yours."

He saw her face flicker—wondering why he said "Matthew" instead of "my father"—but she couldn't catch the thought. Her mind was overwhelmed by her heart. He could read this as clearly as the text on a billboard.

"I don't... I mean..."

Her hands were in her lap. He put his hand on top of them.

"Shh." He said. "You don't have to speak. You don't need words to tell me..."

He kissed her and tasted her longing, and he knew. His other hand ran up her back, to the nape of her neck—So slender! So frail!—then combed through her hair. He lowered it again, feeling her shiver as he caressed her spine. His other hand slid across her thigh, encircling her, and she put her hands on his back, lightly, too lost in bliss to grip with strength.

When the kiss broke he asked, "Do you love me?"

She blinked, he could see tears in her eyes, streaks of mascara on her eyeglasses. "You know I do."

His smile was the perfect image of kindness and passion as he leaned in and said, "Do you remember Sly Deighton?"

She blinked.

"Sly... Deighton? From high school." She frowned, and the glaze around her eyes cleared, a little. "Yeah, I guess."

"Back in tenth grade, he said you had a great ass."

Another blink from her. He could see the mood fading—this wasn't the compliment she wanted.

"I said, 'Yeah, and great titties too,'" Gaviel continued. "'If you put a bag on her head, you could almost fuck her.'"

She pushed him away and stood, but he grabbed her. It was a casual move. He hooked the back of her belt and pulled, and when she tried to step back, her calf hit the sofa. She sat again, hard.

Gaviel popped up as she went down, as if they were on a see-saw. He spun to face her. She tried another shove, but he caught both her arms and raised them over her head. Moving forward he sat on her lap, facing her, his weight pinning her to the couch.

"Let me go," she hissed, voice tight. She was struggling, but she didn't shout. That made Gaviel smile, a smirk that showed teeth, an ugly ivory crack in his handsome ebony face.

Not yelling, he thought. *Still not scared enough to risk the embarrassment. Whoever invented shame must have been on our side.*

"Noah Wallace went to college," Gaviel whispered, his voice low and intimate. "That was his mistake, his weakness. His price. He went to college on his daddy's money, even knowing that the good reverend had been fucking the choir director for years, doing it whenever he could squirrel away some time. Doing it anywhere; any position. Noah didn't want to believe, but he saw it. He went to the church because his dad had forgotten an envelope of social security documents, and Noah saw them fucking like dogs in the choir's practice room."

"What? What are..."

"Noah saw them and was disgusted. He hated his father, and rightly so. But he did nothing. He turned up his nose at

Matthew, but not at Matthew's money. For a while he tried to tell himself that it was maybe just one time, but he kept following and peeping until he knew better. Sometimes, he'd ask his girlfriends to do things he'd seen his father do to his whore, and sometimes they said no to him. That made him mad."

"Noah, you… I don't know what you, you…"

"Noah went to college and he fought against Kierkegaard and Lewis and Augustine. He fought them and defied God and found allies named Nietzsche and Rand and Shaw. He spent all his time, all his effort, on his atheism until he got hit by some bitch in a sport ute who couldn't hang up the phone and drive."

She'd had enough. She drew in breath for a serious scream, but Gaviel jammed her left arm across her face, cramming it against her mouth, muffling her with her own flesh. He clamped his hands together, keeping her arms and head compressed, crushing their bodies together like an anaconda with its prey. He kept on whispering with his lips by her ear.

"He got hit hard and hurt bad, and as he was dying, as his life passed before his eyes, he realized that he still believed. He couldn't help it, and he knew that he still wasn't even half the man his father was. He saw that he was a fool who'd wasted his youth and that he still couldn't admit it. He couldn't release his pride, even teetering on the edge of death, and he despaired, May. His despair was rich and heavy, and it bored a hole all the way down to Hell.

"But he didn't slide down that hole. No. Instead, SOMETHING CAME UP IT."

The arms around her loosened, but she didn't run, she just cowered and stared at the figure of awe and horror and majesty before her. He was flawless, perfect, a radiant angel who should have been beautiful—but somehow his perfection was alien, his flawlessness an offense to the world around it. A grinding grating dissonance of light and matter itself.

"BEHOLD," it said. "THE MAN YOU THOUGHT YOU LOVED. THE MAN YOU THOUGHT LOVED YOU. BUT THERE IS NO MAN, AND THERE IS NO LOVE. THERE IS ONLY I."

Her lower lip trembled, and a thin, compressed "...nooooo..." leaked out of her.

"NOAH DESPISED YOU AS A MAN DESPISES A WOMAN WHO LOVES FOOLISHLY, BUT I DESPISE YOU AS THE SUN DESPISES THE WORM IT SHRIVELS."

She buried her face in her folded hands. "Oh God," she whispered. "Oh God, deliver me from evil. Deliver me from this."

Fuck, thought Gaviel as he felt the power of her whispers cutting into him. *I'd better make this good, and I'd better make it quick.*

"YOUR GOD DOES NOT HEAR YOU, NOR WOULD HE CARE IF HE DID. WHAT ARE YOU TO THE ALLMAKER? YOU ARE NOTHING. YOU ARE A BUNDLE OF GENES AND GERMS, FIT ONLY TO SPREAD YOUR ILK ACROSS THE PLANET LIKE A PLAGUE. YOU ARE AN ANIMAL THAT GREW ARROGANT. YOU ARE NOT FIT EVEN TO JUDGE — ONLY TO BE CAST DOWN."

"Our Father who art in Heaven, hallowed by thy name..."

"YOU DARE CALL HIM YOUR FATHER, WHEN YOU GAVE YOUR HEART TO HIS ENEMY? NOT EVEN IN PRIDE OR DEFIANCE, BUT IN DELUSION! YOU GAVE YOUR LOVE TO A DEVIL BECAUSE YOU COULDN'T SEE BEHIND THE MASK YOU MADE! YOU COULD NOT SEE THE ENEMY OF GOD, FOR YOU WERE TOO DELUDED BY YOUR OWN GIRLISH FANTASIES. NOW YOU MUST WAKE FROM YOUR DREAMS OF ROMANCE. THIS IS REALITY. NOW YOU MUST GIVE UP YOUR CHILDISH HOPES OF A FATHER GOD TO SAVE YOU. REALITY IS ME."

Her prayers trailed off.

Good thing, Gaviel thought. *I'd be done in ten more minutes.* He'd pulled hard on the soul-strings to his puppets—to Renee, to Leotis and Chasney—but the three of them together barely had as much passion and depth to them as May. As this one innocent dental assistant.

"LOOK AT ME."

She did. Her eyes were dull, wet, empty… defeated.

"BEHOLD THE FIRE THAT CONSUMES YOUR ILLUSIONS."

Her body began to shake with sobs.

"YOU CANNOT RESIST ME. BOTH OF US KNOW THIS."

A nod was her silent acknowledgement.

Behind her, a door opened. A bulky man in shoddy clothes stepped into the apartment.

"There is another way," this newcomer said.

Blinking in the glare of angel glory, May tried to focus on him.

"Let me take your pain away," Tim Grady said. "Let me give you solace."

In his hand he held an ice pick.

Chapter Twelve

Lee Boyer Jr. squinted through his scope, thinking that this was a pretty stupid job. No payoff, first and foremost. If there was no payoff, any job was stupid.

Second, it was tough. Tough work and no payoff, that made it stupidly stupid. But he'd said he'd serve, he'd taken the pledge, and whenever he got too frustrated about the dumbness, all he had to do was think of those gray shadow wings enfolding him… think of his parents, writhing in hellfire, finally getting what they deserved, *forever*.

A kid who gets hit a lot learns to hide, and Lee had gotten hit a lot as a kid. Today he was hiding in a field—soybeans or sorghum or some fucking plant, he didn't know. It was all just stumps and late snow now. He was cold, but not too cold. It hurt, it wasn't numb. Pain didn't mean much to Lee, not his own pain anyhow. He could take or leave it. Other people's pain was mostly a tool to get stuff. Get payoffs. But this time there was no payoff.

Well, there was supposed to be a fucked-up angel hidden in the house. So that was the payoff. Whatever. He said he'd serve so… whatever.

If the job had been in Atlantic City or Hackensack or Trenton, it would have been cake. Boyer knew hard cases there who'd shoot first and ask questions never, he could put together a one-time crew of eight guys, kick the door in, waste everyone and be over a bridge into another jurisdiction by the time the dust cleared. For ten Gs he could do it in a weekend.

But that would be in a city, not in the middle of nowhere. Out here, he didn't know any crimeys. And out here, it was a long, lonesome drive in every direction to get anywhere—meaning, it would take forever to get away. Sure, he could hope to kack everyone in the house before they could call 911. If he had a bunch of guys—which he didn't—it would *still* be iffy.

Instead, he decided to let the cops do his work for him.

He'd clocked the house—he planted bugs by the front and back doors at night, just to get a feel for when people were coming and going. When he knew when the activity was, he'd started hanging around and peeping at them with the binoculars. Once he knew who he was looking for, he followed them to work, got an idea of their schedules. It wasn't too hard.

There were at least two of 'em at the house by day, and usually four or more at night. An hour ago, the last of the night-shift angel-hunters had left for his job at the mill. Half an hour ago, Lee had used a cloned cell phone to place an anonymous call to the police, alerting them that a kidnap victim was being held in the basement of 1387 Sawyer Way, off Rural Route 19.

A smile creased his face as he heard a car driving up. His own renter (with that cloned celly) was parked a good mile and a half away. He watched as the brown car disgorged its brown-clad driver, who ambled up to the door and knocked.

Boyer could have listened through the bug, but he didn't bother. He could tell what the trooper was thinking through body language.

Right about now, he's thinking "Well, this is a big goddamn waste of time when I could be pulling over big-boob speeders and letting them off with warnings. Or I could be eating a donut. Ho hum."

The door opened partway and a cautious face peeked out. Lee imagined him saying "Can I help you officer?" all cowed and cringey.

The trooper rolled his shoulders and raised a hand.

"Yeah," he's saying. "Some nut job called in to say you got a prisoner down in your cellar. I know, it's kooky, but I got to check it out, y'know?"

Lee thought the guy in the doorway blanched, but it was hard to tell. The door closed a little and then opened wider—he must have taken off a chain.

Boyer supposed the deputy (or state trooper or whatever the fuck the guy was—bacon was bacon in Boyer's book) might stumble across the truth on his own, but Lee didn't want to take the chance. He shifted his position a little, breathed gently out, pulled the trigger and put a bullet through the cop's back.

He frowned. He'd aimed a little off to one side, but it looked like the entry hole was right on the spine. He could hear screams—distant, but those two Southern boys down on the farm both had healthy lungs on 'em. Then his smile returned as he heard the cop's voice over his police-band scanner, shouting, "Shots fired, officer down! Shots fired! Shots fired!"

"Shawts faihed," Boyer mimicked as he crawled backward. He left the rifle in place—it was clean. When he was out of sight, he stood and started back to his car. He listened to the police scanner the whole way, hearing the mass of cops getting dispatched to 1387 Sawyer. He smiled like a man who's hearing his home team play with nothing but razzle-dazzle. His work was done.

"You've done some vile things, but that was the worst."

"Who cares what you think?"

It was the same dream again. Noah, centered in the darkness. Gaviel, the darkness on the margins.

"Why would you betray May like that? I mean, she's... fuck it, she's *good*."

"Was good. I believe she's lost any moral capacity she once had."

"You *bastard!*"

"Oooh, I'm *so hurt*. The futile intellectual called me a *name*. Why don't you try 'devil'? I got called that once too. Or even better, 'Namaru.' That's more official."

"You wretched, miserable, *evil* piece of shit."

"As the kids these days say—well *duh*. I crawled out of Hell, remember, which does a pretty good job as sewer of the universe. Why are you so upset? May deserved it."

"That's a fucking lie!"

"Oh, very well, maybe she didn't *deserve* it, but she sure left herself wide open to it. You're an educated man, you've taken those Women's Studies courses, read your Germaine Greer and Gloria Steinem. What would they have to say about a woman— particularly a woman of color—who relies on a man's opinion for her image of herself?"

"I'm sure they'd say she deserved to get her eye poked out with an ice pick."

"He didn't poke her eye out, though it was in the spirit of 'if thine eye offend thee, pluck it out.' What he did was scramble her brain."

"Disgusting. And all because you were too scared to face Avitu."

"That's absurd."

"I don't think it is. For all your talk about 'the war,' I don't see you stand and fight much. Whatsername in Los Angeles, you shot her in the back."

"I wasn't familiar with guns then. If I had been, I'd have shot her in the head."

"You didn't go face-to-face with the Darkness of the Deeps, you used tricks on that old man Lasalle, and even on those gangbangers. And when that demon showed up at the hospital, shit…"

"Let me remind you that I'd just taken a nasty fall."

"That you got running away from two of us mere mortals."

"There's nothing 'mere' about humans imbued with demonic power."

"Say whatever you want, I know the truth. You're a bully. When real trouble comes along, you run like urine down a coward's leg."

"I can't believe I'm getting this lecture from *you*. You betrayed May long before I did."

"What?"

"You knew how she felt in high school. Surely your comments to Sly weren't meant as a compliment."

"Hey, there's a difference between a high school kid saying something stupid and, and *auctioning off someone's soul!*"

"It's a difference of degree, not type. Both were acts of calculated cruelty. Both were perpetrated against an innocent, and both were performed to appease others. The only difference is that I had the balls to dive deep into betrayal, while you just dipped in your toe."

"It doesn't take courage to do what you did."

"To go head-to-head with a woman of real faith, all on the strength of a bluff? To negotiate as an equal with a creature that could simply crush me and my brood of thralls like a spider in its web? I think you underestimate me. What would *you* have done in my position? Nobly taken your blows to protect her?"

"I guess we'll never know, will we?"

Gaviel woke up grinding his teeth. As he composed his expression, he wished he could do *more* to Noah, do something worse than steal his body.

Zola? He thought. But he felt tired and decided against it.

Several days later, the Reverend Matthew Wallace took to the pulpit with a somber look on his face. He looked out over the crowd, at the camera, he frowned and coughed into his fist.

This prompted a muttering in the audience.

It wasn't much, that little cough. In most congregations it would have been ignored. But Matthew Wallace wasn't an average minister, wasn't bound by the normal limitations of public speakers. He didn't cough or stammer or lose his place.

Watching him cough was like seeing Gregory Hines trip over a crack in the sidewalk.

"Y'know," he said, "Usually my sermons are very polished. I work on them. Practice, practice, practice, in front of the mirror usually. People say it sounds spontaneous like I'm just, just up here talkin' off the top of my head. I'm not."

He gave a little smile.

"It takes a lot of practice to make it look spontaneous."

There was a little murmur of chuckling through the crowd.

"Today I was planning on speaking of one of the seven deadly sins. I was going to talk about gluttony. Y'all know gluttony, right? It's not a major-league sin. It's not anger, poking at you, saying, 'Why don't you dress him on down? Why don't you shut her up with a smack? Why don't you go out to the car, get that gun, take him to town?' That's anger. We see it all over, in the news, in the wars."

He sighed.

"Anger's a serious sin. Or greed, that's another one in the big time, greed tellin' you, 'Just take it, why not?' Or telling you, 'No one will miss a little money here or there, a little more or less.' It's telling those CEOs, those CFOs, 'Fire 'em, who cares? They ain't no one, just little people, working class, gettin' 'em out of the way will puff up your stock options, make you another million bucks!' Greed gets in the news, big frauds, bank scams, all kinds of crazy schemes with the stocks and bonds. Serious sins.

"And there's lust." He looked at the camera and let his eyes twinkle a little. "I'd tell you what lust says all the time, but this here's a family program.

"Up against those, gluttony doesn't seem so bad. It's bush league. All it says is 'Aw, one more Twinkie ain't gonna hurt no one.' And so what? Gluttons aren't bashing people like the wrathful, they ain't stealing like the greedy or the envious. They just get fat, and who doesn't like a fat man here or there? My own grandpa Morley was fat as a Christmas ham, and you wouldn't meet a sweeter man anywhere. What's wrong with a glutton?

"You see, I had my sermon all planned out.

"But then May Carter disappeared."

He paused to let the crowd murmur.

"Three days ago, May Carter left her apartment, locked the door, got in her car and drove off. No one knows just where she went, or just when. She lived alone. There's a message on her answering machine. The police know she was gone at 6:30 when that call came. She was gone or not answering the phone.

"Her car was found miles away in Maryland Heights, doors unlocked, key in the ignition. There was no sign of a struggle in her home or in her auto. But there's no sign of May, either.

"Most of you know this. Most of you know May. And those who don't, maybe some of our TV viewers, are wondering what this has to do with them. What it has to do with gluttony. And I know, there doesn't seem to be a connection. I'll try and make one." He licked his lips. "I'll try.

"May was no glutton. She was a moderate woman. I don't know that May was a victim of any of the seven deadlies. She was, near as I know, modest and forgiving, generous and cheerful, kind and even-tempered.

"Now she's gone. We don't know if she ran off on her own. Doesn't seem likely. More likely she got taken, and not by a glutton. If she was, it was... it was lust or wrath or..."

He looked down and away, composing himself.

"...or someone with them all twisted together. If she was taken, she fell victim to one of the big sins. Not gluttony.

"That's why it's easy to ignore gluttony. It doesn't seem like you're hurting anyone. Maybe you're hurting yourself, but even then, it doesn't *seem* like it. The pleasures of gluttony are immediate, and the downside, it's way off in the future. The fun part's now; the bad part's later. It's not like wrath, where you pay as you play, it's... subtle. It's easy to ignore.

"That's its power."

There was a pause, silent.

"*That's* its power."

A few murmurs from the crowd, but they weren't lit up yet, this wasn't the usual Matthew Wallace Express. He was switching between two tracks and each one was half as fast, but the words still worked. They had power. The pauses and repetitions were familiar, and people listened up almost in spite of themselves.

"It's easy to *ignore,* and that's its *power*. It gets you one donut at a time, one burger at a time, one full-fat venti latte coffee drink at a time. It adds up, it's sin with compound interest. It sneaks up on you ounce by ounce until one day you wake up and realize you're fifty pounds overweight—sixty pounds, *eighty* pounds! You're walking around with your layers of sin wrapped around you, it's like an overcoat you can't take off. It makes you sweaty, and it makes you breathe heavy, and it makes it hard to get up off the couch or push yourself away from the dinner table.

"It makes it hard," he said, "to do anything but be more gluttonous and more slothful."

He paused.

"You know," he said. "There's children here in America who go to bed hungry."

He said it quietly. He didn't elaborate on it... yet. He just said it again.

"There are children, *here*. In *America*. And they go to bed *hungry*."

The crowd started to hum with him. They got this, they understood this, they could see where he was going.

"America is the land of plenty. You drive up north to Chicago, west to Kansas City, drive down south or east, and all you'll see is fields of grain, fields of wheat, fields of corn. You'll pass by hog farms and cow farms and soybean farms. You'll go by ostrich and emu farms, cranberry bogs and fish hatcheries and dairies and orchards full of fruit. This country is full of food. It's overflowing with God's abundance, food enough for any nation. Food enough for the world!

"But those kids go hungry. Here in America, they go hungry.

"And it's worse elsewhere. You know this. How could it not be worse? There's countries where the fields aren't full of rice, they're full of unexploded landmines. There's countries where most of the ground don't grow nothin' but sand. Countries that are nothin' but dust devils and scorpions. Countries where it's not just the kids going hungry, it's everyone.

"Where's all that food going?"

"It's the gluttons!" someone shouted.

"Amen," Matthew said. "It's the gluttons. And they don't *want* to starve any kids. They don't want to starve anyone. If those kids were *there*, were in their dining rooms, I got no doubt those gluttons would share. They'd give 'em a slice of pie, a nice big sandwich with all the trimmings, couple of slices of that Meat Lover's Deluxe pizza. They would. Most would. Why not? Gluttony's not greed, it's not envy — why not share?

"If those kids were right there, they'd share.

"But of course, they're not there. They're... somewhere else. It's always somewhere else, isn't it? Far away, where the po' folk live. Ethiopia or Angola or Afghanistan, somewhere foreign and distant and hard to find on a map. Somewhere with a name that sounds made up. Out of sight and out of mind."

He paused, letting the boom mic pick up the indignant muttering of the congregation.

"My fat grandpa Morley..." He paused, and let the crowd noise die down, let them get attentive again. "My fat grandpa, he was a kind man. He'd carry a pocketful of sweets and give 'em out to any kid on the street. An' I remember when I was young and collecting money for the pagan babies—any of y'all remember pagan babies? Am I just too old, outta touch? I was collecting money for the hungry children in China, and I remember him giving me a sad sad look and sayin', 'I just hate to even think about that.'"

He paused.

"I don't remember," he said, slow and distinct and significant, "if he gave any money. I don't know if he donated or if he just said, 'I hate to even think about that.'" He frowned, seeming to meditate.

"Out of sight, out of mind."

Silence.

"'I hate to even think about that.'"

"Tell it, Rev'ren'!" It was a lone voice.

"We put it out of mind, the hunger and suffering, and then it's got us."

The silence broke with a seething sound.

"Then, it's got us."

"Amen!"

"Then it's *got* us, because then we're in the habit of putting suffering out of mind. And when you can put those hungry kids out of your mind, you can forget all about 'em, and it's sad. You *hate* to *even think* about it, so you don't think. You unwrap another Twinkie, and you like that sugary filling and you *don't think*, and that lets it keep happening! You don't think, and you keep buying those pork rinds at the grocery store. And the man at the store doesn't think, he just rings 'em up for you. The man packing the pork and selling it doesn't think. The farmer, why, for all he knows, the pigs he kills are going to hungry people. He doesn't think about it. We've all got plenty in the land of the full and the home of the brave and those invisible Ethiopians, we *hate to even think about them!*"

"Amen!"

"Tell it, preacher!"

Matthew spoke again. "And now May," he said.

The crowd rumbled before him.

"Now... May. This poor, pure girl just fades away, near us all, right here in St. Louis, right here in Maryland Heights, and how many of us hate to even think about it? How many? I do. Lord knows I do! I hate to think about that—kidnapping, murder, whatever her fate might be. I got a daughter; it doesn't take too much imagination to picture her on a milk bottle, on the TV news, part of the re-enactment on *America's Most Wanted*. Not too much imagination at all, just the *right kind*. We can all see our selves, our children, our families in May's tragedy, and we *hate to think about it*.

"But we have to.

"Those of you here in person, you each got a flyer when you came in. It's in there, in behind the hymn of the day, and it's got a picture and a number to call. And all you at home, in just a minute you're going to see her, see May's picture, and you're going to see that number too. One of you might see *her*. You might see something. You might hate to think about it, but you *got* to think about it, because you might be her only hope. You, thinking about it, watching, could be God's way to save her. If you let Him work through you.

"I'm sounding, I know, like that fellow on *Cops*, but we got something those cop shows don't have. We've got something the police don't use. We've got something that May loved and that loves May very much. We've got the Holy Spirit, people."

"Amen!"

"We've got the spirit, and we've got prayer!"

"Tell it!" "Amen! Hallelujah!"

"I want each of you to close your eyes and pray now, pray for the safe return of this poor girl. And I want each of you to *open* your eyes and *watch* for the safe return of this lost child of God. And I want each of you to keep your *mind* open. Think about sin. Think about that hard route to God, think about doing right.

"Even when you hate to think about it."

"Wow. You're famous."

When Rabbadün didn't reply, Hasmed gritted his teeth and exhaled.

The other demon's mortal shell was a wreck. The humans who'd nabbed him had really done a job. They were either utterly hate-filled or utterly paranoid. Or both. They'd put tourniquets on both Rabbadün's arms and both his legs. They'd left them on for days, starving the limbs of blood until they died and became gangrenous, at which point they sawed them off. Police were still searching for them.

They'd also cut out Rabbadün's tongue. Maybe they'd been afraid to hear what he had to say. Maybe they knew he might invoke aid if he could speak. Maybe they just made a lucky guess, Hasmed didn't know. But finding a kidnapped John Doe—horribly mutilated—in the home of a quiet and law-abiding Presbyterian couple—after a shootout with the cops—

and with other suspected "cultists" still at large... well, it was more than a media circus. The Los Angeles quake situation was finally coming under control (or, at least, was out of control in boring and predictable ways), so the talking heads were happy to have some new gabble fodder.

(One telegenic sociologist with dubious credentials had even posited a link between this latest atrocity and the murder of Clara Caulter by Joellen and Black Hawk O'Hanlon. He mentioned Faulkner and *A Streetcar Named Desire* and talked about a rich vein of violent perversity running through Southern culture. No one mentioned demons, however.)

Hasmed could feel how tenuous Rabbadün's grip was, but he didn't seriously consider letting him return to Hell.

What would I tell Vodantu? "Oops, he slipped"? This dumb fuck gets trashed by mortals, and I'd get the blame for not saving him.

Instead, he blew soothing air on Rabbadün's fever, calmed the trauma of his remaining tissues and restored the demon's tongue.

Rabbadün's eyes flicked open. "Hasmed?" he said thickly.

"Hey there, fucko."

"Where...?" He rolled his head left and right, and then tentatively smiled. "You did it! You got me out of there!"

"Yep. I wasted a bunch of my time and effort, and I risked one of my best vassals to save *you* from a pack of dumbass *mortals.*"

"They weren't just mortal, man, they... they knew stuff, knew about us."

"Gee, ya think? You suppose that your running around carving up hookers and getting your ya-yas out might have had something to do with that?"

"No, it was more than that."

At that moment, the door opened. Hasmed frowned, concentrated, and the nurse who walked in simply ignored him.

"Remember that you can't speak," Hasmed hissed at Rabbadün.

"How are you doing today?" the nurse asked. The patient moaned and acted groggy.

"It's great that you're awake—Dr. Mehta will be really excited. Ooh, and you'd probably like your dressings changed, huh?"

Hasmed gritted his teeth while she prattled and swaddled and wiped. When she was finally gone, he unveiled himself again.

"Hasmed, you gotta fix me up," Rabbadün said.

"Oh, I gotta?"

"Come on man, you're not just gonna leave me here, are you? Leave me like this?"

"What's in it for me?"

"Vodan—"

Hasmed's fist lashed down and across Rabbadün's jaw before the cripple could finish saying their master's name. Rabbadün's eyes widened, and his stumps moved helplessly as Hasmed's hands closed over his mouth.

"You say that name, and you're done, got me?" Hasmed shifted so that his left hand was on the point of Rabbadün's chin, he leaned in to keep it closed as he produced a switchblade with his right. A brief click, and the point was right under Hasmed's left hand.

"Here's the script," he said. "I let you speak, and the first thing out of your mouth is your True Name."

The sounds the imprisoned demon made weren't coherent, but from tone Hasmed guessed it was something like "Fuck you."

"I know what you're thinking," Hasmed said. "What's the worst I can do? Kill you? Shit, you've been in Hell before, and once you're there, the boss will call you up and you'll rat me out, right? So you think I'm bluffing. You think I won't do it because I'd just be shooting myself in the foot. And that's right. But my foot's on your face right now, asswipe. How many years were you in the Abyss? Hundreds? Millions? It felt like eternity, didn't it? You got *one* chance in eternity, one chance to get out and walk again. You think another chance like that is gonna come along quick?" He leaned in close, until his horrible scar and eye of blood were only inches from Rabbadün. "Even if you were only there *ten minutes*, it would feel like a billion years... wouldn't it?"

He saw the realization in the other demon's eyes, and he raised his hand off Rabbadün's mouth.

"Five syllables," Rabbadün said. Hasmed barked with laughter.

"Still negotiating? Pardon the pun, but you ain't got a leg to stand on." He licked three fingers on his left hand and reached back to slap a thigh stump for emphasis.

"Still, it's a start. Let's have 'em."

"Look, the boss wants you to fix me. He's got *your* Name."

"You've got a lot of faith in house loyalty, pal. Put yourself in the archduke's shoes. On one hand you've got a guy who's got Mob backing, thralls, a growing power structure. On the other there's a fuckup who got his legs chopped off by *six measly humans*."

"They weren't—"

"Oh, they were *special*, they *knew* stuff, it's *not my fault*," Hasmed said in an insultingly whiny impression. "How well d'you think that's gonna to play? Fuggeddaboudit."

Rabbadün was sullenly silent for a moment, then the tones flowed forth, his movement in the cosmic symphony.

"That's swell," Hasmed said, and stood up, dusting off the front of his pants.

"Hey, where you think you're going?"

"Eh, dunno. Maybe I'll go invoke up a Slayer or Defiler or something, see what they'll give me for five parts of an oracle's identity."

"You fucker! You do it and I'll—"

"You'll what?" Hasmed cupped a hand by his ear. "Go to the boss? Start a whole 'he said, she said' dispute? Let's not forget who *started* this whole True Name game, fucko. You were the one who extorted me. Don't cry 'cause you got caught on your own hook."

"You'll pay for this!"

Hasmed snickered. "Aw, you sound like y'r mama when you say that. But in the end, she always gave it away free."

The insult shouldn't have stung, much. Angels don't have mothers. But Rabbadün was frustrated at needing rescue, annoyed by Hasmed's contempt... and behind it there were resentments going back to the war, and secret jealousies from even before that, all housed in a damaged and tortured body, guided by a bundle of bad brain wiring marinated by years of drug abuse.

And to be honest, Rabbadün's term in Hell hadn't done much to improve his impulse-control.

"Fuck you!" he shrieked. "Fuck you and your gangland cronies and your money! Fuck your whole Second House, you're all a bunch of cowardly assfucks! You may have the boss fooled but not me! Not me, *Asharu*! You don't have the guts or the vision to go all the way. You may pretend you don't care about them, but I've *seen* you, Hasmed. I *know* you're still a defender deep down."

"Tell that to Vanessa—remember her? Or how about Sal Macellaio's kid, hm?" Hasmed heard rapid footsteps outside and absentmindedly, he made himself unseeable.

"It's even sadder that you'd hurt them without really believing. You didn't really want it. I could *tell*. You just went through the motions. If it was that shaky little bantamweight you hang around with, or your curly haired little girl..."

"What?"

But Hasmed didn't wait for clarification. As soon as he realized that Rabbadün had been spying on Tina, his course was set. The knife came out and he killed the demon he'd rescued, slicing the throat so hard and fast that the blade grated against the spine.

He spoke the Enochian words that were Rabbadün, and his knowledge was imperfect, his control imperfect. Rabbadün's spirit fought bitterly, but at its core, it was less afraid of annihilation than of going back to Hell. In the end, it gave in. In the end, Hasmed ate Rabbadün's soul.

Shit. That's a revolting development, he thought, just as the door burst open. A doctor and nurse didn't even pause to wonder how this could happen—they were that good. They just tried to resuscitate a nearly decapitated body, while its killer slipped out the door behind them, lost in thought.

Gaviel struggled to pay attention. He *seemed* very interested, of course. Appearing to care was easy.

"I haven't seen you here before," he said.

The girl in front of him kept her head hung low, her long beaded braids dangling in front of her face like a curtain. Her name was Zoe.

"Chasney said..."

Gaviel smiled, and it felt thinner to him than he wanted it to. *Focus*, he told himself. *This shit's starting to pay off. You've got a Judas goat leading the others into the slaughterhouse.*

"Yes?" he prompted.

"He said you could help," she whispered.

"Do you need help, Zoe?"

She shrugged, nodded.

This would be so much easier if they didn't make me strong-arm them into saying what they want.

He knew, of course. He could feel how faint her faith was. It was pounded thin, weak as a cobweb. It could barely hold the weight of a struggling fly. She didn't believe in him or God or herself; she didn't believe in America or education or hard work or perseverance. Just about all of her had been hollowed out. She was just a shape around a void of self-loathing and self-pity and fear, fear, fear.

"I thought," she said, "That maybe if I lost some weight..."

"Why?"

"You makin' fun of me!" She turned aside and huddled herself closer in, as if trying to reduce herself, trying to compact herself down to a Size 4.

She was large, yes. A little fat—not obese. If she were a man, she'd be hefty, regular-guy heavy. The sort who might crouch on the football field as a linebacker. She had a little double chin and maybe a bit of jiggle and sag under her upper arm when she waved. She was a little bit overweight.

In her eyes, Gaviel knew, she was a monster. Every crude joke and snicker and comment magnified her, until in her own mind she was gigantic, grotesque. A human garbage dump sprawled on the landscape like an acre of suet.

It would not be hard to bind her to him. She was desperate for hope, and for that hope she would happily destroy her mind or soul or body. Why not? There was nothing about her that she valued.

Her watery faith would be a slender payoff, Gaviel was well aware. *But beggars can't be choosers*, he thought.

He drew in breath to speak his honeyed words and then paused.

When did I become a beggar?

"Snap out of it," he said.

Her head jerked up like she was a marionette on a string.

"If you want to lose a few pounds, start doing some calisthenics. Or you could just accept that 'large' is one of the sizes human beings come in."

Her eyes were wide, and they looked painted like a puppet's.

"You only feel guilty about your weight because you let people define you. You only feel bad about your color because you let others describe you to yourself. You only feel vulnerable as a woman because you believe others when they call you weak."

These were not revolutionary concepts to her, nor to him. Simple truths, so obvious and oft-repeated that they'd become clichés, part of the background noise of culture. But spoken in the voice of a Messenger of the Lord, the phrases lost their sheen of glibness and struck her mind with the force of hammer blows.

"You can take charge of your life. You can define yourself. You can reinvent yourself if you have the will and the courage. It's not easy. It's not comfortable. It's not fun. But if you do it, you'll live by your own strength instead of the tolerance of others. Now go."

She got up, looking stunned, and turned toward the door. Following some obscure drive, Gaviel stood and kicked her in the seat of the pants. She stumbled forward, recovered, looked back at him, then left without a word.

There, he thought, *a literal kick in the ass to go with the metaphorical one.*

He'd given her a gift, awakened some of her dormant drive and pride and ambition. It would wear off in a week, maybe less. He wondered if that jumpstart would be enough to let her switch her life onto a new track.

He wondered why he'd bothered when there wasn't any payoff.

Chapter Thirteen

The skeleton of a second building was up at Avitu's compound. It was poured concrete blocks with a tile roof. Solar panels were coming later—one of Teddy's ideas. Just a shell, it was empty of everything but dust and Tyvek wrappers, but it was protection from the sun, and Joellen asked Blackie to meet her there.

"Mason's still in the cabin?" Black Hawk asked, wiping his forehead. He was dressed in a T-shirt and shorts. After getting a big dose of money from Gwyn, he'd gone shopping with a woman named Pamela Creed, another follower of the Tree. She'd got him a snappy suit and some dressy shirts and ties. He spent more money on two suits and five shirts than he'd spent on clothing in the last five years. He got new shoes and silk boxers and, in the end, found that he was more comfortable in boots and jeans and flannels.

In a way, his old stuff was comforting. When he looked in the mirror, he saw a stranger's face. But at least the clothes were the same.

"Yeah," Joellen said, worry lines forming dents on her new face.

"Still in a sulk, huh?"

"It's not a *sulk* son, show some respect for your daddy!"

He shrugged.

"He's... he's in a..." Joellen raised a manicured nail to her lip, remembered that it was carefully sculpted, and reluctantly lowered it unbitten. "I have to do something for him," she said. "And for that, I have to go away."

"Yeah?"

"I'm afraid so." She told him her plan.

He gave her a flat, skeptical look.

"Mama…" he said.

"Blackie, I have to do this thing! It's not just for us, not just for me, it's for the Goddess too! Her property is, is missing and I have to get it back. That's all there is to it."

"You're talking about a federal crime."

"Pah. I'm already a fed'ral fugitive, ain't I? The FBI, to hell with them, they're useless. Can't catch anyone, less he's backed into a hole and they outnumber him ten to one." He heard the bitterness in her voice, saw the distance in her eyes, and he knew she was back at the farmhouse, back with her dying relatives, getting ready to surrender and save him.

"I just… I worry."

"I can take care of myself, and the Tree can take care of me. We've come this far, ain't we?"

The building had no door, just a taped-up tarpaulin to keep the dust out. Before Black Hawk could answer her question, a massive hand pushed the tarp aside and Tim Grady entered.

"Do you mind?" Blackie said. "We're having a private conversation here."

Grady looked at him with blank eyes. Grady's eyes were always blank.

"Avitu told me you were here," the Hollywood Ice Pick said. His voice was as flat as his stare.

"Oh."

"What do you need, Tim?" Joellen's voice was always patient and clear when she addressed him—as if she were talking to a young child.

"I have a new sacrifice."

"Teddy is in the cabin, Tim. You can take the sacrifice to him. He'll do the cleansing."

"She's already been cleansed. I did it myself."

"That's very good, Tim. When Gwynafra comes, you can give her the sacrifice for processing."

"We shouldn't process this one."

Again, Black Hawk felt a tingle of unease. He didn't like to talk about "processing" the people who'd lost the curse. Afterward, they were like morons or children or dogs, they moved about like they were really drunk, or like they were zombies in a movie. They didn't talk, just grunted or worse — moaned. They needed diapers.

Gwyn or Pam or one of the other followers usually brought sacrifices from Las Vegas — people who'd lost it all on gambling or drink or some other despair, people with nothing left to lose but their minds. Teddy would... fix them... and then they'd hang around a day or two until Gwynafra could take them back. The mud woman took them somewhere, and they were never seen or heard from again. That was the "process."

"Why not?" Joellen asked.

"Gwyn said." That was enough for Tim.

"So what do you want us to do about it?" Blackie asked.

"Take care of her," Tim said. He turned his head, looking at someone outside the building. "Come here," he called.

A young black woman wandered up to the door. She had the lost look of a sacrifice recently "cleansed." Her right eye was clouded with blood — Tim must have scratched it performing the ritual.

(When Teddy did it, there was no outward sign of injury.)

Tim took her hand and led her inside.

Joellen looked at her son and frowned. "You'll have to do this," she said. "I have to leave."

"But mama..."

"I'm sorry son, but we have duties and obligations. I love you." She kissed his cheek and hurried out the door, not looking at the sacrifice.

"Her name is May," Tim said. He gave her hand to Blackie like he was handing over a dog's leash.

"But… what am I…?"

Tim turned and left.

Blackie looked at May.

"Well damn," he said.

She made a soft keening sound in the back of her throat.

"I don't see how you can stand to eat that crap," Sabriel said, curling a lip at the bucket of Kentucky Fried Chicken on Gaviel's dining room table.

"If it was just the skin and breading, I'd eat *that*," Thomas Ramone said around a full mouth.

"The secret ingredient is MSG," Gaviel added, his own mouth similarly greased and stuffed.

Sabriel picked at a biscuit, and suddenly Gaviel saw Thomas's eyes narrow and his nostrils flare.

"In fact, you were eating this 'crap' when you had me tied up in your fucking basement, weren't you?" Thomas said.

Gaviel glanced between them. Sabriel gave an idle shrug and said, "Yeah, and it turned my stomach. It's too oily, and it gets all over your fingers."

"YOU SHOULD LET BYGONES BE, THOMAS," Gaviel said.

Ramone's eyes got hazy for a second, and his face relaxed a bit.

"IT'S COOL, MAN," Gaviel said. "IT'S ALL GOOD."

"Yeah," Tom said, his forehead clearing. "It's all good."

"Y'know, I've got *Yo Homie* for the PlayStation on rental 'til Thursday."

"Yeah? Y'mind?"

"Be my guest." Thomas rose and went to the living room. Behind him, Gaviel gently shook his head.

"Didn't shield him from suggestion, huh?"

"The greatest chef in the world can't make a ham sandwich if all he has is turkey. He got what he bargained for."

"I'm sure. What was that business about your basement?"

"Hey, I didn't entice him into my house. He entered of his own free will. Let's leave it at that, 'kay?"

"All right. I'm just a little uneasy—reasonably so, I think—with your thrall knowing where I live and my celestial name and so forth... holding all that information in a brain with all the resistance of wet toilet paper."

"I keep him on a tight leash."

"I guess so."

Neither spoke for a moment. Gaviel tore into the chicken with gusto, wincing when he heard the PlayStation hip-hop pinging from his living room.

"Why does he always turn the music on?"

"He probably doesn't know it bugs you," Sabriel said.

"You'd think he could figure it out, since I turn it off on every single game."

She rolled her eyes. "In case you hadn't noticed, Thomas isn't exactly a rocket scientist. He's about as sharp as a sumo wrestler's thigh."

More silence, marred only by the moist sounds of Gaviel tearing a chicken wing apart, and the tinny sounds of Thomas's game.

"So," Sabriel said, pushing her coleslaw away uneaten. "About the Keeper of the Twin—"

"Uht-uht-uht!" Gaviel held up his hand to stop her. "I'd prefer to eat in peace and discuss business after."

274 / GREG STOLZE

"Oh *fine*."

"Are you going to finish that slaw?"

"Help yourself."

When Gaviel was finally full, he wiped his mouth, washed his hands in the kitchen sink, then came out and said two words in Enochian.

Sabriel raised an eyebrow. "What's that?"

"Two components of the Keeper's True Name."

"Two? That's all you got?"

There was the barest pause before Gaviel said, "That's right."

Gaviel left the pause to make Sabriel think that he had more, was holding back, and didn't want her to know about it. In fact, he'd told her all he knew but figured she wouldn't believe him if he told her that truth, or if she did believe, would feel that he hadn't gotten enough power to really put Avitu in check.

Sabriel frowned. "Well, it's better than nothing, I suppose."

"Considerably better, I would think. And the Reaper of Souls? Is he on as short a leash as your dim human friend?"

(Usiel was, at that moment, making his way up the coast of Italy. He'd robbed another bank, bought a car and was planning to visit Vatican City. With no passport, he had to sneak around national borders, either by physical stealth or by taking painful shortcuts through the lands of the dead.

(He was still upset and confused by his most recent talk with Lucifer. That was on top of his confusion about Sabriel and his confusion about Glenda Fielding. All in all, he was very confused indeed, and he hoped for some divine guidance to help straighten him out.

(Then he heard Gaviel the Namaru discussing him—and not in flattering terms.)

"Don't worry about him. I'm pretty sure I've got his number," Sabriel said.

She said this with some conviction, but not with blithe assurance. She knew Gaviel would see right through a show of total confidence. In actual fact, she hadn't seen the Reaper in days, and he wasn't responding to her invocations. She was worried, but she didn't think it would do any good at all to share her concerns with Gaviel.

"What number is that? Six six six?"

"Regardless of his punishment and his wrath, the Reaper of Souls isn't like you and me, Gaviel. I don't know that you could properly call him a demon at all."

(As she spoke his title, Usiel began to hear her side of the conversation as well. He pulled over by the side of the road. Clive Keene's stolen heart was beating uncomfortably fast in Usiel's chest.)

"Despised by God, cast down into Hell, returned in the stolen body of a mortal to wreak havoc on the realm of the living? Sounds like a demon to me."

"Unlike so many demons—you, for example—he still wants to do the right thing. He's still vulnerable to the temptation of virtue."

"From what you've told me of the Keeper, she wants to be virtuous as well—undo Lucifer's work, strip mortals down into the cattle they were meant to be and renew the world as an Eden of ignorance."

Sabriel sighed and sat. "For all I know, the Reaper would back her if he knew. But he's uncertain, now. He hesitates."

(Sitting in his parked car, Usiel wondered who the "Keeper" was. Did they mean Avitu?)

"Thanks to you, I presume?"

"I guess."

"I'm impressed. Hoodwinking one of the Lord's most fearsome avengers is quite the coup. You must be delighted."

Sabriel wasn't. In fact, she felt a deep disquiet when she thought about how she'd treated Usiel. She wasn't sorry, exactly... after all, if she hadn't stopped him, she'd be back in Hell, and there was no way she was going back without a fight. But nevertheless... it made her feel petty and dirty and small. All the things she hated about being human. In the same way that she despised having to eat and sweat and moisturize the dried skin on her elbows, she despised having to wheedle and cozen an angel. It was acceptable treatment for riff-raff like Hasmed and Gaviel, rebels and losers and bums like her... but Usiel was something different, and it made her sad to play him that way.

But she was sure Gaviel wouldn't understand, and she couldn't show him anything he might interpret as weakness anyhow. So she smiled a wicked smile.

"The Reaper, the *angel*, had a weak spot for one of my fellows. Did you know Haniel?"

"Never had the pleasure," Gaviel glibly replied. He knew that he might well have met her, or even had a lengthy friendship, but his memories of the time before the Fall were weaker than he wanted to admit.

"She and the Reaper were lovers, and I simply acted like her."

"How melodramatic. Did she rebel or remain loyal?"

"Neither. You remember God's offer to explain his treatment of humankind?"

"'See as I see to know what I know'? I remember something of the sort."

"She took him up on it."

"Ah." Gaviel gave his head a sad shake. "And so the Allmaker unmade her for her hubris?"

Sabriel shrugged. "Who knows?"

"No one but God, I suppose, and He's not talking. So that was the Achilles heel of Heaven's champion? The ghost of affection for some simpering Oceanite?"

"I'll thank you to speak of my sister with some respect. She had the courage to seek the truth. Shit, for all we know, she found it."

"Mm. Good for her."

"Ever wish you had?"

"What? Took up the Almighty's offer?" Gaviel shrugged. "When I was in Hell, sure. I would have picked annihilation over that in an instant. I'd have leaped at the chance. But I didn't regret rebelling during the war, and I don't regret existing now. I only felt bad about anything when I got caught and punished." He smiled. "I guess that makes me like a human, doesn't it? Anyhow, no, I don't envy Haniel her fate, whatever it is. Maybe she's with God now, but I doubt it. I think she's become nothing at all, while I'm still around to enjoy cigarettes and *Yo Homie* and fried chicken. It's not Paradise, but I'll take it over Hell any day."

"I'd only been Christina for a few weeks before I heard from the Knight of the Bounded Infinite. Remember her? Well, she's got this plan to restore the world. You know, rebuild it in our image now that the loyalists are all gone. Or maybe it was that she was going to free humankind to rebuild it in *their* image. Something crazy, ambitious like that."

Gaviel laughed. "Screw that. If you let them run things, we'd be like the 'human' exhibit in a zoo run by chimps."

"Well then, what about the other idea? Risen angels protecting their charges, making up for the war and the Fall by restoring the world?"

"Yeah, 'cause we did such a *great job* the last time we tried to take the moral high road. I don't think well-meaning demons are going to do better with the world than humans would. We'd probably just create epic problems instead of petty ones." His eyes got distant, and his sneer was all the uglier because it sat on such a handsome face. "Hell, even *God* couldn't build a cosmos that worked right. Allmaker, Almighty, all-powerful...

and Lucifer, the best part of His design, trashed the rest of it. If the Ancient of Days couldn't get it right, what chance do we have?"

"Couldn't get it right... or chose not to?"

"If God *chose* to make a doomed universe, we're in even *worse* shape." He shook his head. "Look, no one's going to come in, fix stuff, pat our cheeks and tuck us into bed. We can make ourselves a comfortable existence—get some thralls, a little power, some security—and I think that's about it."

"That's all?" Sabriel stood up so she could stare down at him. "When did you get so lazy?"

"When I realized that there was nothing attainable that was worth all that much effort. Why? What's your big plan?"

"The humans have to pay, that's my plan."

"Oh, vengeance. *That's* a great way to spend eternity. Once they're wiped out or lobotomized or enslaved or whatever, exactly what reason does God have to leave the cosmos running, hm? Ever think about that?"

"I don't want to turn them back into animals, not like the Tree, but... the ones who think they can *create*. The ones who think they're *like us*, they... they *nauseate* me. Every piece of music you've heard, Gaviel, some human made that. You can't stand it, can you? Their pathetic, puny attempts at mirroring the True Song? Doesn't it make you want to smash their instruments, burn their songbooks and kill the composers?"

Gaviel gave a light laugh. "It makes me want to turn off the radio," he said.

His air of unconcern was almost perfect. Almost.

"You're *scared*," she said.

He laughed again. It was less perfect. It was brittle. "That's ridiculous. I've got some concerns, certainly, but fear doesn't factor in. I wasn't built for fear. I was made for mastery, and you know it."

"Like you've mastered the Keeper. And your Foe to the east. And the Reaper."

"The Keeper's off our backs. My Foe is stymied. And *you* seduced and befuddled our scythe-wielding friend."

There was a moment of silence.

"Isn't there anything else you want?" Sabriel said, and she was surprised. She knew she was being stupid, being vulnerable, but she couldn't shake the distressing feeling that there had to be *more* to it, that there had to be a *reason* they'd escaped the Abyss, a better reason than simple comfort and just getting by.

Before he could reply, Thomas stuck his head around the corner. "Dude, this thing is *awesome*. I read that the Big Pimpin' scenario is really cool, but it's multiplayer. You guys almost done?"

The next day was Friday, and Gaviel went once more to the high school to mentor. There were three new students this time, one a girl who sat by herself in a corner. She had on tight jeans and a clingy T-shirt, but her inviting garb was at odds with her forbidding expression.

He talked to the other new students a bit afterward, but he deemed them incompletely ripe. Maybe in a week, or a month. All the time, the third girl sat and sullenly watched. Now and then, one of her hundred-dollar sneakers would tap impatiently on the floor.

Gaviel could tell she was making the other two nervous, but he didn't much care. If anything, it amused and interested him. When they'd finally given their last, over-the-shoulder looks at her, they rose together and scurried out.

Gaviel sat, unmoving.

She sat, silent.

He enjoyed this. She was testing him. She was waiting for him to get up and walk over to her and try to draw her out of her shell. He intended to do no such thing.

After ten minutes of the silent treatment, she rolled her eyes, stood up and stalked over to him. She stood in front of the desk, hands on hips, and looked at him like he was something from the bottom of her shoe.

"So what you do to Renee?" she asked.

Gaviel smiled thinly.

Waited.

Waited.

She shifted her posture, and he said, "I'm afraid you have the advantage of me. Your name is…"

"I'm Jewell."

"Ah."

"What you do to Renee?"

"Beg your pardon?"

"Don't you try'n play me! One day she ain't *nothin'* — just some dumb bitch always lookin' 'round with her stupid google eyes — an' then she turns into queen shit overnight? Nuh uh. This ain't no movie where the librarian takes off her glasses, put her hair down and she's Catherine Zeta Jones. You did somethin' to her."

"You're clever."

She rolled her eyes once more, as if to say *well obviously*. He laughed out loud.

"Why do you care?"

No answer, but the first little crack in Jewell's rock-hard façade started to show.

"This is about Leotis, isn't it?"

"Leotis? Fuck him. Fuck that stupid-ass played-out wooly-head meatball. This about Renee thinking she's all that, ac'in' like she can look down on *me* and play me the fool before everyone."

"You're better." Gaviel didn't say it with even a hint of mockery in his voice. Neither was there a trace of flattery. He said it because it was true.

"Damn straight," Jewell replied.

Jewell was no May or Matthew, but she had a bright, sharp soul. If she ever found something bigger and better to believe in, she might give those two a run for their money. But unlike them, Jewell didn't believe in God. She believed in herself, and while that made her strong and smart and let her bully her peers, it ultimately limited her. Until she could believe that much in something outside herself, her growth was limited. But Gaviel knew she wouldn't want to hear that.

"Since we're on the same page there, you must be wondering why Renee can now… succeed where you… well… don't. Yes?"

She just glared a bitter glare.

"You were right to guess she had help. You were right to guess that she had *my* help. And if you want, you can have my help too."

He invited her to go somewhere with him, but she said he could say his piece right there in the school well enough. It made him smile again.

He laid out his proposal and explained his terms.

She thought it over.

"No way in hell," she said.

"No? May I ask why not?"

"'Cause I don' need nobody's help to be me. And if you're helpin' be somethin' else, I don' want to be that."

He gave a good-natured nod.

"Okay, well, if you change your mind, you know how to find me."

"Uh huh." She turned her back without the courtesy of saying goodbye.

"One more thing. TELL NO ONE ABOUT THIS."

She didn't turn back, but at the sound of his true voice she froze. Not for long, she started walking away again quickly, but in that moment he saw something in her posture that had been absent before.

Respect.

It wasn't her soul, but he'd take it.

That night, while the mortals of Los Angeles had nightmares of demons—as many of them had had ever since the quake— Gaviel once again had a nightmare about a mortal.

"Sabriel really pissed you off, didn't she?" Noah asked. "When she said you were afraid, I mean."

"I see no percentage in contemplating the judgment of some salt-water slut. Besides, haven't we already gone over the issue of our relative cowardices *ad infinitum*? If I gave you your body back, would you have the guts to tell your father everything? To explain that it was your jealousy of his sexual conquests that left you open to my 'dark influence'?"

"That's... that's an oversimplification and you *know* it."

"If I gave you a second chance, you'd piss it away just like your first."

"That's an 'if' of gigantic proportions. You wouldn't let go of my body in a million years. You're too scared of Hell, too scared that you misjudged me, too scared that I'd beat you in a fair fight and *take my life back*."

"If I'm scared of anything, I'm scared that you'd squander my careful gains of cash and power and reputation before you despaired, once more, and surrendered your shell to me."

Gaviel was tired. He was even *dreaming* that he felt tired, tired of bickering with Noah and wishing he could just be *done* with the whiny little punk once and for all. Awake, with his full power to bear, he could squash Noah's bleating with little effort—every day spent basking in the regard of Leotis and Chas and Renee made him stronger, made it easier to grind Noah down. But at night...

And then he woke up.

It took him a moment to realize what had awakened him, because it was not something natural to him. It was an alien power, one he had stolen in Los Angeles, the power of foresight and fate-sense. He'd used it dimly, partially, sensing small movements of local things. But where before he'd used it like a magnifying glass, it was now like a telescope, letting him see something distant... and large.

It was the Reaper of Souls. And he was coming for Gaviel.

Surging through the underworld on wings of ash and anger, the Reaper of Souls gritted his teeth.

The Namaru first, he thought. *Gaviel sun-lord, liar, deceiver and mocker of God. He'll get the punishment he deserves. And after...*

There was a flicker of doubt as he thought about Sabriel, but the memory of her contempt stung him.

After him, the Defiler. For her kindness before the Fall, I'll delay her day of reckoning. And perhaps I'll ask about this Keeper before I finish what I started.

He felt better once he'd explained his decision to himself, and he continued to surge through the tempest of the death-realm's wreckage.

Angels and demons do not, as a rule, study psychology, and Clive Keene's grasp of it was minimal at best. So Usiel didn't pause to connect his decision to kill Gaviel first with a memory that kept coming to his attention, over and over, as he traveled. A memory of the war...

They hadn't had a decent battle for weeks, only a series of skirmishes, each more petty and inconclusive than the last. The forces of the fallen were on the run, trying to get the Mountains of Morning between themselves and the warriors of the Holy Host. It was a smart delaying tactic—many angels could no longer fly. Even those who could might be vulnerable to wind and chill at the heights if they took physical form—and physical forms were needed for much of the hardest fighting.

Usiel was in command, and he pushed his soldiers hard, piling angels and loyal humans into a valley, chasing the demons into the pass, but it was too slow. The demons had abandoned their followers in a rearguard maneuver. While the humans fought, the angels had to wait and the demons could escape.

At the entry of the valley, Usiel stood, dark and vast as an anvil thunderhead. He looked across and could see—see!—one of the defiant Namaru holding the pass, warming the blasphemers with his summer glory, urging them to greatness against the worshippers of God.

Usiel knew that rebel. Gaviel, once Archangel of the Summer Sun, now styled the "Lord" of the same. He longed to wing across the valley and smite the blasphemer, but while he was a match for the devil alone, he could not face Gaviel and his comrades. And Usiel could not bring his own troops in while the humans clogged the valley.

As he tried to think of an answer, he saw something.

He saw the way the demon-worshippers turned to their patron, and he saw the love in their eyes. More than that, he felt it, felt their adoration and trust and hope, and it stung him. He was no lofty Angel of Light to inspire with grandeur. An Angel of Decay, all he'd ever seen from them was fear, and to feel their regard flowing to one of God's Exiles...

He had a plan.

It made sense. His army would lose its human followers, but there were more where they came from. The important thing was that they would deny the demons that same resource, the scarce nourishment of human devotion. It would be sad for the angels, but ruinous for the demons.

He consulted no one, but moved across the field like fog. Everywhere his shadow fell, men and women, loyal and rebel, all died alike.

Usiel dodged around a more turbulent part of the storm, trying to keep his mind focused on navigation, on finding Gaviel and making him pay. He kept telling himself that he was punishing the rebel for his disrespect toward the Allmaker.

He kept trying not to think of the look of horror and disbelief that had crossed Gaviel's face as Usiel slaughtered the faithful, so many years ago.

"Hi, Mom? Yeah, I'm sorry to call you so late, but it's really important. Can I talk to Dad? No, don't... could you just put Dad on the line?"

"I'm sorry honey." Zola's voice was nervous and apologetic in Gaviel's ear, even filtered through the tinny tones of his cell phone. "He's doing the late shift at the shelter tonight."

"That must be why his phone's off," Gaviel said. "I'll just try him there."

"Son, what's... What's going on?"

"It's not *trouble*, Ma, just... I just have to talk to him."

"All right."

Her disappointment—her hurt feeling that he couldn't trust her with his problem—it was so clear, even over the phone, that if Gaviel hadn't been concerned about being sent back to Hell, and *soon*, he might have felt a pang of sympathy. But he didn't have energy or attention to spare for that. Instead he disconnected and dialed Gina Parris's number.

"Late shift at the shelter my ass," he muttered as he listened to it ring, checked the clock, checked the gas meter, checked the speedometer as he rocketed down the road.

He got her answering machine—she *sang* her message, which would have made him wince, but he didn't have time to wince—and after the beep he said, "Pick up! This is Noah Wallace, I know my dad's there, put him on the phone unless you want *everyone* to find out. Pick up!"

"What?" Matthew sounded panicky. "What is it?"

"Get to the church. Right away. It's an emergency."

"That's, it's a thirty-minute drive from here!"

"Then you better drive *fast*. It's a matter of life and death."

Gaviel saw flashing lights in his rearview mirror. He started to pull over.

"What's going on?" Matthew asked.

"Just do it, Reverend. I'll explain later."

When the police officer told him to roll down his window, Gaviel looked him in the eyes and said, "I'M A POLICE DETECTIVE. UNDERCOVER. I NEED YOU TO COME WITH ME, RIGHT NOW, SIRENS OFF, DON'T ASK QUESTIONS."

The policeman blinked thickly and said, "Yes sir!"

When they arrived at Matthew's chapel, Gaviel barely felt a sting as he pushed the doors open. Had the site come to respect him, or at least tolerate his presence? Had he developed some sort of resistance from constant exposure? No way to know, and it didn't matter now.

"You've got a shotgun in the trunk, right?" he asked the cop.

"Yeah, but I really ought to call in—"

"No! The guy we're after has a scanner, we can't tip him off."

"What about calling the dispatcher on the phone?"

"There's a very good reason we can't do that. Just do it my way."

Again, the cop's eyes lost focus, and he fumbled the trunk open to get the shotgun.

As he was doing that, Gaviel was setting up a weapon of his own.

Noah the grad student hadn't had any idea where to get serious firepower, of course. He'd known a girl who had a brother who smoked grass, though, and the brother's source knew a guy who ran with the gangs, and so forth. Simply by talking to each person's least-reputable source, Gaviel eventually found a man who could sell him a fully-automatic AK-47.

He didn't expect it to do all that much good, but every little bit helped.

The Reaper is stronger, he thought as he loaded the weapon. *But can he last? If he doesn't have thralls, he'll wear out pretty fast.*

If he'd wanted to communicate his feelings to anyone, he'd have smiled. The cop wandered back in, shotgun at port arms.

"Stay ready," Gaviel told him. "This could get real ugly."

"Who—"

"When you see him, you'll know."

And then, with a blast of stale air and ice wind, the Reaper of Souls emerged from the underworld.

His wings spanned fifteen feet, ragged and dark behind his bone shoulders. He raised his scythe of shadows in charcoal fingers, advancing...

...and bursting into flame.

Gaviel smirked. The chapel was holy ground and had been long before Matthew chose it for his own. Maybe it had once been a frontier chapel or a burial mound for the natives. Whatever it was, it was a wellspring of human power, awakened again by Matthew's flock.

The church was of men, and men didn't like demons. Gaviel had felt the site's smoldering anger even when he took Noah's shape. Coming in the form of an angel cast down, Usiel had fanned it into blinding rage.

"Welcome to church, Usiel!" Gaviel stood up behind the altar and emptied the Kalashnikov into the Reaper of Souls.

"ONCE AGAIN, YOU PROFANE THE HOLY!"

The assault rifle was empty, but Gaviel had a second clip taped upside down on the first—a "jungle clip." He pulled off the empty, spun it and slammed the full one home.

As he did, he spared a glance for the cop, who was simply staring. He'd gotten as far as pointing his weapon, but fear and awe and disbelief had jammed up his mind like too much hair in a shower drain.

The Reaper sprang forward as Gaviel barked a word of Enochian. It was addressed to the dormant flame sleeping in a shotgun shell, and he woke it to instant life. The pellets slammed through the Reaper, but Gaviel saw his wounds closing as soon as they appeared, like tiny flames going out in the rain. Nevertheless, he knew well the effort such healing took.

Every little bit, he thought, and emptied the second clip.

Usiel restored himself once more—

(In Illinois, Glenda Fielding woke from an uneasy slumber. She felt a sudden chill, even under her blankets.)

—as his terrible releasing tool swung through the air at Gaviel. The devil parried with his rifle, deflecting the blade's flat sweep up over his head. Usiel pulled back hard, and the gray edge of the scythe parted the Kalashnikov's wooden stock as if it were made of cheese.

Where the hell is Matthew? Gaviel wondered as he jumped back, rolling backward into the choir stalls. "SHOOT HIM!" he bellowed, and the voice of celestial command was enough to jar the cop into action. He pulled the trigger, remembered that the gun had already fired, then cleared the chamber and sent another blast of buckshot into the Reaper's ashy wings.

This time, the wounds closed more slowly.

(Glenda Fielding clutched the blankets to her. This was a peculiar chill. Usually, her hands and feet and ears got cold first, whatever was exposed and farthest from her heart. But this time, the cold seemed to have started at her very core.)

Usiel turned to the policeman, raising his scythe—but instead of striking, he simply spoke.

"SEE YOUR DEATH," he said in grating tones, while turning the eyeless sockets of his black skull to face him.

The police officer never told anyone about that night except for his wife and, later, his son. Even to them, he never told exactly what he saw in Death's eyes. But his hair turned pure white, and he served the force fearlessly for four more years, and one warm day in June he hung himself in his garage, facing a calendar with pictures of next year's Fords. His note simply said, "It's time."

He saw what the Reaper showed him, and he ran away as fast as he could.

When Usiel turned back, Gaviel was no longer hidden, and he was no longer human. His bleak angelic beauty shone forth like a beacon, even as the flames of angry faith blackened the tips of his fingers and smoldered smoke in his hair. A sweep of wings, and he was up by the ceiling, shining, calling out in the tongue of angels, the language of creation itself.

But his speech was no blessing or benediction. Instead he sang destruction and hate, he sang corrosion and treachery. He sang words that stained the world, and each barbed tone struck the Reaper like an arrow.

Usiel howled, and his ribs popped open like the fingers of a grasping hand. Inside, his imprisoned spirit slaves leaped free, streaming into the air as he bellowed, "ATTACK!" The ghosts of

Tommy Jenks and Gordy Hines and other shades or mortals who had gotten in the Reaper's way sprang out.

All but Jenks were new ghosts, and weak, unaccustomed to the ways of death. Hines tried to possess Gaviel's body, but the devil's spirit was too firmly in charge for that. Others tried to strike him physically or distract him with visions of maggots and flies, but the worst they could do was harass and annoy. Jenks, on the other hand, had the power to call flames and turn them to his bidding—even against a creature that had once been their unquestioned lord.

Gaviel resisted the fires of death as he'd fought the flames of faith—

(Chasney Shaw struggled in his sleep against a bad dream, a dream where he was laughed at and helpless.)

(Leotis Grant got up for a glass of water, trying to recover from a wash of sorrow and despair that seemed to fall on him with leaden weight.)

—and instead of fighting Jenks's ghost, Gaviel fixed him with a brilliant glare and said, "RESIST YOUR ENSLAVER!"

Braced by the courage of that radiant command, Jenks struggled... and was free.

He had only enough time to turn and lunge before the Reaper's releasing tool swung through him, consigning him to oblivion, but it bought Gaviel time again, time to fly away, dodge the scythe, scream more words of wounding at Usiel.

(Glenda was huddled in her bed, electric blanket on full, covers over her head like a child afraid of the closet monster. She clutched a cross and prayed, prayed, prayed, and she could not see that her breath was steaming from the icy chill that was creeping along her bones.)

The church was an enclosed space, and Gaviel could only run so far without leaving, without losing the edge that his slight resistance gave him. He fled and fought, but Usiel's scythe swung wide and fast, and eventually struck the summer-lord's wing.

Gaviel fell.

(Renee DeVries' dreams turned into a nightmare of sorrow so swiftly that she was jerked awake, already sobbing.)

Usiel descended upon him. Gaviel blocked one blow of the scythe, and he seized the Reaper's hands with desperate strength, digging in his fiery claws and struggling to keep the blade from getting close; fighting to keep Usiel from drawing back for an unstoppable blow. He could smell the Reaper's charnel breath and feel the chill of its hell gaze. His probing fingers dug into the strange scar on Usiel's hand, the Slayer howled and weakened just long enough for Gaviel to sit up.

(Glenda started to pray to her angel, pray that he would save her again, not knowing it was his need that was stealing her life.)

The scabbed-over scar re-opened and continued to bleed, angry embers inside it. Gaviel saw and realized that Usiel was weakening. If he could only keep pushing...

The ghost of Gordy Hines picked up a music stand and swung its base into Gaviel's head.

The grip slackened, and Usiel tore his hands loose. The scythe rose and fell, a killing stroke—

(Leotis Grant suddenly hunched over the sink and vomited, puke coming out his nose, feeling like it was pressing his *eyes*, burning, and when he looked down, he saw blood in it.)

(Chasney fell out of bed screaming about the fire, the fire in his chest, and lights popped on up and down the hall as his parents, his sister and brother slammed open doors and ran into his bedroom.)

(Renee felt her sobs change into thrashing, an uncontrollable shuddering as if some giant dog had her in its jaws and was shaking her. Her teeth slammed together and apart with clattering speed, chattering hard enough to bite through tongue and lips.)

—but Gaviel survived, saw the shaft falling again.

If it hits, he thought, *It's either me or them.*

His thralls had trusted him, and he wondered if he would go back to Hell to save them.

He threw his arms up, making a cross before his face, and the haft of the scythe struck his forearms. He saw the Reaper leaning down, saw the ghost's makeshift weapon raised for another strike.

Gaviel grinned.

"Okay, Noah. Show me what you've got."

And suddenly, Usiel was contending against merely human strength. His foe was no glowing apparition, just a young black man in a nice coat. The blade's cruel tip dipped, steam rising from its chill plane, but he stopped it a scant millimeter from Noah Wallace's forehead.

Noah screamed, and it was a human scream. It was a full-on wail of terror and despair, and Usiel knew no Demon of Pride would cry like that, even at the point of death.

Gordy Hines started to slam down the music stand, but with an indrawn hiss Usiel recaptured him. The metal framework fell to the floor.

"WHERE'S GAVIEL?" the Reaper hissed.

Okay, Noah, the demon's mocking voice echoed in his brain. *You wanted a chance to strut your stuff, play the hero, fight against impossible odds. Ta da.*

"Nooooo!" Noah shrieked. "Come back! Please, come back, help me, save me!"

"Noah?"

Both man and spirit turned at that voice. A human voice, but a voice of command, the voice that had awoken and focused the holy ground on which all three stood.

It was the voice of Reverend Matthew Wallace.

"Dad! Help me!" was as far as the son got before Gaviel rose up in him again.

Too late, Noah. You had your chance, just like before. You gave in too quick, just like before. And now you're mine.

Just like before.

Gaviel grabbed the Slayer's injured hand and dug in, shoving the scythe back. The Reaper barely noticed.

"I cast thee out!" Matthew shouted.

Usiel's shriek of rage was unearthly. He wrestled his releasing tool free of the devil's grip, raised it for a final blow…

"I cast thee *out!*" the Reverend repeated, striding forward, his belt unbuckled and shoes untied and shirt untucked beneath his jacket. But he was in his church, in his element, and he was doing the Lord's work.

Usiel stumbled back as Gaviel scuttled the other way, toward Matthew; toward his savior.

"HE'S USING YOU AGAIN! YOUR SON IS HIS CAPTIVE!"

"Silence, demon! In the name of Jesus Christ, *I cast thee out!*"

Usiel could strike him, kill him, the work of a moment, and then finish the devil off, but he knew it would kill Glenda too, and she was praying to *him*, he could hear her in his mind and heart.

Burning black wings clapped together, and in a crash of stained glass, the Reaper of Souls fled.

"Thank you," Gaviel panted, looking up at the minister.

Matthew's return glance was searching and cool.

Epilogue

Mitch Berger was surfing the Internet. He drummed his fingers as an image slowly clarified, thinking, *Maybe I should spring for DSL*, knowing he couldn't really afford it.

He heard a buzz from his door.

With a grunt, he grabbed his cane and struggled to his feet, then clumped across the floor to the intercom.

"Who is it?" he said, partly annoyed at the interruption, partly glad that someone was maybe visiting.

And hell, he thought. *I can always save Miss July to the hard drive.*

"It's Chuck."

"Chuck? Chuck Rodriguez?"

"Uh huh. You wanna let me in?"

"Yeah! Yeah, just… hold on… aw, hell with it." He pushed the button, then hustled back to the computer. He got the image saved and the browser closed out just in time to hear the knock on his door.

"Just a second!"

He peeked out and could barely believe his eyes. He undid the chain and the security shaft, turned the deadbolt and lock and opened the door.

"Chuck. Damn."

"Heh." The other man smiled. "Been a while, I guess."

"I'll say. Shit, where you *been*?"

Chuck opened his mouth, closed it, shrugged. "Searching," he finally said.

They were quiet for a moment. "You doing anything?" Chuck asked.

"Naw, I was just... I'm off work, y'know, workman's comp. All that stuff. Disaster relief, just like everyone else around here. What about you though? Last I heard was when you were getting yelled at on, like, Larry King and everything. Then nothing. I mean, I called, I sent you letters and... I mean, nothing." He looked down at his feet, turned his aluminum cane this way and that. "I was *worried* about you."

"I'm fine. You wanna go get some coffee? I'm buying."

"Yeah, sure. That'd be great!"

As they walked down the stairs, Chuck first, the two men started to speak at the same time.

"Did you ever get that book deal?" Mitch asked.

"There's some people I'd like you to meet," Chuck said.

They paused, stopped, then continued down the stairs in silence.

"The book thing fell through," Chuck said.

"Damn shame. What people?"

"Well, they're people I met working on the book, actually."

"Yeah?"

"Mm hm. Here okay?"

"Yeah, sure." They walked into the local Starbucks franchise. Mitch was a little surprised to see it so empty—just a woman and her daughter at a table. No drinks, no one around behind the counter.

Must be cleaning up, he thought.

"These friends of mine," Chuck said. "They're... pretty special."

"Special how?"

"They're interested in what I saw. What *we* saw."

"You mean the…" Mitch glanced around, saw the pair at the table looking neutrally his way and lowered his voice. Months had passed, but there were still some words you didn't say lightly in Los Angeles. "…the Lucifer thing?"

"Exactly."

"C'mon, I was… you know I was all messed up, drunk, ripped to the tits on that dilaudid stuff."

"But I wasn't. I know what I saw."

"That's more than I can say about me."

"Still. You were present. You gave witness."

It was the woman. She'd stood up and come by their table. The little girl was with her.

"Mitch, I'd like you to meet Mukikel and Shadrannat."

"Those are… interesting names," Mitch said, awkwardly standing. He told himself he wanted to be polite, but something about the way the two of them looked at him—even the little girl, calm and mature and much too thoughtful—it made him want to stand, ready to fight. Or run away.

"We are seeking those who have seen the Morningstar. Who know the truth. Who can testify to his glory." This was the older one—Mukikel, Mitch thought.

"Who can testify to our glory." The little girl said that. What was she, twelve? Thirteen?

"Uh, like I said, I'd like to help you guys, but…"

"Mitch." Chuck's hand was on his arm. "It's okay, man. Trust me."

"Let's… let's get coffee, huh? Yeah, some coffee. Who's a guy gotta know to get a double espresso, huh?" Mitch's jocularity was strained and forced, and he privately thought that the second to last thing he wanted was some caffeine. But the *last* thing he wanted, suddenly, was to hear what Mukikel and Shadrannat were about to say.

"We sent them away," Mukikel said. "It will make our revelation easier."

"Revelation?"

She raised her arms over her head, as if stretching after a long nap. Shadrannat hugged herself and ducked her head and then...

Mitch stumbled backward, cane falling from numb fingers. He tripped on the edge of a chair and tumbled to the floor.

Mukikel was a radiant ebony figure, wings plumed with brilliant red autumn leaves. Eight-inch obsidian claws tipped her hands.

"BE NOT AFRAID," she said.

Shadrannat was tall, stick slender, with a butterfly wingspan that stretched all across the small room. Her face... Mitch couldn't look at her face, couldn't look away. Was she the loveliest, saddest, most austere woman he'd ever seen? Was it utterly alien, insectile, terrifying in its pure utility? Was it both?

He realized that the hand she held out to him was glowing slightly, like a firefly, and her voice—a chorus of bees and crickets—said, "WE SSSEEEK THE MORNINGSSSTAR. HEEE WILL LEEEAD USS TO GREATNESSS AGAIN, AND WE WILL EXALT HIM ONCE MORE."

Instinctively, Mitch started to kneel, but Chuck stopped him.

"No," he said, his eyes bright with a zealot's perfect confidence. "Save your praise for Lucifer. We worship him."

About the Author

In the course of his life, Greg Stolze has had the glasses punched off his face by a police officer, has fallen in love, has ridden an elephant, has sat around with three blonde women discussing their underwear, has danced badly, has gotten drunk, has danced while drunk and has written novels. Only the writing, the love and the elephant were as exciting as you'd think.

Curious about other Crossroad Press books? Stop by our
website: http://crossroadpress.com
We offer quality writing
in digital, audio, and print formats.

Subscribe to our newsletter on the website homepage and
receive a free eBook.